EVIL CHILD

"My baby," the Doll-Maker moaned. The pale green light of the moon sketched the terrible agony on her wide trembling face. "My Mary . . . is sick. Sick with hate, the fury of an evil one. A child of darkness has taken my baby's loving soul and soiled it with cries of vengeance!"

The huge old woman slid off the small, vinyl-covered bench, her big fists pounding her skull in torment.

"It is not fair," she cried in the stillness of the trailer. "My best, my most lovely creation."

Again, she sensed the sudden sharp, twisting pain. The vision of the doll's arms being twisted, tortured to purposely hurt an innocent child, exploded in her mind.

My doll's powers were not made for that! Sinking down onto her knees, the woman prayed the life-power, the wish-giving away from the most precious of all her creations.

But the evil one, the blond child whose face haunted her dreams, tearing apart her heart like a meat-grinder, was too strong.

She knew, then, that the child's life-force had already entered the doll, was growing inside it like a killing vine.

And she could do nothing to stop it. . . .

THE DOLL

BY JOSH WEBSTER

ZEBRA BOOKS
KENSINGTON PUBLISHING CORP.

ZEBRA BOOKS

are published by

Kensington Publishing Corp.
475 Park Avenue South
New York, NY 10016

First printing: March 1986

Printed in the United States of America

Prologue

Ya está, she thought. You are complete. The only thing left is the child's touch. The touch of life.

"*Mi bebe*," she said out loud, hugging the small muslin doll against her massive breasts. "All my life. Years beyond counting, I have made the dolls. The special dolls. But none as perfect as you."

The old woman's lips spread back across her black-gummed toothless mouth, revealing a broad unabashed grin of victory.

The dolls were her pride. And this one was her greatest achievement. She could feel its power radiating against her.

Holding the doll at arm's length, the great folds of flesh around her bones trembling with anticipation, she inspected the doll one final time. A child's joy, born of innocence, unmarred by time or tragedy, glowed in her deep-set gray eyes.

"I will call you . . . Mary. For the Virgin Mary. The Christians' mother of God. She, too, created life without the seeds of life, the man's seed. Like me, she created life through faith. And love. And the ways of the spirit-world."

The old woman's massive, sausagelike fingers caressed the doll's blond woolly hair with incredible gentleness, like the touch of angels' wings.

"My baby," she repeated, "you are the youngest and most precious of all." Opening her tree-trunk thighs, she sat her soft-sculptured, hand-sewn creation in the hammocklike dip of her brightly colored dress.

Slowly her mighty grin faded and her gray, ageless eyes clouded over with sadness. Yet beyond the sadness, the love of a mother, nurtured by the understanding that all things, even children, must be freed, framed her dark face.

With a calm born of a lifetime of similar tragedies, she sighed. "Mary, oh, my Mary. I am but the Doll-Maker. My power is now within you. I feel it stirring, but it is only the seed. I am not the gardener. It is not for me to nurture my dolls and make them grow. I am only the Doll-Maker. Whatever is to be planted inside you, to spark your true awakening, is the duty of another, of the child for whom you are chosen, whose wish you will fulfill in exchange for their caring and love. That is the soil you need in order to have a full life. Wait, my precious, for the child's touch of joy will be, to you, the water of life. And the child's love, the good rich soil for your ancient roots."

Pushing against her tremendous bulk, the old woman arose from the chair like a great breaching whale.

"*Yo te amo*. I love you," she said, placing the doll carefully on the long plastic table extending the entire length of the room. Other dolls, siblings quite similar yet uniquely individualized, were lined in a neat row on the table. "All of you. But I must let you go." She gazed slowly down the row. "You are for the children. I have prepared you. But I am only the Doll-Maker. The maker of the seed. It is for the children to do the planting. They are the true growers of life."

Stepping back from the table, the desert sun beating down on her through the clean glass window, she reached deep between her canyonlike cleavage and exhumed a gold, three-headed amulet; two abstract jaguar skulls, snarling in profile, framed the sides of a grinning, death-mask face.

"Ometéotl, mother of the gods, and father of the gods, whose sons are earth, air, fire, and water, the generative force of all living things, your dolls are completed. Bless them all. Through you, with the materials thy sons have given me, they shall live. I am your servant. The vessel through which you work. But the children are your true love. The dolls are ready!"

The old woman pressed the ancient amulet reverently to her lips, then dropped it back into the cavern between her breasts.

Her hands began to tremble.

It was now *el tiempo de dar*, the time of giving. She could put it off no longer.

Or, as the factory salesman called it, filling the adoption quota.

She did not care for his gringo words, it showed he did not understand. But his meaning was clear.

To her, the Time of Giving was sacred. Closing her eyes, she meditated on the power of giving . . . Ometéotl's power. Her power. The dolls' power. Soon the human children's power as well.

It was extremely difficult to concentrate on the two-thousand-year-old mantras of her priests. She had never felt as much power in any of her dolls as she had in the one now called Mary. It was her Doll of Dolls. The most perfect of all her creations. It hurt to think of her doll being crammed into one of the dark, coffinlike boxes to be shipped off to some big American city and bought for one of the spoiled American children.

"Ayee," she stammered, pounding her temples with both fists.

It was wrong to mar the Time of Giving with selfishness and lies.

"Forgive me," she cried, shaking her head. "It is blasphemy to speak against the children. Any children."

But my heart, she wept inside, feeling it crumbling like a great stone temple in an earthquake. My heart is not clean. I love one of my dolls too much.

That is a sin. A sacrilege to Ometéotl and to my mother, who entrusted the power to create the sacred living dolls with me, as her mother had with her dolls, and as her mother with hers, for a hundred generations.

Quickly the woman knelt before the window. Beads of sweat poured down over her huge body while she prayed fervently for forgiveness, for her heart to open fully to the giving. Never, in all her years, had it been so hard to let one of her dolls go.

Yet if she did not, the doll, Mary, would never truly be born, merely exist in horrifying limbo between the world of the living and the world of ghosts.

* * *

8

The skinny young man pushed back his long black hair and obediently followed the foreman, hoping their conversation was finally over.

It wasn't.

"Juan, I must know," the foreman asked. "I will not call the authorities. You know that. We, *pochos*, stick together. But you must tell me so if the gringos come, I will know what to do."

Juan's dark suspicious eyes met the older man's gaze, and he knew that his foreman was sincere. *And what choice do I have?* Juan concluded fatalistically. *I have come to the U.S. illegally. I have no work card, no papers. Nothing.*

After checking up and down the factory corridor, Juan sighed. "Sí. I am illegal, a *pacho*. I came across three days ago."

Pedro Gonzales patted the young man's shoulder with his thick, calloused hand. *He is hardly more than a boy,* he thought sadly, *yet he must act as a man. He is in a foreign country filled with light-faced people who do not want him in their land. Yet to live, he must come.*

Pedro started walking again. "Have you any relatives here in this country?"

"Sí, two cousins and my uncle are in Los Angeles. But I have a sister here in the factory. Victoria. She is one of the apprentice sewers of the dolls. It was she who told me of this job."

Again, Pedro halted, this time by two large blue metal doors. "Do not worry. It is safe here. Come. We will get more carts and boxes and finish crating the dolls before the truck comes from the city."

Juan nodded absentmindedly. He had been crating

9

dolls all morning. It was boring work, but not heavy labor. Boredom was easier to accept than the swollen aching muscles of migrant farm labor.

But if the work was relatively easy, the strange alien motif of the factory still haunted him.

The two front offices, where his sister had taken him to be hired, looked like hospital nursery rooms, with rows of showcase dolls in cribs behind long glass walls. All the women who worked in the offices, as well as in shipping, wore standard white nurses' uniforms. The men wore the tunics and trousers of hospital orderlies.

All that, just to make the dolls more expensive for the rich Americans, he thought, a little disgusted.

What bothered him most, however, was that the young women who sewed the dolls were not allowed to speak to him while they worked.

He was a handsome boy, quite popular with the girls in his village, but when he tried to flirt or tease or make jokes here, the women ignored him completely.

It is like working in a monastery, Juan decided. Even the pretty ones act as if it is sacrilegious to speak or to reveal the slightest passion of their youth.

But this is not a sacred place, he reminded himself. It is only a factory. A workshop to make stupid little dolls. Even if they dress up the factory to look like a children's ward and pretend the dolls are real live human babies, they are still only dolls.

It will be a long, cold winter, Juan thought sadly, if the girls here keep acting like nuns.

Shoving back the big swinging doors, Pedro rolled out two double-decker metal carts full of boxes and playfully kicked one at Juan. The young man deftly side-stepped it and caught the handrail with the grace of an aspiring toreador.

Pedro laughed loudly. "You're lucky it had no horns," he jested. "Or you would have been gored in the belly."

The young man smiled, a trace of good-natured defiance in his eyes. "I have run with the bulls. I am too quick. The hairy beasts never touched me. And I was in the back of the crowd, right with the bulls, all the way to the arena."

Pedro grinned, enjoying the foolish courage of youth. "In this country, the gringos have another meaning for the word bull. It is that kind of bull I think you give me now."

As the older man guffawed raucously, Juan fiddled with the corner of one of the cardboard boxes, trying to imagine what other meaning Pedro could possibly have meant.

After Pedro finished chortling at his own joke, he put a finger to his lip. "We must be quiet now." He pointed at the last door in the corridor behind Juan. "Normally only I pack the dolls in that room. But we are running late and the truck from San Diego is due any minute." Holding his hand up as if he were being sworn in at court, he reiterated a previous warning. "Remember. Be careful with these dolls. Be gentle. Lay them in the boxes as if they were fresh eggs from your favorite hen."

Juan shrugged. "But Pedro, they are only dolls. I have crated hundreds of them already. Why do you make such a thing of it?"

Pedro waved the question away. "Enough. It is not for you to question."

11

"But . . ."

A sudden stern glance from his new foreman stopped the young man from finishing his objection.

Slowly Pedro opened the door, with Juan close behind him, staring over his shoulder.

"*Con permiso*, Doll-Maker. We have come for your dolls."

The young man tried not to look shocked as he followed Pedro into the stark, sun-bright room. It was not like any other he had seen in the factory. It looked more like an Indian's one-room adobe hut. It even had a fireplace in the wall. But the room was not nearly as startling as the woman by the window. She was wider than both men together, standing shoulder to shoulder, with breasts like watermelons and hips the breadth of a mule's rump. But it was her face that shocked him most. She looked exactly like the unearthed statues of Aztec royalty Juan had seen in the museums in Mexico City. Her nose was long and straight and hooked sharply just below her big, dark hawklike eyes that perched upon high, protruding cheekbones.

Juan unconsciously genuflected as soon as her powerful eyes met his.

It made the old woman grin.

"*Vamonos*," Pedro ordered. "Start at the other end of the table. Remember to check each box to make sure the name on the adoption certificate coincides with the name on the doll's tag."

Juan could feel the woman watching his every move as he pushed his cart to the edge of the table and opened the clear plastic lid on the first box.

The adoption papers and birth certificate in the box

called the doll Mary. Checking the first doll in the row, he saw the name on the tag was the same. He quickly tossed the doll into its box and flipped the blue and pink container into one of two larger shipping crates on the bottom shelf of the cart.

"Ayee!" the woman screamed.

The sudden, terrible cry caused Juan to spin around and trip on the corner of the cart, almost knocking it over.

Before he could raise himself from his bent position, the huge woman attacked.

"Doll-Maker, please!" Pedro called from the other end of the room. "He did not mean to be so rough with . . ."

"*Mi bebé!*" The old woman's wide face twisted ominously. "He treats my baby like a stick of firewood. My Mary, named for the Virgin Mother of Christ."

Suddenly the young man found himself being swept off his feet. Dangling him like a bag of laundry, the woman held him in the air with one bearlike paw. Everything began to spin. A sharp pain shot up his spine into the base of his skull.

Pedro dashed from his cart, knowing that Juan's back could snap like a twig under the incredible strength of the Doll-Maker.

"Please, Holy Mother. Doll-Maker. He is young. He did not know of your children. Only of dolls. And of a job in a strange land with strange ways. You must forgive his ignorance. He is young and from a small village. He knows not of your ways."

A terrible darkness encircled Juan. His throat began spasming. Air no longer infiltrated his windpipe.

Pedro swung himself under the old woman's arms and faced her squarely.

"Please, Doll-Maker. I will send him away. He will never touch your children again. Holy Mother, let him go. Show him mercy."

Juan's limp body crumpled to the floor. Like bursts of steam venting from an old iron heating pipe, his high-pitched gasps echoed in the still, hot room.

Pedro quickly knelt and helped the young man to his feet.

He could feel the aftershocks of terror racking the boy's limbs as he dragged him out the door.

Chapter I

"We'll eat in here," Barbra Foster announced, slicing the three BLT's corner to corner, "at our new breakfast table."

"Can't we eat in front of the TV?" Gretchen whined, her eyes glued to the set. "Spider-man is about to . . ."

"You've been watching that thing since you got up," her mother stated. "Now get off your fannies and come in here."

The ten-year-old twins glanced at each other momentarily, then slowly arose from the floor. Mary clicked off the set. As they strolled into the kitchen, Gretchen hesitated by the counter, lightly tapping her fingers on its smooth metal edge, and Mary accidentally bumped into her, shoving her forward.

"Don't push," Gretchen sniped, purposely blocking her path.

"Well, what'd you stop for?"

Barbra poured milk into their glasses and scooped a handful of Fritos onto each plate. "Quit dawdling and sit."

Mary circled cautiously around her twin and

plopped down in her chair. Although they had only lived in their new house three days, Mary had already established her place at the table. She had staked her claim by putting her favorite glass there, the one with a picture of E.T. on it.

Gretchen hovered by the counter, pouting. "It was my favorite cartoon."

"It is not," Mary argued, her upper lip rimmed with milk. "You like Scoobie Doo best."

"Not anymore," Gretchen blurted out defensively.

"They're all your favorite when it comes to turning off that darn set," Barbra concluded. "Now sit down and eat."

After a long, righteous sigh, Gretchen did as she was told. Barbra hid her amusement, waiting for Gretchen's eyes to light up as she peeked under the top layer of toast.

"Hmmmm. BLT's."

"Can I have more Fritos?" Mary asked, deftly stealing a few from her twin's plate while she was busy inspecting her sandwich.

"Quit it." Gretchen quickly shifted her plate out of her sister's reach, catching her glass of milk with an elbow. It rocked precariously on its edge and Gretchen froze. Luckily it didn't tip over. Gretchen breathed a sigh of relief.

"Almost." Mary giggled.

Both twins burst out laughing.

"What is it with you two today?" Barbra asked, not really expecting an answer. Mary carefully picked the tomato and bacon from her sandwich and began munching on the top piece of toast. As Gretchen devoured hers, she spied a hand nonchalantly creeping toward her Fritos and slapped it away.

Barbra finished her sandwich and leaned back in her chair. "After lunch, I think you both should go outside and play. Maybe that will get rid of some of this excess energy."

"But it's raining out," Gretchen objected.

"It's been raining ever since we got here," Mary added.

"It's just a little drizzle, honey. You can't stay cooped up in the house all winter waiting for the rain to stop. Not here in Washington."

Gretched shrugged. "I don't mind stayin' in."

After two long days of driving from San Diego to Seattle in a Monte Carlo packed to the roof with clothes, the twins in the front seat constantly bored and irritable, then two more hours driving northeast the third day, through who knows how many small, gray, dirty towns to their new home in Canaan, population 1,633, a mill town as dank and unlovely as Barbra had feared it would be, then another day directing a couple of neanderthal movers with all the physical dexterity of two blind water buffalo in heat, followed by two more days assessing the carnage of nicks and dents while hunting for missing paraphernalia inevitably stuffed into the last place anyone would think of to look, Barbra had about had it. One quick glance was all it took to convince the twins to step lightly for a while.

When the doorbell rang, both girls bolted from the table to answer it. Barbra was too exhausted to care, at that point, who their first official visitor might be. All she wanted was to escape to the sanctuary of a long, hot bubble bath to be followed by an uninterrupted nap, an impossible luxury for a recently divorced, working mother of ten-year-old twins. To her chagrin, Barbra Foster suddenly felt as if she had truly passed the peak of her life-span and was now on the downhill slide to old age. In another six months, she would be forty, but at this moment she felt closer to eighty. Every muscle in her tall, long-legged body ached.

"Mommy, there's a package for us," Gretchen yelled, dashing into the kitchen. "It's from Daddy. But you have to sign something first."

The U.P.S. carrier stooped over to show Mary exactly where her mother should sign the receipt sheet. He arose as Barbra approached.

"It's for all of us, Mommy." Mary beamed. "Says so right on the package. To Mary, Gretchen, and Barbra Foster."

Barbra signed the sheet and thanked the carrier. After herding the girls away from the door, she tried to shut it, but the carrier didn't move. Barbra opened the door again.

"Is there something else?"

"Excuse me, ma'am, but aren't you the lady that's gonna be the new vice president at the mill?"

"That's right." Barbra smiled. "How did you . . ."

"Canaan's a small town. We've all heard about it. Caused a lot of talk, actually."

"I hope not all bad."

The carrier stared awkwardly down at his shuffling feet. "My brother, Jake, works in shipping at the mill. Jake McClusky." He peered up at her, an odd trace of defiance in his dark eyes. "Jake's a good man, Mrs. Foster," he stated, as if defending his brother's integrity in a court of law.

"I'm sure he is." Barbra retained her smile as she attempted to close the door. The carrier blocked it with one hand. Instinctively Barbra pushed her children behind her.

"He ain't got much seniority. Only been at the mill a year. But he works harder than all the others put together down there."

"I'm sure he does. Is that all?" Barbra asked coldly.

"It's just that seniority shouldn't always be the way to judge who gets laid off and who doesn't." He turned and headed for his truck. "They should be judged by the work they do."

Barbra closed the door. So it's already begun, she thought. The rumors. Sudden, whispered innuendos. Coffee break chatter in every nook and cranny of Hopkins Lumber. Probably in every bar and greasy spoon in Canaan as well. After all, it was a mill town. Canaan was born a mill town and it would die a mill town. Hopkins Lumber and Canaan, for all intents and purposes, were synonymous. And both were dying. The lumber business was in an unprecedented slump, one that would take radical measures to revitalize. Although the nation's unemployment was heading for ten percent, the mill towns in the Pacific Northwest were averaging thirty percent. Radical measures, however, were Barbra Foster's forte. In the last nine years, she had taken three failing companies, all bought at bargain prices by Lexon Corporation, her employer of the last fifteen years, and turned them around. Now it was Hopkins Lumber Mill's turn. And she was ready. But was the town ready? Things would get worse before they got better, that was always the way. They knew that, too, she concluded, because the rumors were true. More people would be laid off very, very soon.

"Mommy, this tape won't rip," Gretchen said, anxiously tugging at the big package.

Barbra turned from the door and knelt on the floor with her daughters. "We'll need scissors."

"I'll get them." Mary ran into the kitchen, only to realize she had no idea where they might be. She started opening drawers and banging them shut. "Where are they, Mom?"

Barbra thought for a moment, then shook her head. "Lord only knows, honey. Take a knife out of the wooden block. We'll use that."

There were three gift-wrapped packages in the box. Housewarming gifts "for his girls," the note from Barbra's newly divorced husband read. The twins eagerly tore open their presents, but Barbra just stared at hers. Being included as one of "his girls" was not very palatable. It merely evoked bitter memories.

"Look," Gretchen squealed with unabashed delight. "An Adoptable Doll. Just like Daddy and I saw in the store." Reverently, Gretchen lifted the doll from its box and held it up. "Oh, she's beautiful."

It was uncanny how much the soft-sculptured, sewn face looked like the twins. If one was to sculpt a caricature of the girls between ages one and two, that doll would be it, Barbra thought.

Gretchen was totally captivated by her present, almost mesmerized by it. She couldn't take her eyes off it. The rest of the world, her mother, her sister,

20

everything seemed to fade away into some obscure recess of her consciousness as she stared at the doll. Concentrating on it with all her will, she could almost hear the doll speaking, its soft, distant voice like the strange sealike echoes of the conch shells she used to cup over her ear on the beach in San Diego.

Noticing the odd look on Gretchen's face, Barbra gently tapped her arm. Gretchen twisted, then slowly, almost painfully, withdrew her gaze from the doll. Glancing at her mother was like looking through the wrong end of a telescope, everything around her was so vague and far away. It took a few moments for Gretchen to mentally revert back through that strange visual tunnel into the real world again. She actually had a sense of sudden disconnection, as if something within the doll had reached out and caressed her very soul with its powerful presence.

Mary peeked at her own present, then closed the lid. Attempting to hide her disappointment, she forced herself to smile at her sister's joy. "It's really nice, Gretchen."

Gretchen hugged her doll, just twitching with delight. Waiting until she had her mother's full attention, she stated offhandedly, "Daddy always knows exactly what to get me."

The daughter's underlying sense of defiance was not lost on her mother.

"So what did Daddy send you, Mary?" she asked, to change the subject.

Mary's bright blue eyes gazed morosely down at her present. Opening the lid reluctantly, she extracted a frilly pink apron. She held it up, almost apologetically, and Barbra read aloud the words inscribed on the front. *"Mommy's Little Helper.* That's very pretty, Mary."

Gretchen snorted through her nose to contain her amusement. Mary glared at her sister as Gretchen shoved the doll's box closer to her mother. "Look. There's pictures of the nursery where the doll was born. And ah . . ." She held up the two fancy gold-rimmed documents.

"Adoption papers," Barbra told her. "And a birth certificate. It says the doll's name is . . ."

"Mary." Gretchen laughed. "I already knew that."

"And how did you know?" Barbra asked, startled.

"She told me," Gretchen answered, holding up her doll.

Mary glanced up at her mother, hoping it wasn't true. "That's not her name, is it, Mommy?"

"Says so right here." Gretchen pointed at the paper triumphantly. "Maybe we should put your apron on her," she snickered. "Mommy's Little Helper Doll."

Mary shoved her present back in the box and slammed the lid. "That's not funny."

"I think so." Gretchen sat the doll next to her and stroked its blond hair. "Little Mary, quite the fairy, how does your garden grow?"

"That's not the right words," Mary objected, humiliated.

"They're my words," Gretchen bantered.

Turning her back to her sister, Mary looked pleadingly at Barbra. "So what did you get, Mommy?"

In all the commotion, Barbra had forgotten that she, too, had received a package. She wished she hadn't. She knew whatever it was, it would be a sarcastic bit of trash. Noting her ex-husband's cruel display of favoritism in the disparity between the twins' gifts, she was convinced of that.

"Open it." Gretchen insisted.

Barbra swallowed her growing apprehension, to retain a festive decorum for her daughters, and undid the wrapping. Inside was a brown and blue striped tie. Gaudy little gold dollar signs dotted it randomly. She held it up, disgusted.

"A tie?" Mary was confused. "You don't wear ties, Mommy. Why would Daddy . . ."

Barbra folded it neatly back into its box. "It's your father's idea of a joke, honey."

"I don't get it," Mary decided.

"Neither do I," Barbra lied.

The twins' bedroom was done in a charming rainbow of pale yellows and light blue. Blue was Gretchen's favorite color, yellow, Mary's. In the corner by the closet, the five-foot panda bear Matt had given Gretchen two years ago for her birthday sat as the official watchdog of their room, one eye dangling on its cheek by a thread. Above it, discarded dolls and stuffed animals, now out of favor, filled two long shelves.

Propped against the headboard of her bed, Mary pretended to read while secretly eyeing Gretchen as she played with her doll on the floor by the panda bear.

"Come look at the pictures of the nursery," Gretchen implored, knowing her sister was watching.

"I can't. I'm reading now." Mary held the book up in front of her face like a newspaper.

Scooping up her doll and its box, Gretchen carted them over to her sister's bed. "Look." She shoved the pictures between Mary and her book. "They have a whole nursery. There's the babies in the beds. And there's a nurse. And there's a doctor. And see that. The names of the babies are on the beds. That's where Mary was born."

"It wasn't born. It was sewn together," Mary said bluntly.

"Was too born." Puffing out her chest, she shoved the adoption papers forward. "See. It says she was born December 12, 1981. She's only a month old." Cuddling the doll, she murmured, "She's so darling."

Mary closed her book and curled one leg under the other. "It's just another doll, Gretchen."

"She is not," Gretchen objected angrily, hugging the doll closer. "She's just like me. She was born and there were doctors and nurses there just like at the hospital where I was born. She's alive. She told me so. And she's all mine because I've adopted her."

Mary rolled away from her twin and opened up her book again.

Gretchen shook her sister's leg impatiently. "Want to play with us? You can be a nurse. I'll be Mary's mother."

Mary slammed her book closed and flipped back over. "I'm Mary. That's a doll."

"She's not a doll. She's my new sister. I told you I adopted her."

"That's stupid."

"You're stupid." Gretchen jumped off the bed, even more agitated. "Why don't you put on that stupid pink apron and go help Mommy like you're supposed to." Taunting her sister was one of her favorite pastimes and she could tell she really had her going this time. "And get off Mary's bed. She wants to take a nap."

"It's my bed."

"It's Mary's bed. My Mary's bed. Not yours. Daddy and Mommy agreed to put you up for adoption now that I have my real sister here."

"You're really looney-tunes, you know that?"

Gretchen grinned triumphantly. "I can't hear you, you know. You're not real. Only my Mary is real. And she loves me more than anything in the whole world, just like Daddy. She's going to make me happy again. Why don't you just crawl under a rock where you belong and leave me and my sister alone?"

Mary's eyes shot toward her twin angrily. She left without a word, knowing if she tried to speak, she would have started crying.

Pleased by the level of torment she had inflicted, Gretchen smiled at her doll.

"She doesn't understand, does she?" she cooed coyly. "But I do. I know how special you are. You're not just another doll, like she says. You're alive. I can feel it. And you're all mine."

Barbra poured the bacon grease into a coffee can and put it back under the sink. She could hear the twins arguing in their room and knew it must have something to do with the doll. The more she thought about their gifts, the more incensed she became. Matt was a lot of things, but he certainly wasn't naive, not when it came to the twins. He had to have known

25

exactly what he was doing. She could understand about her gift. There was no love lost between them anymore. But why purposely choose to hurt Mary, too? If it was just to get back at her, the man was really sick. Barbra had to wonder if he really loved Mary at all. Was it possible Gretchen was the only one he truly cared about now? Barbra had seen that same quiet pain wash over Mary often enough over the years to know even she understood who her father's favorite was. Yet she never once had complained, which was more than she could say about Gretchen. But the incongruity of the twins' presents today was, by far, Matt's most blatant display of favoritism to date. To Barbra, it was absolutely unforgivable.

She picked the tie box up off the counter and stared at it in disbelief.

How could he?

The sound of the twins' arguing dimmed as her mind wandered back to that fateful night when all her hopes, her dreams, her foolish misconceptions that somehow things might change, that there was still a chance to salvage their badly battered marriage, had been utterly destroyed. It was like coming home to discover your house was burning and, while praying desperately that the brave firemen could save it, suddenly the furnace explodes, flames devour the walls, and the entire structure collapses into a charred heap of rubble.

Six months ago, she thought. Almost to the day. As soon as she had arrived at the office, she had felt something was wrong. It was impossible not to notice the quick looks of pity or the sudden hush as she passed the small group of salesmen. Finally, her friend Helen, the receptionist, had broken down and told her why.

Barbra had gone home early that afternoon and immediately packed the twins off to a friend's house for dinner. Then the lonely vigil of waiting began.

Matt finally lumbered in a little before nine, loaded on gin martinis as usual. Even in his clouded state, he had sensed the tension as soon as he closed the front door. The house was deathly still. He immediately called for his favorite little girl, but this time Gretchen didn't come running into his arms. His only greeting was the cold, empty silence.

"Where are the kids?" he asked, going straight to the liquor cabinet. A cupboard door slammed. "Barb? Where's the twins?" He buried two ice cubes in a glass of gin, then spotted Barbra leaning against the door to the den, arms crossed, one eyebrow tilted.

"Why didn't you answer me?" he asked brashly, stirring his drink with a finger. "I suppose my dinner is in the oven again?"

"You bastard," she sneered.

"God, it's good to be home," he said sarcastically.

Barbra's trembling hands dug into the flesh of her upper arms. "You had to do it, didn't you? You had to take that little bitch to the Blue Lion." Her eyes burned fiercely. "You shit."

Matt threw up his hand innocently, making sure not to spill his gin. "What the hell are you talking about?"

"Leta Coolige," Barbra answered through clenched teeth. "You took her to the Blue Lion last night. From what everyone in the office says, you were just about ripping her clothes off in the lounge."

"Come on, Barbra." He waved it off as if it were inconsequential and started toward her.

"Keep away from me." Barbra slid around toward the fireplace. "God, Matt, how could you? You know that's where all my salespeople hang out. It was the one place that would embarrass me most. That's why you went there, isn't it?"

Matt gulped down his drink and quickly fixed another. "What's the real problem, Barb? Is this going to jeopardize your brand-new promotion?"

"So that's it." She slowly shook her head. "I should have known."

"So what is it? The fact that I'd rather go out with a woman than a corporate genius?"

"That's not fair, Matt."

"Not fair?" he scoffed. "Not fair?"

"You can't stand it, can you? What the hell did you want? A cute, brainless, giggling little secretary for a wife? One who tells you how brilliant you are no matter how much you screw things up? A walking clone without the briefest flashes of ambition or talent? Jesus God, Matt, why didn't you marry that cheerleader Betty whatever-her-name-was with the bouncing jugs for brains if that's all you ever wanted. I'm good at what I do. I always thought you'd be proud of me. But you never were. You've never said one encouraging word to me about what I do."

"I don't give a damn about your fucking success." He bowed mockingly. "Two promotions in the last year alone. A salary that now doubles her pitifully inept husband's." He put a finger to his lips. "Drinks too much, I hear. Once was the captain of the football team in college, though. A real shining star that was

28

going places, that's what they all said. Wonder whatever happened to old Matt Foster?" He drained the bottle into his glass, turned and stumbled, but caught his balance on the liquor cabinet. "Heard he married that tall blonde who was always in the library. Turned out she was really a transvestite. Miss Manly Woman, class of '64."

Whatever semblance of pity or love Barbra Foster had once had disappeared forever then. The awful fact that the apparition swaying across the room as if the floor was slanted was the father of her children became abhorrent to her.

"You're nothing but a burned-out college jock who never wanted to grow up. You've never taken responsibility for anything. You blame me. You'd blame the whole damn world for your own inadequacies rather than face them."

"The world?" Matt slammed his glass on the end table by the sofa. "Not the whole world, Barb. Just you. You've made a career out of castrating me and every other poor slob that has to work with you. You should go to Denmark and get the operation you so dearly deserve."

"Jesus." Barbra sighed, dropping her head onto the arm resting across the fireplace mantel.

"Don't play pious with me, God damn it!" Matt screamed, drumming his finger against his chest. "You're the one who's driven me to drink. And you drove me to another woman, too."

"And I caused you to get fired three times in the last six years, I suppose?"

"That's right. How could I compete with . . . the girl genius? I had to fail just to let you look good."

29

Barbra couldn't believe this. "Sick, Matt. Real sick."

"Sick?" He heaved his glass against the wall, shattering it. "I'll tell you what's sick. Having a wife you haven't made love to in almost a year. That's sick!"

"And that's . . . my fault too . . . right?" Barbra stuttered, fighting to keep back the tears. "You're the one . . . who couldn't . . . do it. You're the one who quit trying. Who pushed me away, over and over again. You, Matt. You!"

"Bullshit!" Matt howled. "I have no problems getting it up for sweet, silly little Leta. Or any of the others, for that matter."

There was nothing more to say then.

Twenty years, Barbra thought nauseously, her insides wrung dry by his words. Twenty years hoping a spoiled child would become a man.

And now . . .

Nothing.

Her stomach spasmed, and she swallowed to keep from throwing up.

"Get out," she whispered, too weak, too hurt, too destroyed inside to scream anymore. "Just get out, Matt. And don't ever come back."

Barbra Foster crumpled the tie up and tossed it in the garbage can under the sink.

"She's mine!" she heard one of the twins yelling. "You can't touch her. She's mine! All mine!"

As Barbra trudged down the hall to check on the girls and hopefully establish some kind of truce, the disgust, the sheer waste of it all, filled her again to the breaking point. In the last six months, she had had to contend with the gut-twisting abhorrence of that night by reminding herself of the good years, the happy times, the love that had once existed, but the memories seemed so blurred now, so far away, as if they weren't her own memories at all, merely something she had read in her youth, a sad, silly story too fanciful to ever have been real.

"Play with your stupid toys," Gretchen snapped. "And leave us alone! What did you come back in here for anyway? No one wants you here."

Barbra stood silently in the doorway, unnoticed.

"I just wanted to hold it for a second. I don't see why you have to blow a gasket about it. It's just a stupid doll."

"You'll hurt her."

"I will not."

"You will. You hate her. You got a stupid present and I got her, and that proves Daddy loves me and not you and you hate her."

"He loves me too," Mary insisted, deeply hurt by the accusation.

Gretchen inched away from her sister, protecting her doll with both arms. "Then why'd it say *Mommy's Little Helper?* He hates you just like he hates Mommy."

Mary started to point at her sister and object, but her hand fell limply back to her side. A tear rolled down her cheek.

"That's mean and untrue, Gretchen Foster," Barbra scolded, shocking both girls with her sudden presence. "How could you say that to your sister?" Barbra drew Mary into her embrace. "Now come over here and apologize."

31

Gretchen squinted maliciously and stood her ground. "No. I won't. It's true. Daddy loves me best. He's always loved me best. It's true. It's true. It's true."

Clinging to her mother, Barbra felt Mary's small shoulders heave as she began to weep.

"It's not true, baby," she whispered, scooping her up into her arms. Gretchen nervously backed away. "As for you, young lady, you're not to leave this room until you apologize. And you're damn lucky I'm too tired to throw you over my knee for a good spanking."

Barbra carried Mary to the living-room sofa and sat her down on her lap. "Gretchen was just being mean, honey." She gently wiped the tears from Mary's chin. "She's full of anger because Daddy's gone, and she was taking it out on you. But she didn't mean it. Daddy's always loved you. You know that."

Mary pressed herself against her mother's breast, as if hoping, by osmosis, to sink back into her mother's womb for comfort. Barbra patted her head lovingly.

Cracking the bedroom door slightly, Gretchen Foster stared down the hall at her mother and sister. Her fingers tightened around the edge of the door. Her breath shortened until she was literally snorting with rage, then she turned and grabbed her doll. A corner of her lip curled savagely.

"I hate her," she told it, glaring at her twin. "She made Mommy get mad at me again like she always does. If it wasn't for her, Mommy would love me. But she doesn't. Only Daddy loves me. And they made him go away. They hate me. And I hate them." She squeezed the doll against her chest, caressing it the way she had just seen her mother stroking Mary. "You'll help me get back at her, won't you? After all, you're my sister now." She rocked the doll gently. "My twin." Slowly she began to twist a clump of the doll's hair absentmindedly, lost in her visions of revenge. "You came here to make me happy, didn't you?"

A strand of hair suddenly snapped off in her hand, but she failed to notice. Looking down, she became instantly hypnotized by the doll's big black eyes. They seemed to grow larger the more she stared, like pools of spreading oil, glistening in a swirling rainbow of changing colors.

"And you know what would make me happiest of all?" she whispered, as if in a trance. "Getting rid of Mommy's Little Helper. For good!"

Chapter II

Anxiety again reared its sleepy head Monday morning and engulfed the Foster household. It was the twins' first day in a new school and Barbra's first official day at work. When Mary opened the garage door, the dark, overcast sky seemed especially gloomy to her. Thick fog oozed down between the tall, big-shouldered mountain slopes into the small river valley, hiding the four-block area of downtown Canaan and the surrounding houses in its gray, ethereal fingers. Like some dark, monstrous apparition, the cold, heavy mist curled and heaved through the moss-heavy, black-green forests, devouring everything in its path. Visibility, as Barbra drove to the old one-story, eight-room grade school, was almost zero.

After meeting briefly with their teacher to reassure herself her children were in good hands, Barbra headed for work. As she passed through the barren, unkempt streets, bits of storefronts peeked in and out of the ghoulish haze, giving her the eerie impression she was driving through a town in its final death throes. A ghost town before its time, silently whispering to its inhabitants to flee before it disappeared forever in that primordial mist.

Turning into the Hopkins Lumber Company parking lot, the same frightening premonition persisted. Was it the way the fog clung to the massive stacks of lumber outside? Or how it seemed to seep right out of the huge old mill itself? Or was it just nerves? Barbra asked herself as she parked the car. After another quick survey of the cluttered grounds, she realized it wasn't any of those things. It was something else. Or, more specifically, the lack of something. Something extremely important: Pride. There was no sense of pride here. Like the squalor of a refugee camp, the mill lay in disarray, as if waiting, defeated, to die.

Barbra Foster sat in her car and waited, too. Waited for the gray, ominous mood that had surrounded her to slowly dissipate while she steadied herself for the task ahead. Things will change, she coaxed herself. She would change them. If necessary, she would be the Pride-Maker. The Resurrector. She would bring this archaic mill back to life. That was her job. She had done it before. She would do it again, here.

A quick tap on the steering wheel and she opened the door. Hopkins Lumber . . . watch out. Your corporate savior has arrived.

Mrs. Bixby introduced the twins to her fifth-grade class. They were absolutely awed, never having seen identical twins, live, before. Thinking back, she realized it had been ten years since she had last had twins in her class. She was glad these two didn't wear matching outfits like the previous pair. She remembered how she had been able to detect minute physical differences in the other twins the first time she had seen them. But not with these two. It was uncanny. They were exactly alike in every detail. Assigning them permanent seats would be the only way to distinguish them until she learned their different personality traits.

As she marked them on her seating chart, she noticed the shy, smiling glances among the boys. These two will certainly break some hearts when they get older, she thought, amused. Those big blue eyes, demurely framed with long, fluttering blond lashes, those pixielike noses, the full arching of the lips and clear radiant skin: a couple of little blond dolls just ready to bloom.

Her first impression, however, was quickly shattered.

It started during the art project. The class had voted, last week, to make a miniature replica of their town for Parents' Day. Each of them was to build a model of their own house, plus one store in town. Using an aerial photograph of Canaan, they planned to put them all together on the large piece of plywood lying on four desks in the back of the room. Add moss for grass, tiny branches for trees, cut out a few paper roads and sidewalks, and it would be complete. Any materials handy could be used to erect each structure. Some worked with cardboard, others chose clay or even the tongue depressors Jamie's father, the town dentist, had donated for the project.

The class loved the concept. A wonderful sense of unity, of community spirit, immediately surrounded the project. Everyone helped everyone else. It would also be a good way for the twins to make friends and feel a part of the class, Mrs. Bixby concluded.

In Mary's case, she was right. She quickly had been swept up in the spirit of the project and was busily helping the two girls who sat in front of her.

But Gretchen did not want any part of it. She had instantly built a wall of isolation around herself, snapping at anyone who tried to offer her assistance. Mrs. Bixby decided to give her time, hoping one of the kids could break her out of her shell.

None could.

To her dismay, she watched Gretchen slowly inch her desk toward the window, away from the rest of the class. For a half hour, she just sat at her desk, sadly gazing out at the playground.

"What kind of material would you like to use, Gretchen?" Mrs. Bixby inquired, easing around to sit on the windowsill. Gretchen shrugged, staring at her desk. The heavyset, gray-haired woman moved closer, leaning one hand on the top of her chair. "How about cardboard? You could draw the walls of your house and cut them out and . . ."

"I don't want to," Gretchen mumbled without looking up.

Mrs. Bixby smiled kindly, knowing the difficulties a ten-year-old faced on her first day in a strange new environment. "Look." Her hand swept out toward the rest of the class. "It's fun. Even Mary is enjoying herself."

Mary heard her name and glanced back. "Gretchen, come work with us. We'll help each other make our new house."

Gretchen glanced out the corner of her eye at her twin, then looked up at her teacher. "I don't want her help."

"That's fine," Mrs. Bixby cajoled. "You can work by yourself. Or do you want me to help you?"

"Maybe," she conceded.

"Okay. Let's start with the drawing." Mrs. Bixby laid a sheet of cardboard on Gretchen's desk and picked up a pencil. "I'll start doing . . ."

Gretchen yanked the cardboard into her lap. "I'll do it alone. I don't need anyone's help."

The teacher straightened up. "It's up to you. But it is a class project. And everyone has to participate."

Gretchen began randomly cutting out selections without even drawing them first. When she Scotch-taped them together the structure made no sense at all. Having no symmetry or purpose to its design, it looked more like a bad piece of modern sculpture than anything resembling a model home.

Mrs. Bixby had been watching her as she checked on the other children's creations. The hostile way Gretchen worked frightened her. Her little hands literally shook as she angrily forced one wall against another and taped them. Upon completion, Gretchen shoved it to a far corner of her desk, crossed her arms, and eyed the other students defensively, as if daring any of them to make a remark.

"All right, class," Mrs. Bixby announced, circling back to her desk. "Put your projects on the back counter by the sink. We'll pick up where we left off tomorrow. It's time for our spelling test."

The class groaned as they slowly gathered up their utensils and started putting them away.

All except Gretchen. She just sat at her desk and stared at her misshapen cardboard structure.

"Gretchen?" Mrs. Bixby raised her eyebrows and nodded toward the back counter. Gretchen didn't move. After the others were back at their seats, Mrs. Bixby approached. "Gretchen? Please put your project back with the others."

The room was suddenly quite still. Gretchen gripped the corners of her seat and didn't budge.

"I'll put it back for you," Mary volunteered, rising from her chair.

"Sit down, please," the teacher commanded. Mary reluctantly did as she was told. All eyes glued to Mrs. Bixby. "Did you hear me, Gretchen?"

A defiant, upturned face met the teacher's stern gaze.

"It's not right," Gretchen stated emphatically.

"What's not right?"

"That." She pointed at her project. A few in class giggled, but that ended abruptly when Mrs. Bixby's eyes swept over them.

Mary squeezed her hands between her thighs, wishing there was something she could do. She hated seeing her sister singled out like this, but Gretchen's stubbornness was forcing a reprimand. Why did she always have to put herself in these spots? Mary wondered. If only she would just let herself be happy for once. And quit making people so mad at her. Especially their new teacher.

"I know the first day is hard, Gretchen, but you still have to follow the rules like everyone else. Now put the . . ."

Gretchen's open palm flew out suddenly and smashed her project. Just as suddenly, she hopped out of her seat, swept up the squashed remains, and put them on the back counter.

Mrs. Bixby tried not to appear shocked. She didn't want to alienate the girl on her first day, but she had to maintain discipline or utter chaos would quickly reign supreme in a class full of fifth graders.

"I think we should have a little talk during recess," she stated before returning to the front of the class.

For the rest of the morning, Gretchen Foster refused to speak except when asked a direct question by her teacher.

A special executive meeting had been scheduled for ten o'clock in the conference room of the newer, more "modern" extension of the mill complex. Modern, for Hopkins Lumber, meant it had been built thirty-one years ago as a showcase office building for the late H. R. Hopkins, Jr. It was an odd, almost schizophrenic blend of Gothic, turn-of-the-century industrialist grandeur and early fifties post-war modern. The conference room took up most of the second floor and connected directly to the president's office. The style and decor were opulent to the point of gaudiness, a fitting symbol of the Hopkins line's need to feel aristocratic. To Barbra, it was merely another sign of an antiquated corporate philosophy, a grand but silly behemoth, a dinosaur too stupid to know it already had become extinct.

In a polite, diplomatic way, Barbra had expressed just those views to a silent, obviously distrustful group of executives at the meeting. Who was this intruder? What did she know about lumber? She could sense those questions in the continued rush of whispers and unsubtle nods. While weighing the reactions, Barbra was not surprised to see only one or two faces under fifty among the group.

As she continued to present her plan to revive the company, the shocked glances turned into grumbling objections. An immediate layoff of another ten percent of the work force? But we've already snipped away fifteen percent, cut back three shifts to two. We've never had the mill just sit idle, even for one shift. Idleness is a cardinal sin in the world of business. Listening to their pompous, backward ideas, how they equated the Bible and business in ridiculously trite analogies, Barbra had the strange feeling she suddenly had been transported back in time.

But she had done her research and argued her points knowledgeably. The key was to incorporate new, state-of-the-art technology. Computerize the mill. Import Japanese robotics capable of cutting more board feet per log, more precisely, with less waste, using only two-thirds of the original work force . . . retrained, of course.

Their grumbling turned into shouted objections. This town depends on Hopkins Lumber. The mill is its life blood. It's been that way for three generations. We can't just abandon our people like that.

"We don't abandon," Barbra interceded. "We retrain."

They were visibly shaken. It was clear they didn't like being told their ways were antiquated. Or that foreign technology was an indispensable key. Why, that was downright un-American!

Before the meeting turned into a shouting match,

Mr. H. R. Hopkins III intervened, asking the different section heads to discuss her plan with middle management and prepare short reports to be presented Wednesday morning.

Barbra returned to her office to sort out exactly what had transpired. As senior vice president, she had the only other office on the top floor. It was a dull, monstrous room that equated size with power and echoed with unwarranted class distinction. Barbra found its grandeur both ugly and embarrassing. But that was not why she felt so uncomfortable at her large, hand-carved mahogany desk. She was trying to decide whether it was really her modernization plan that had riled everyone at the meeting or if it was the fact that a woman had presented it. As she gazed out the twelve-foot-tall windows at the vast expanse of buildings, trucks, and piled lumber, she was dismayed to realize she hadn't felt quite this defensive about being a woman in years.

Except with Matt.

I'm the only woman executive here, she thought. And they hate it. She had sensed animosity the moment she had stood up to start the report.

Men! Barbra sighed heavily. Between Matt's obnoxious gifts yesterday and the blatant prejudices that had confronted her today, she had about had it with men. She slowly inhaled, pulling the loose reins of her emotions back before they ran wild and tried to think logically. She hadn't felt so ill at ease, so out of place in a business environment, since she had first taken the job of assistant personnel manager at Lexon's home office in San Diego fifteen years ago. Sexism was almost expected back then. Hell, the word hadn't even filtered into the vocabulary yet. But times supposedly had changed. At least in most places, she thought with growing frustration. But not here. Not in Canaan. Not at the lumber mill. All the old anger, the anger of the late sixties she thought she had purged a long time ago, came seeping back into her consciousness. She knew her plan was sound. And they knew it too. They just couldn't stand to admit it. Not to a woman, anyway.

H. R. Hopkins III knocked once, then opened the door to Barbra's office without waiting for a response. "Well, that should give the boys something to chew on for a while," He laughed, dragging his sizable bulk to a chair by her desk. Barbra watched him slowly lower his rotund body down into the seat, huffing as if it were a great strain, as though his body were a cumbersome prison in which he had found himself unfortunately trapped. He pulled out a cigar and held it out. "Do you mind?"

She did, but shook her head no.

"I hope you don't think it was inappropriate, my cutting the meeting short," he said, gnawing on the cigar. A line of saliva dripped from the corner of his thick blue lips onto his chin.

"It had ended before then, anyway," she stated. She wanted to say more, but decided it would be best to let him set the tone of this encounter. She had the strange feeling it was not going to go any better than the meeting had.

"They'll need time to hash over the details of your report. I'm afraid they're a little. . ." He slowly chewed the cigar around to the other side of his mouth. "Shall we say . . . old-fashioned?"

43

"Weren't copies of the report distributed last week? I sent them more than . . ."

He held a pudgy hand up and grinned. "We thought it best if we waited until you arrived. Let you present it in person. It is a bit radical, to say the least. Some of my boys don't take to change too easily."

Barbra did not like his use of the royal "we" or the patronizing way he called men over fifty "his boys." "Mr. Hopkins, time is of the essence. I've already been working out the deals with two Japanese firms and . . ."

"Mrs. Foster, please." With great effort, he pushed himself up out of the chair. "We, Hopkins, have been running this mill for three generations." He stepped around the desk and leaned on her chair. "I realize a talented girl like yourself, used to the corporate hustle of a multinational firm like Lexon, may be a little impatient with our ways, but . . ."

Barbra tried not to dwell on the insult of being called a girl as she listened to him tell her, again, how "his boys" would need time to adjust to her and her ways, as if she were a completely different species, totally alien from them. Cigar smoke bellowed around her as he crowded her chair.

She coughed. "Mr. Hopkins, I came here to do a job. Now if some of the personnel can't seem to . . ."

"Now. Now." He shook his head and bent down closer. "They'll come around. I just think you and I should work more closely together on this at first. To help them adjust."

Barbra didn't like the way this was going at all. Pulling her chair up toward her desk, she arose and tried to make her way around what she was beginning to consider a cigar-chomping cretin. Before she had taken two steps, she felt a hand pat her rump.

Too livid to speak, she turned and glared. His foolish grin disappeared abruptly.

"I think we should reassess exactly what our positions are, Mr. Hopkins," she stated in a metallic monotone, purposely slurring his name, as if addressing a servant. "First," Barbra pointed a finger in his face, "If you ever dare touch me again . . ." She swallowed and, staring icily, shook her head and dropped her hand. The point had been made. "Second, I don't give a damn about 'the boys' adjusting to me. Or you, for that matter. You fail to understand our positions. You are not my boss. Lexon is. Lexon sent me here to turn this prehistoric mill into a model of modern technological efficiency. They, as you know, are now the majority stockholders. Not you. You mortgaged yourself into a hole so deep even Lexon had trouble bailing you out. In the last two years, this mill hasn't had one quarter which showed a profit. If it wasn't for Lexon capital, you'd be shutting the place down in less than a year and you know it. Your personal resources ran dry six months ago. That's why you sold out to us. And that's why I'm here. My title as senior vice president is one of mere courtesy to you. Actually, I'm in charge. And you'd better understand that. You enjoyed today's little debacle because you hoped it might alienate me. Let the jackels nip at her heels to scare the poor little girl and put her in her place. So I'd feel I had to work through you in order to get anything done. Then when it got testy, when it looked like I wouldn't back down, like I might have to exert my full authority in the meeting, you cut it short. Why? Because you were scared. Scared this little girl wasn't going to take any shit. Scared I might spill the beans about who the real boss is here now. You couldn't stand that, could you, Mr. Hopkins?"

His red face paled. The cigar almost fell from his lips. "I just wanted to . . . help. Help you adjust, Mrs. Foster. They can be a tough group and I . . ."

"You are being kept, Mr. Hopkins, as a figurehead. Your debts have been paid off and you will retain your salary and your title until you retire. Those were the provisions entitled you in the contract. But please don't misread that. I run the show here. And if you don't like it, or if you, in any way, try to make things more difficult for me, I have the express permission of Lexon to let the mill go under. And you with it. If I can turn this place around, Lexon will be pleased. If I decide it's not worth the investment, that's fine, too. Lexon needs tax write-offs. They look at this mill as a no-lose deal. If it becomes profitable, well and good. If it doesn't, that's money in the bank, too."

Barbra stomped to the door and opened it. "Do we understand each other now?"

H. R. Hopkins III slinked past, nodding his bald head.

Pacing her large office, Barbra attempted to calm herself. It wasn't like her to make power plays. She was used to forging alliances when mutually satisfying benefits could be afforded each ally, a type of inner-office bonding, not by dictatorial mandates, especially

46

when its basic premise wasn't even true. Lexon had no inclinations to use Hopkins Lumber as a tax write-off. Her job was to modernize a typically cumbersome, failing lumber mill. If the experiment was successful and if the economy remained stagnant, there would be other mills willing to sell well below their potential worth. Then modernize and wait, hopefully not too long, for the revival of the building industry and the profits to come rolling in.

A defeated man was not the best of allies, but she was pretty sure Mr. Hopkins would back her now, if for no other reason than to save face. His position was too dear to him to risk such an embarrassing confrontation in front of "his boys." It was definitely a form of blackmail, she thought, but so what? He had showed his true colors.

And although he had turned her stomach, she needed him. If it was necessary to rule through fear in order to establish credibility, so be it. He obviously had wanted her to be discredited at the meeting, having purposely not prepared management by holding back her advance report. He had hoped the shock of her plan would unite his colleagues against her and reestablish him as their leader, the one with whom she would have to unite in order to function. It had been his game, but she had won.

Yet the victory held no satisfaction for her. It was not the way she had wanted to establish her working relationship in this firm. She now felt an underlying defensiveness that had to be breached. She did not need that as a constant in her work environment. She loved her work, the challenge, the tactics, the rewards of success, but suddenly that joy had been stolen. Her

47

victory would ring hollow as long as it continued to mire her love for her work.

But it wasn't just H. R. Hopkins III who caused her to feel so alienated and angry. Or the men at the meeting. Or even Matt. It was simply men in general. She had had it with them. She knew hers was a dangerous and unfair generalization, but logic had nothing to do with it. It was just how she felt.

And it scared her.

"Excuse me." A voice echoed in the vast expanse of her office. Barbra's eyes shot toward the door. The young executive smiled awkwardly when confronted with her quick scowl.

"Yes?" she asked curtly.

"I knocked twice, but . . ."

"Sorry, I was thinking." Barbra recognized the face. He was the one she had seen taking notes at the meeting, the one who kept nodding to himself, as if in agreement and not formulating an argument. Barbra found herself ready to jump down his throat, too, and fought to relax. "What can I do for you, Mr. . . .?" She cocked her head, waiting for a name.

"Striker," he said, approaching. "Michael Striker."

She nodded and they shook hands. He was in his mid-thirties, with a tough, pleasing face that seemed almost out of place in a suit and tie. He would make a good model for the rugged Marlboro man ads, she thought. Before she could assess him further, she was startled by a sudden burst of laughter as he glanced back at the closed door. If she hadn't been so upset, his laughter might easily have been contagious. Watching curiously, she almost smiled anyway. The bright, honest twinkle in his dark eyes, his broad grin

48

as he shook his head, clearly delighted by something, started to break her defenses.

"What's the joke?" she asked.

He shoved his big hands into his pants pockets, gazed at the floor, then met her eyes, openly searching. Barbra couldn't help but smile when he grinned again.

"I've been waiting years to hear something like that," he announced.

"I beg your pardon?"

"I came up to discuss a few ideas I had, relating to your report. I . . . I overhead your discussion with . . ." He tried to hold in his amusement, but couldn't. "It was fabulous. Putting Old Man Hopkins in his place like that. Absolutely great."

"And no one's business but his and mine," she injected, walking back to her desk. "I hope you understand that." What was Striker's game? she wondered. It would have been better office politics to pretend he hadn't heard, so why would he say that? Maybe he was kissing ass. Having discovered, by eavesdropping, that she was the real boss here, it might make sense.

"I'm not part of the rather extensive grapevine in the mill, I'm afraid." He followed her to her desk, pulling a chair along with him. "I'm not one of the inner circle, so to speak." His eyes danced, unhampered by her warning. "Don't even play golf."

"Golf?" she asked, puzzled.

"Can't rise into the upper echelon unless you play golf at the club with Old Man Hopkins. That's one of the basic rules."

Barbra shook her head, still not sure what to make

of him. Whatever his motives, she could tell he wasn't one to be easily intimidated. "Sit down, Mr. Striker. I believe you said you had a few ideas you wanted to discuss."

Drawing his chair closer, he slipped down agilely and leaned one arm on her desk. "I read your advance outline a week ago. It was . . ."

"I thought no one had seen a copy until today."

"Meg gave me a copy. Mr. Hopkins's secretary. Hell, she runs the show, as far as I'm concerned. Without her, he wouldn't know how to tie his own shoes."

"That's rather a harsh testament, don't you think? I can see why you're not part of, as you put it, the inner circle. What exactly is your position here, Mr. Striker?"

"I'm the head of shipping. Worked my way up from driving a truck when I was nineteen. I'm the only senior executive without a degree." He said it with a boyish sense of pride that touched Barbra. Either this guy is crazy or he knows exactly what he's doing, she decided. His initial introduction was risky, but he seemed so damn sure of himself.

Michael Striker knew he was being scrutinized, but had decided last week, after reading her report, that this woman was the one who was going to change things here and that was something he wanted to be an integral part of. She was the vessel sent out in this recessionary storm to rescue a sinking mill and he saw no reason not to row out and meet her halfway.

"I'll be perfectly honest, Mrs. Foster." He sat back and folded his hands. "This company is foundering. Has been for years. I was born and raised here. My friends and neighbors work here. I don't want to see it die. I came up from the ranks, so my allegiance is with them." He pointed at the window. "All those guys that need their jobs to feed their families. Management, here, is stagnant. As stagnant as Old Man Hopkins's bourbon-soaked mind. I realize what I'm saying is out of place, but I'm taking that chance. I hope what I say will be as confidential as what you told Mr. Hopkins. You need an ally. But not one based on fear. And I'm it. Because I need you, too."

"I can choose my own allies, thank you, Mr. Striker. Now why don't you quit the working-man's patriotism and tell me why you're really here."

"All right." He was beginning to wonder if he had made a crucial blunder, but the hand was dealt now and he had already bet his job. There was nothing more to lose.

"Perhaps I shouldn't have been so outspoken. But if things keep going the way they are, this company will fold in six months. Looking for a job in another lumber company would be impossible in times like this. My credentials are good here, but without a specific degree, moving to another industry would be difficult. So I decided I had nothing to lose by saying what I did. But it isn't just for me. And it isn't bullshit blue-collar patriotism. I meant what I said." He adjusted himself in the large leather chair and scratched his cheek. It was time to get down to business. "After I read your report, I got in contact with Petterson Brothers, a major shipping firm in Seattle. They do a lot of business with the Japanese. They even have some ties with Tashito, one of the electronics, high-tech firms you mention in your report. It seems Tashito has a rather large construction company as a subsidiary. They are planning to build two new plants. Both of which will have complete housing facilities for all their employees, as well as gymnasiums, a small theater, etc. What they're planning, in essence, is to erect two corporate towns to house their employees and keep them happy, contented, and close to the factory. All very paternal. And very Japanese. The point is, they'll need lumber. And we need their robotics. And Petterson Brothers would like to get the contract to ship both. The Tashito people already realize that Lexon, if your little experiment works, may begin to buy up and modernize a whole fleet of mills. One little mill isn't worth a damn to Lexon. So that's the only possible reason for your being here. Old Man Hopkins's ego may not let him see that, but they have. Assuming they are correct, they may be interested in forming a long-term alliance. At least that's what Petterson Brothers speculate. Lumber in exchange for technology. The Pacific Northwest has been shipping logs to the Japanese for years. But they always did their own cutting. To open up the cut-lumber trade with them would really be something. This type of exchange could be the key. And a lucrative one at that. For all involved. You can modernize mills all you want, but without a strong market, what's the point? This will give us that market, at least until the recession wanes and housing starts are up again in America."

Barbra was impressed. The man had done his homework. The idea was brilliantly simple and extremely intriguing. But she was still leery of Striker's intentions. He could definitely be a strong ally. Or a

52

powerful enemy. She just wasn't sure which it would be.

"Come on. Let's climb this one," Mary suggested.

Janet, a tiny, black-haired girl and her friend, Linda, readily agreed. Janet, the smallest person in the class, was a spelling wizard and always helped Mrs. Bixby correct papers. She had been elected the unofficial tutor of the fifth grade and was always willing to aid anyone with their reading assignments. Mary liked her immediately, having discovered they both shared a deep affection for books.

Linda, Janet's next door neighbor, was extremely tall and lanky. They went everywhere together, the Mutt and Jeff of the fifth grade, but were more than happy to adopt Mary into their small clan after she had helped them with their art projects.

They skipped together toward the largest jungle gym, a huge, square pyramid of dissecting bars. Mary halted momentarily. The others stopped and waited. A pretty, sad-eyed little girl in a frilly yellow dress was hovering nearby. She was in their class, too, but Mary's two new friends seemed more than willing to ignore her.

"You want to play with us?" Mary offered. "We're gonna climb to the top."

The girl barely gave her a second glance. "How childish," she muttered, sauntering away.

"La-dee-da," Linda parodied, trying to look ultra-sophisticated. "Little Miss Snotty Pants." Her buddy chuckled. Linda was the reigning queen of comedy in the fifth grade. To the girls in her class, she had no equal. Even Tommy Potts, the official class clown, couldn't match her joke for joke.

Mary watched the sad-eyed girl flirt with two sixth graders, then run off by herself, laughing.

"Don't worry about Becky," Janet said. "She thinks she's too good for everybody. Her daddy, Old Man Hopkins, owns the mill."

Linda donned her snobbish pose again. "This Christmas we went to Hawaii for two weeks. Daddy has a condo on the beach." She pointed a long finger under her chin and curtsied.

Janet burst out laughing. Mary wasn't quite sure what to make of it. Tugging her new friend closer, Janet explained. "Becky's a showoff. Always talking about money and new clothes and vacations. She doesn't really have any friends." Making a face, she added, "She likes boys. She's always flirting."

"Boys." Linda shook her head as if that said it all. Janet nodded in agreement.

Mary skirted to the top of the gym and waited for her new friends to join her. The clouds broke and the sun peeked down at her momentarily, then disappeared again. The metal bars were still moist, but the girls didn't care as they climbed up next to Mary. Playing in the winter rain was like playing in the snow to their counterparts in the Midwest or Northeast. Together, all three watched the swarm of children below, scurrying about in a dozen different directions.

When they first had been dismissed for recess, Mary had waited in the hall for Gretchen. Janet and Linda had found her there and told her it would probably take a while if Mrs. Bixby was having one of her famous little talks. All the kids liked Mrs. Bixby, but she wasn't one of those teachers you could take advantage of. Poor Gretchen was finding that out right now, Mary had thought sadly.

After peeking in the window from the playground to see how it was going, Mary had finally given in and trotted off with her new friends. She felt sorry for her sister, but what could she do? Gretchen was always getting in trouble like that. She did it to herself, time and time again, but it still made Mary sad. No one, not Mary, not other teachers, not even their mother, could make Gretchen behave if she didn't want to. There was just something in Gretchen that made her like that, Mary had decided years ago.

Gripping the top rung tightly, Mary curled her legs up over it, braced herself, and swung upside down, dangling with no hands. Janet gasped at her sudden acrobatics.

"I'd never do that," Linda announced, edging next to Mary. "I'd scrape my head on the ground."

They all laughed so hard Mary had to grip the bar with her hands to keep from dropping off. In her topsy-turvy position, she suddenly spied Gretchen heading toward the jungle gym.

"Get down from there!" Gretchen cried, screeching to a halt at the edge of the gym. "Mary. Quit it! You'll hurt me."

"I'm okay," Mary protested.

Gretchen tugged at the lower bars, her small body jerking furiously. "Mary. Don't!" Janet and Linda glanced at each other, stupefied. "Mary, you might hurt me. Get down!"

To the girls' surprise, Mary pulled herself up and scampered down the gym.

Gretchen peered up at the two girls staring at her oddly, then focused on her sister. Janet thought she was about to cry.

"You did that on purpose, didn't you?"

Mary reached out to her sister. "I was just playing. It's no big deal. Just an old jungle gym."

"You were trying to scare me," Gretchen accused. "Make me look like a baby in front of the others. You shouldn't be up there. You know what happened the last time."

"Gretchen, I was only . . ."

Her sister backed away. "You don't want anyone to like me." Yanking her backpack off her shoulders, she clutched it to her chest like a shield. "You did it on purpose. To make me scared. So I'd look stupid again."

Mary sadly watched her sister run away. Janet and Linda climbed down and stood beside her.

"How could you hurt her from up there?" Linda asked. "It'd be impossible."

"Yeah." Janet agreed. "She wasn't standing under you or anything." She touched her new friend's arm, suddenly worried by Mary's downcast gaze. "What did she mean by all that?"

Mary sighed. "Nothing. She didn't mean anything. She just worries about me. That's all."

There was no reason to tell them the truth.

No one had ever believed it before, Mary thought. Not even Mommy.

Gretchen opened her blue backpack and carefully extracted her new doll. Hitching the pack up over one shoulder, she held the doll in both arms like a newborn baby and drifted aimlessly along the fence, keeping as much distance as she could between herself and the other kids in the playground.

"They don't like me," she whispered, cuddling the doll. "They all think I'm weird. I could see the way those two girls looked at me." She rocked the doll slowly. "The whole class laughed at me this morning. Now Mary made me looked like a nerd. She knows what happens if either one of us gets hurt. It's just not fair. She's always swinging or jumping down hills and hurting us. She knows she shouldn't. I've told her. But she likes being mean like that. Teasing me just to make me look like a jerk."

Becky Hopkins pointed Gretchen out to the two boys she had flirted with earlier. She didn't like the twins. They were new and different and had stolen her spotlight. Because no one had ever seen twins before, except on TV, they were the talk of the school. But she knew better. Her daddy said their mother was "one of those big city bitches that dint' know her place." He had said other things too, dirty things that Becky didn't understand but that had made her mother blush. But his meaning was obvious. And if Daddy didn't like their mother, she saw no reason to like the twins.

"Look at her," Becky said. "She's talking to a doll."

"Geez, they do look exactly alike, don't they, Billy?" Both boys shook their heads in amazement, infuriating Becky even more.

"She's crazy, you know," Becky stated emphatically. "She couldn't do her art project, so she smashed it to pieces, right in front of Mrs. Bixby. Then she refused to talk to anyone. Check her out now." The boys obeyed her command. "She's chattering away like a monkey. Maybe she only knows how to talk to dolls."

The boys let that sink in for a moment. It was strange, they had to admit that, but what was the big deal? Why should Becky care one way or the other?

"Let's go over there." Becky took both their hands. "Come on. I want to hear what's she's saying."

Mary spotted the threesome circling around her sister, trapping her against the wire fence.

"Becky's boyfriends," Janet explained, noticing her concern. "She leads them around like she owns them."

Mary could see the frightened expression on her sister's face. What else can go wrong on our first day? Mary wondered, leading her friends toward the fence.

"Leave me alone," Gretchen snapped, shoving one of the boys in the chest. "I wasn't bothering you."

"She is nuts." Jack laughed, spinning his finger around his ear for emphasis.

Billy flipped his baseball back and forth in his hands. "What's the doll got to say for itself? Did it wet its pants?"

Becky broke into a forced guffaw. "Maybe her twin got all the brains."

Gretchen backed against the fence, using a puddle to separate them from her. "Why don't you go soak your heads in a toilet?" she quipped.

"Oooohhhh," Billy said, wiggling his hands like spiders. "A tough guy, huh?"

Jack grabbed the baseball from his cohort. "Wanna play catch?"

Gretchen turned her head and tried to ignore them.

Jack nodded for Becky to take a few steps back. "Here, catch." He chucked the ball as hard as he could into the puddle, splashing Gretchen's pants.

"She's not much of a ball player." Billy chuckled.

Becky was too busy gloating to notice the three girls running up behind her. Mary shoved the boys apart, leaped over the puddle, and swooped up the ball. She had seen the whole thing and knew who the real instigator was. She would have liked to slap the smug look off Becky's face, but had a better idea.

"Hey, Becky," Mary called. "Is this yours?"

Becky frowned uneasily. "That's Billy's. Give it back to him."

"Here. You give it to him." Mary tossed the muddy ball at Becky.

A stream of water splashed against her dress when she tried to block it. Becky stared down at the line of mud crossing her chest. Her mouth dropped open in shock.

"She's not much of a ball player either," Mary quoted.

"Why you . . . you . . ." Finding herself at a loss for words, Becky took off to find the teacher on duty. Without her there to prod them on, the two boys picked up the ball and left quietly.

"Alll . . . rrrright!" Linda exclaimed, slapping Mary on the back. "You really got her good."

"She deserved it." Mary put her arm around her sister. "Are you OK?" Gretchen said nothing as Mary bent down and flicked the thicker pieces of mud off her pants legs.

"Don't worry," Janet reassured her. "We'll tell the

59

teacher it was an accident. You were just tossing them back their ball."

"That was really something," Linda said. "Did you see the look on her snotty little face?" She exaggerated her imitation of the expression and the girls giggled.

All except Gretchen.

"Let's head over by the kickball game," Janet suggested.

Gretchen watched them go, but didn't follow. Mary was being tugged along in a flurry of congratulations, but pulled away when she noticed they had left Gretchen behind.

"Come on, Gretchen," she called.

Tucking the doll under her chin, Gretchen just stared.

Mary stared back. "Don't you want to come?"

"No," Gretchen barked. "Just go away, OK?"

Mary knew, by experience, there was no sense trying to convince her sister to join them if she didn't want to. "It's up to you," she sighed, trotting off to catch up with friends.

Once out of earshot, Gretchen sarcastically mimicked Linda. "Alll . . . rrrright. Got her good." She kicked a clump of mud into the puddle. "That was realllly something." She snorted angrily and bent down to pick up a rock from under the fence. "Big deal. I didn't ask her for help. She just did that to show off. Make me look like a big chicken or somethin'."

She began tapping the rock against the hollow metal fence post. Soon she was cracking the stone into the post with all her might. It rang out in a high-pitched wail, like the sound of a rock skipping across a frozen lake.

"Just because she knows I can't hurt her without hurting myself too, she thinks she can make a fool out of me anytime she wants."

Again, the rock cracked into the post, denting it.

"But you won't let her keep doing it, will you? You hate her just like me. You and I have the same feelings," she told the doll, snuggled against her cheek. "We're real twins, you and me. Whoever I hate, you hate. I can tell. I can feel it. The hate growing in you. My hate. That's why I know you're my real sister. You and me, we think alike. Together, we'll fix her good. I know it. I just know we will."

Chapter III

Barbra arrived home minutes after the school bus
had dropped off the children living on her street. The
sky was completely clear, a first since the Fosters had
moved there. Highland Road rose steeply into the
foothills and dead-ended in a cul-de-sac three houses
past Barbra's. The homes were surrounded by tall,
erect fir trees, sentinels of the past looming huge
above the densely packed, tropical foliage like giant
soldiers standing guard, protecting the land from the
civilized creatures that sought to tame it. Always wet
and glistening, the forest was a fitting place for
imaginations to run rampant with visions of fairies or
lurking demons in the farthest reaches of perennial
darkness.

But with the sun shining, Barbra found she had
never seen a more beautiful land. The massive, hard-
edged mountains twinkled silver-white above the snow
line, the brown-green trees rising near their peaks like
ragged coveralls hitched high onto their mammoth
shoulders. Having parked the car in the garage,
Barbra paused to drink in the full grandeur of the
landscape. Below, past the sharp, spearlike tips of the

fir trees in the ravine, she could see the whole valley, a winding expanse of lush green pastures, a few cows dotting the farthest fields, the wide Snohomish river twisting along the edge of the northern foothills, the small, matchbox town, the one, large, open park to the east along the banks of the dark, muddy river. In the northwest corner, the huge red mill pulsated in the brightness like a severed heart torn from the valley's trembling chest.

As soon as Barbra opened the front door, she heard the incessant cackle of the television.

"I thought we agreed? No TV before dinner during weekdays," she said, hanging her coat in the hall closet.

"I was just gonna watch it while I ate." Gretchen scooped a large knifeful of chunky peanut butter and slicked it across the top of her half-eaten banana.

"It's a gorgeous afternoon." Barbra peeked in the kitchen. Mary was busily consuming Fritos. "Junk Food Mary," she teased.

The little girl crinkled the bag up and put it back on the shelf. "I was just eating a little. Gretchen took the last banana."

"There's apples in the fridge."

"I'm not that hungry."

"Not after half a bag of Fritos," Gretchen announced, her face glued to the TV screen.

"I think you both should go out and play," Barbra suggested. "Meet some of the neighborhood kids."

"There's three girls in our class that live on Highline," Mary quickly added, hoping her mother had chosen to ignore Gretchen's accusation. "They were on the bus."

"Big deal." Gretchen turned up the set.

"Don't you want to make friends?" Barbra asked.

"No." Gretchen shoved the knife into the peanut butter jar and stuck it up on top of the TV next to the banana peel.

Barbra sat on the sofa behind her. She had hoped the move to a new environment would help. But it hadn't. Gretchen was still choosing to alienate herself from other kids just like she had in San Diego. "Why don't you want to make friends, honey?"

"Mary makes enough friends for both of us." Gretchen shifted onto her side, keeping her back to her mother. "Besides, I don't like the kids around here."

It hurt Barbra to hear the sadness in her daughter's voice. Gretchen had always been shy and introverted, but since the divorce, she had drawn even further into herself. Barbra bent forward and lightly squeezed Gretchen's shoulder.

"Don't you think you should try, honey?" she asking, trying not to be pushy. "We all need friends." Gretchen inched out of her mother's grasp.

"Let's check it out," Mary invoked, yanking her jacket off the kitchen table. "Come on, Gretchen. Let's go explore. There's a neat hill up at the dead end circle. One of the kids told me there was a horse trail there."

"I want to watch TV." Gretchen sat up and looked back over her shoulder as if the whole conversation was extremely annoying.

Barbra glanced from one twin to the other. She suddenly felt there was something wrong. "Did everything go all right in school? How was your first day?"

Gretchen's eyes snapped toward her sister. Before Mary could say a word, Gretchen had begun. "It was boring. But school's always boring. Other than that, nothing much happened."

Barbra noticed the surprised look on Mary's face as she put on her coat and headed for the sliding glass door that opened onto the back porch.

"I think you should go with her, Gretchen," Barbra cajoled. "It'll be fun."

"Do I have to?" Gretchen faced her mother, her eyes pleading.

Barbra gave up. "No. You don't have to. But either way, you still are going to turn off that tube. That's the rules."

Gretchen punched off the set. "Mary and I are going to our room to play house."

"No, I'm not," Mary said, half outside.

"I wasn't talking to you." Gretchen plucked her doll up off the chair and sat it next to her on the floor. "You want to play with me, don't you, Mary?" she asked it. "That's right. In our room. With your doll house."

It was Mary's doll house, but Gretchen was acting weird again so she decided not to argue the point. Closing the glass door behind her, she trooped off toward the road. Gretchen was the one who had had a bad day at school. If she didn't want to talk about it, that was up to her.

"Gretchen, are you all right?" Barbra asked quietly.

The girl straightened up. "Yeah. Why?"

"Nothing interesting happened in school?"

Gretchen cupped her hand over the doll's ear,

mumbled something incoherent, then put the doll's lips to her ear and pretended to listen.

"Gretchen, did anything . . ."

"Can I go to my room now?" She stood up, cradling the doll. "Mary's tired. She's had a rough day at school."

Barbra decided to go along with the role-reversal. "Why? What happened to her?"

Gretchen sauntered past, whispered to the doll, then turned and stared. "She says she'd rather not talk about it. Not with you, anyway."

Barbra had established an office in the smallest of the four bedrooms. Part of the reason she had accepted the job in Canaan was because she would be able to work at home after three, if there was nothing of dire importance at the mill. That was part of the deal. After having shuttled the children from one day-care center to another for the first nine years of their lives, Barbra felt it was important, to her as well as to them, to be home as soon as they got out of school. Since the divorce, Barbra had spent many long hours evaluating and reevaluating her priorities, especially her dual role as a business-woman and a mother.

She was obviously successful in her career, but was she a good mother? That was the question that had haunted her most over the last half year. The kindest answer she could give herself in all honesty, was a qualified yes, when she was around. But she hadn't been around nearly as much as she should have. She just couldn't deny that anymore. For years, she had put her career on at least as equal a level as her family.

The guilt that realization evoked, as a mother, was difficult to excuse.

But at least she was doing something about it. Whether it was too late was a question only time would answer.

Perhaps if the girls had grown up as normal, healthy ten-year-olds, the guilt wouldn't have been so difficult to bear. But they hadn't. At least not Gretchen. And if anything, she was getting worse.

Barbra found herself shuffling through a backlog of the mill's order sheets, unable to concentrate on their rather dismal figures. Her mind kept skipping to the meeting at work, and to Old Man Hopkins's lecherous innuendos, and to Michael Striker, then back to Gretchen's behavior problems and her final, cruel statement: "Not with you, anyway."

She knew exactly what her daughter had meant. When troubled, Gretchen had always sought the willing arms of her father. Always. There was no doubt the divorce had been especially traumatic for her. She had never made friends, never wanted to participate in anything that Barbra had planned for the girls. All she ever wanted was her father to hold her so she could shut out the rest of the world in his warm embrace. It had become one of the first major stumbling blocks in their marriage. Barbra thought Gretchen should be forced, for her own good, to break out of her self-imposed exile and learn to be a part of the world of children, of parties and games, but Matt hadn't seen it that way. He had thought a little shyness was an appropriate feminine attribute. Rather cute really, the way she always ran into his arms for comfort. The ensuing arguments that created always

67

made Barbra feel like she was the heavy, a cruel ogre in her daughter's eyes, for trying to make her do things that frightened her.

Barbra put the papers into a manila envelope and dropped them back in the file cabinet. She felt so laden with intangibles she knew there was no sense trying to work. Gazing above the clutter of business paraphernalia strewn about the desk, she began to inspect the line of photographs in their silver and gold frames. Highlights of a marriage now defunct. A couple of shots of the kids at different ages. Baby portraits. A lovely family pose in front of the ocean, the surf pounding up in a frozen curl of gray foam, the girls in their baggy little bikinis, their round tummies bulging, the blank space where Daddy had been carefully snipped out of the picture. She had started cutting him out of the pictures of them with friends before the twins were born, but had gotten carried away after they had had that terrible battle in court for custody and had completely eliminated his image, at least from her own collection.

The last photograph in the line was of her best friend, Sue Greening. They were sitting together, arms around each other, on the porch of a cabin in the Sierra Nevadas, a half-gallon jug of cheap rosé snugly resting between them, their glassy-eyed grins a testament to the other empty bottle sprawled at their feet.

Barbra's tightly drawn lips slowly curved into a smile. Sue Greening did that for her. She could always make her laugh. Skinny, redheaded Sue with the metal pin in her knee from a car accident. She used to make it snap at the worst times, just to see Barbra wince. Then she'd burst out laughing. It might not have been funny to anyone else, but to them it was hilarious. Even after two bad marriages and a son with diabetes, Sue Greening thought life too short and too full of wonder to stay sad for more than ten minutes at a time.

Before she knew it, Barbra was dialing her friend's number. The nervousness in her belly dissolved rapidly into giddy anticipation.

Just hearing her friend's voice say "Hello" was tranquilizing. One of the best home-spun remedies for what ails you, Barbra thought. After an initial how-are-the-kids, Barbra told her about Canaan, the mill, that morning's meeting, dirty old Mr. Hopkins, and finally Michael Striker.

"He stopped by the office again just as I was leaving," Barbra informed her. "Wanted to know if I felt like meeting him for a drink after work to talk some more about the project."

"So what'd you say?" Sue pressed.

"No," Barbra stated so matter-of-factly it made Sue chuckle.

"A handsome, intelligent man asks you out for an innocent little drink and you said no?"

"I had to get home. I wanted to be here when the kids arrived. It was their first day in school. You know that's one of the main reasons I took this job in Nowhere, Washington."

"Barbra, why did you call me?"

The question startled her. "I don't know. I was lonely. I wanted to . . ."

"That's the point," Sue injected.

"What's the point?"

"You were lonely. So you called me. An old friend.

Very safe, Barbra. Very safe, indeed."

"Are we playing therapist again, Sue?"

"Damn right, kid. Remember how you felt after your mother died?" There was a long pause. Barbra's father had died of a heart attack two years after she had graduated from college. She had been an only child, a welcomed but extremely late surprise for her parents at the age of forty. Twelve years later, when her own kids were two, her mother passed away in her sleep. The trauma of losing her last parent had torn Barbra from her roots. Her youth, her childhood, even a sense of innocence, had been ripped away that fateful morning.

"I just wish the kids could have known her better," Barbra sighed, pushing back the flood of memories.

"You shut yourself off for a long time, remember? Suddenly the marriage was all-important. It had to work no matter what. That's what you told me for years after that. Even when Matt started drinking more and not coming home, you still kept saying that. You held onto him for dear life. It was tearing you apart, but you refused to see Matt for what he was."

"Hey, Sue," Barbra said. "I was hoping for a little smile and sunshine from my buddy. Do we have to go over all this? It's over. We're divorced. And that's that."

"Is it?"

Barbra stared at the phone as if her questioning gaze could somehow transport itself across the wires. "What's the point, Sue?"

"How many dates have you had since the divorce?"

"Well . . . ah . . . none, really."

"And how often did you have sex with Matt in the

70

last year of your marriage?"

"Sue," Barbra moaned. "This is getting ridiculous. You're going around in circles and getting nowhere."

"Not once, right?"

"You know that as well as I do. So what?"

"It's not healthy, kid. You've shut yourself off from men. From sex. For too long a time now. You may be divorced, but Matt's ghost still haunts you. You're a good-looking lady. You're not the spinster type. You sure liked the proverbial roll in the sack before things got bad. So now you start a new life. A handsome young man, someone you attest you find somewhat intriguing, asked you to have a simple drink with him. And you said no. Come on, Barbra. I knew he's not the first handsome man to have asked you out since your separation. But you've refused them all."

"I was in the middle of a divorce, Sue. I just couldn't deal with it."

"And now?"

Barbra sighed. "I don't know."

"Barbra, you're my best friend. I love you. And I'm worried about you. So please don't think I'm being too pushy or out of line, but I think you're scared. Scared of men at this point. Did you ever think maybe you're hiding behind your career and your kids now, to protect yourself from what you need most? The way you hid behind your marriage after your mother died. Just because Matt was an immature, self-centered asshole doesn't mean they all are. You're too young, too healthy, too full of . . ."

Barbra sighed. "Vim and vigor?"

"Lust, honey. Lust."

"Sue, I only just met the guy. And he's a business

associate. And I'm not sure I trust him. Besides, it's not good to mix business with . . ."

"There's always an excuse, isn't there? If you want to find one. Personally, kid, I think it hurts the old libido, frazzles the nerves, not to get laid once in a while."

The bawdiness of the conversation increased during the next few minutes and then it was like old times again. Sue was never one to retain a sense of decorum when it came to discussing erotica in delightfully graphic detail. By the time she hung up Barbra was holding her aching belly, she had laughed so much.

But the blunt questions Sue had brought up earlier, questions Barbra had been trying to ask herself but kept stuffing back into the recesses of her consciousness lingered in her mind.

Was it true? she wondered. Was she really scared of men? Was she hiding?

"You really like this dollhouse, don't you, Mary?" Gretchen asked, setting the doll closer to the two-story miniature home. "It was your favorite toy two years ago."

Gretchen removed the five-inch mother doll from the master bedroom upstairs and flipped it across the room.

"I don't want her in our house," she said, gently picking the father statue up out of the dining room, its one hand bent up in a permanent gesture of either hello or good-bye, depending on the child's fancy. "Now that Daddy ate, he's tired and is gonna go to bed." She laid him on the blue plastic canopy bed.

Carefully she perused the inside of the house, then crossed her legs and leaned back on her hands, confident that all was well inside.

Outside the window, she could hear children's voices yelling and laughing. Then, above the chaotic din, her twin's voice rang out. Gretchen sneered, grabbed her doll, and stood up. She despised the fact that other kids liked her sister.

Gretchen suddenly cocked her head and looked questioningly into the doll's eyes.

"What?" she asked it, turning her ear toward the soft-sculptured mouth.

Although it had begun as a "pretend" game, Gretchen was beginning to believe the doll really could communicate with her. If she concentrated, emptied her mind of everything but the belief that the doll was a real, living creature, she could hear things she knew weren't just pretend. The more she concentrated, the clearer the words became, words she was no longer making up herself.

"Yeah, I could do that." The girl frowned, still listening intently. "But why? What will that do?"

Suddenly she pulled her head back and shook the doll as if it were a broken, static-ridden portable radio.

"Answer me!" she growled.

Again she shook it, then glued its face against her ear. After a while, she sighed in frustration and let the doll fall to her side.

"If you don't wanna tell me, fine. I'll do it anyway."

Gretchen placed the doll on Mary's dresser and picked up her twin's hairbrush.

"Geez, it's stuffed full with hair." She glanced

down at the doll. "How much do I need?" She quickly shrugged. "Still not talking, huh?"

Taking a fine-tooth plastic comb, Gretchen began to force it through the blond tangles in Mary's brush. Soon she had a wad of silky hair the size of a golf ball.

Scooping up the doll, she sat down on the corner of her bed and drew out the longer strands of her sister's hair. Smoothing out a lock of the doll's hair, she began to braid it with her sister's.

As she worked, the girl began to hum an odd, high-pitched tune. She had never heard the melody before and yet it seemed to pulsate within her, as if something or someone was singing along with her.

Sometimes, she could even hear the words of the song, but they were in a strange foreign tongue.

The little girl had no idea it was one of the sacred chants of Ometéotl. A prayer two thousands years older than herself.

It was the song of birth.

The Doll's song.

In the tongue of the Nahuas, the People of the Cranes, the true Aztecs, the chant song of gratitude to the child-mother for the gift of life.

But more than that, it called to the powers beyond, the powers of Ometéotl's children on earth, to fulfill the wish of the life-giver, the child-mother called Gretchen.

As Barbra finished washing the dinner dishes, she felt a pair of eyes watching her.

"Want me to dry the pans?" Gretchen asked, grabbing a towel.

Barbra tried not to sound surprised. "That'd be nice. Thank you." Gretchen never offered to help with anything. It was a battle just to get her to do her chores. Although Barbra truly wished this was an act of kindness, she couldn't help wondering what Gretchen's real motive was.

Gretchen stuck to her mother like a shadow after that. Walking into the living room, her daughter close to her heels, Barbra picked up the new *Time* magazine and was about to sit, when . . .

"Mom. Can we call Daddy? To thank him for our presents?"

So that was it.

"You remember the area code?"

"I know his new number by heart."

Barbra nodded, smiling. "I think it would be a good idea. Tell your sister. You both can call from my bedroom."

Gretchen dashed toward the hall, only to stop suddenly and turn. "Should I call collect?"

"No, honey. That's all right. Just call."

Barbra sat down and began thumbing through the magazine, but found herself too busy listening to the girls' voices in her room to read. Mary was trying to tell her father all about Canaan, but suddenly stopped in mid-sentence. Then Gretchen was talking. Barbra didn't have to be there to know what had occurred. Unable to control her excitement, Gretchen had literally ripped the phone out of her sister's hand. It happened every time they called Daddy.

Mary climbed over the arm of the sofa and plopped down onto the soft cushion by her mother. Barbra realized she would have liked to talk longer with her father but would never try to wrestle the phone away from Gretchen. She knew how much her father meant to her twin.

"How's Daddy?"

"OK, I guess." Mary rolled over onto her belly and played with a loose thread on the cushion.

"I hate school," they both heard Gretchen state emphatically. Mary's face jerked up.

Gretchen had moved the phone to the bottom of the bed and was standing in the doorway shouting down the hall. "The teacher picked on me, Daddy. She made the other kids laugh at me. Even Mary laughed."

"I did not," Mary said, slamming her feet against the arm of the sofa.

"And some boys splashed mud on me." Her voice grew louder. "I hate it here, Daddy. I do. I wish I was there with you. I love you so much, Daddy. It's no fun here without you."

Barbra's head slowly bowed, her eyes blankly fixed on the magazine. Mary huffed angrily, knowing what her sister was trying to do. It wasn't the first time. She could picture Gretchen's face all twisted up into that nasty little gloat of hers. Mary could forgive her sister for most things. After all, they were twins. And she loved her, as hard as that could be at times. But not this. This was pure meanness.

"Mom?" Gretchen called. "Daddy wants to speak to you."

Mary bolted off the sofa in time to catch the smirk on Gretchen's face as she handed her mother the phone. Tapping her fingers on the wall, Mary waited for her sister to walk by, then followed. "That was really gross, Gretchen."

"What was?" Gretchen asked casually.

"You know what." Mary trailed her to the TV. "You said that stuff just to hurt Mommy."

"What stuff?" Gretchen turned the channels absentmindedly.

Mary's little hands balled into fists. Her sister's catty indifference increased her rage, but there was no use trying to discuss it now. Gretchen was not about to admit anything. Mary darted down the hall and stood outside her mother's room.

"What do you mean?" Barbra snarled defensively.

Mary leaned against the doorway and peeked sadly at the bed. They're gonna start fighting again, she thought. Mom's already starting to pace.

"I didn't know anything about it, Matt. Neither of them told me." Barbra stopped pacing. Her hand squeezed the phone until the knuckles whitened. "Oh? And I suppose you could handle it better?"

Mary could hear the fast, angry blur of accusations flooding into the receiver. Twice Barbra tried to get a word in but failed. Then Mary felt her sister beside her, listening, too.

"If the court had agreed with that crap, you would have gotten custody. But they didn't. And neither do I." Barbra stopped for a moment, but cut Matt's next statement short. "You're the one who made it worse. It wasn't me that kept spoiling her, letting her get away with murder." Barbra froze, her back to the girls. "Hell, Matt, you can't deny it. Look at the presents you just sent, for God's sake. A little disparity in my opinion, Matt." She paused. "Well, if things are so tight, how could you afford a one-hundred-thirty-dollar doll in the first place? You're full of shit, Matt." A sudden outburst forced Barbra to hold the phone away, then she started in again. "Damn it, Matt, you haven't sent one fucking support check. Not one. But you blow the wad on a stupid doll. Sure she has special problems. Yes, Matt. I understand that. They both need love, Matt." Suddenly Barbra sat down on the edge of the bed. "They cut your territory again. What did you . . ." Another pause. "Oh, Matt. I'm sorry." The twins could hear their father's voice again. Barbra shot up off the bed. "That's fine with me. You don't deserve pity anymore. You did it to yourself, Matt. Oh, you think so, huh? The judge knew how much we both made when he decided on payments. I'd better see a check soon or you can forget having the twins down there for Easter." With that, Barbra slammed the phone down.

"You can't do that," Gretchen cried, kicking the open door against the wall. "I want to see Daddy. I want to see Daddy."

Barbra was in no mood for another tantrum. She had just gone through one with Matt.

"You'll see Daddy, honey. Don't worry. I was just making a point."

"You don't want us to see him. You hate him. And you hate me, too, because he loves me."

"I love you too, honey." Barbra tried to pull Gretchen into her embrace, but the girl fought her way free.

"Only Daddy loves me!" she screamed. "Just Daddy!"

"Honey, you know that's not true."

"It is!" Gretchen elbowed her way past Mary and

ran into the living room. "It is! It is! It is!"

Barbra hurried after her and Mary followed reluctantly. She had had it with her sister's games.

"You'll never let us see him again," Gretchen yelled, kicking the sofa. "Never!"

"Gretchen, that's not so. Now quit this screaming so we can talk."

"It is so." Gretchen spun around, smashing a sculptured china lamp with her fist. It shattered on the rug. As if running in place, she began to stomp on the cloth shade.

"That's enough of that!" Barbra scolded, clutching her daughter's wrists and pulling her toward her. "Gretchen, I want you to see your father. I know how much you love him. We all love each other. I just . . ."

"No! No you don't!" Gretchen tugged desperately, but couldn't break free. Her foot shot out and Barbra felt a sudden pain erupt in her skin.

"That's it." Barbra swept her daughter up and carried her, dangling upside down, to the nearest chair. "You've gone too far, Gretchen. You don't kick me or anyone else. Ever!"

Gretchen suddenly found herself helplessly draped, belly down, over her mother's knees.

"Mommy, don't!" Mary cried, tugging the arm of the chair. "Please don't spank her, Mommy. Please."

"She's got to learn. Now don't interfere, Mary. I have to do this."

Mary backed away, trembling. Tears streamed down her cheeks. "Please, Mommy, don't."

As soon as Barbra's hand smacked against Gretchen's rump, both twins cried out simultaneously.

With each successive smack, Mary felt the pain

shoot through her own buttocks as if she were the one being spanked.

When it was over, Barbra dragged Gretchen by the arm to her room. Her howls of protest echoed through the entire house.

"Now you stay in there until you're ready to apologize. And no radio. And no toys. You're to sit on that bed and think. And that's all. Your behavior is intolerable. You'd better think long and hard, young lady."

Mary was standing by the broken lamp, rubbing her behind, when Barbra returned.

"I'm sorry it upset you, honey," Barbra said. Mary clasped her around the waist. "I hate having to do that. God, I hate it. But this time she went too far. You can understand that, can't you, Mary?"

"You shouldn't spank her like that," Mary whimpered, squeezing herself against her mother. "It hurts me so much."

"It hurts me even more to do it," Barbra comforted, crouching down toward her daughter.

"I don't mean like that, Mommy," Mary sighed. "I mean it hurts me. Really hurts me, too."

"I do understand." Barbra gently clasped Mary's face against her cheek. "I love her, too. But I had to do it."

Mary saw the pain in her mother's eyes, but knew she didn't really understand at all.

No one did.

Except Gretchen.

"I'll stay in here for the rest of my life," Gretchen

told the doll, propping it up against the pillows on her head. "I'll never apologize. I'd rather die. Starve to death right here on the bed."

Gretchen heard her sister talking to their mother and yanked the doll up angrily.

"Poor Mary," she sneered. "We don't want to hurt Mommy's little Helper, do we?"

Holding it around the neck, Gretchen punched it in the stomach.

"That's for you, Mary, you little crybaby."

She punched it again.

"I hate you."

Then again.

"I hate you more than anything."

Suddenly Mary twisted out of her mother's arms and gasped.

Barbra straightened up. "What's wrong? What . . ."

"My stomach." Mary doubled over, her face contorted with pain. "It hurts awful."

"Too much emotional excitement after a big dinner," Barbra soothed, rubbing her back. "Just try and and relax. Does it hurt like cramps or does it . . ."

"It feels like . . ."

Mary gagged as if the wind had been kicked out of her.

"Mommy? Mommy, I think I'm . . . I'm gonna . . ."

Before she could finish, she threw up all over both of them.

Running frantically to get paper towels and a wet

rag, Barbra did not notice her other daughter watching, shocked, from the hallway, her curious eyes darting, back and forth, from her sister to the doll.

The Doll-Maker's old gray-white Winnebago squatted at the far south corner of the trailer camp, its symmetry slightly tilted to the east, as one wheel slowly sank, day by day, into the bank of the dry riverbed beside it. The camp had all the modern conveniences of a trailer park. There was water and electrical hookups for the trailers and even a game room, a large shack really, with a pool table, pin balls, and two card tables for the migrant workers' enjoyment after their twelve-hour shifts at the factory. Everyone knew that the owner of the factory was making a tremendous profit, but no one ever complained about their meager wages because the vast majority of the labor force were *pachos*, illegal aliens. The only satisfaction the workers had was the fact that even the owner, a legal Mexican immigrant, bowed to the whims of the Doll-Maker. Not because she sewed the finest dolls in the factory, but because he, too, knew the legend of the Doll-Maker. Although, for years, he had held only scorn for the foolish old Aztec legends, legends for dumb mountain Indians and senile old women, he no longer scoffed, for he had seen her magic with his own eyes.

As the red desert sun set over the Sierras, Victoria Martinez stood outside the rusty old trailer, counting what money she had, hoping it was enough not to insult the Doll-Maker's pride.

To ask a favor of the Doll-Maker, to request her

powers, was a frightening thing, not something to take lightly. If her daughter, Juana, was not so deathly sick, Victoria never would have considered coming to her this night.

Warily Victoria knocked at the aluminum door.

"Victoria, *entre*," the Doll-Maker's voice beckoned. "Do not be frightened. I am merely a mother, like yourself."

Victoria nervously pushed open the door and stepped up into the cabin of the Winnebago. It was dark inside. One gas lamp flickered above the propane stove. The interior was sparse and the strong smell of marijuana permeated the air. Dolls of every size and shape, some half-finished, some headless, some so old they looked like they would crumble into dust if touched were scattered everywhere.

"Sit down, *por favor*," the Doll-Maker said, pointing to the bench across the table from her.

Victoria meekly did as she was told. Looking around, bent-headed, she felt as if she were being scrutinized, perhaps even judged, by the gallery of mismatched dolls.

"You have come because of Juana?"

Victoria was not surprised the Doll-Maker knew that without being told. She had expected as much.

"Sí." Slowly she peered up at the massive old woman. "She is sick inside. And has the fever. For two days now, I have sat with her, but it only gets worse. I cannot call a gringo doctor, because my husband and I are *pochos*." Tears filled the woman's big, frightened eyes. "I cannot stand to see my *bebé* hurting so much. It breaks my heart. I have nowhere to turn. Please Holy Mother, Doll-Maker, I plead with you for help.

Save my baby!" Unable to hold it back any longer, Victoria began to weep loudly. As she did, she poured her money out on the table. "It is all we have. Until the day of payment, it is everything. Take it, please."

The old woman leaned back against the bench and scratched just below her overwhelming breasts. For a long time, nothing was said. Victoria watched the Doll-Maker puff on her stone pipe. Smoke circled around them and drifted up toward the dim yellow light.

"You come with humility? And without doubts?" the Doll-Maker asked suddenly, harshly.

The woman nodded, unable to meet the Doll-Maker's probing eyes. Staring down at the edge of the table, she spied three bulbous fingers pushing the money back toward her.

"Use that for food. And for good tea. And for tequila. It will help the child. I have no need for it."

Terrified that she had insulted this powerful woman of magic, Victoria stammered, "I am sorry. I did not mean to . . ."

"Enough. It was good you offered something as precious as the last of your money. For that, I will be honored to help."

Unable to speak, Victoria grabbed the old woman's hand and kissed it.

With great effort the Doll-Maker slid out from the table. "I have a doll," she said. Her voice was soft and soothing. She opened a cabinet next to the sink and took out a doll not much bigger than her hand. Its brown face was smudged with dirt and its straight black hair was tangled into two large wads. "Have you brought the things of your baby for me?" she asked, slipping back onto the bench with a grunt.

"*Sí.*" The young woman pulled the handkerchief out of the pocket of her thick-ruffled skirt. "I have a lock of her hair. And here, this handkerchief is wet with her tears. And also I have . . ."

"It is enough. I need no more," the Doll-Maker interrupted, scooping up the two articles. She tied the handkerchief like a toga around the naked, then knotted the human hair to both tangled clumps of dyed sheep's wool on the doll's head.

Victoria hoped it was just her imagination, but the interior of the trailer suddenly began to grow brighter. And with it, a surge of heat. Perspiration rolled down her ribs, making her blouse stick to her firm, milk-heavy breasts.

"Do you know of the ways of the Dolls? And of Ometéotl?" Without waiting for her answers, the old woman continued, her voice growing stronger, more virile, as the strange brightness increased. "All things of this earth are alive. And have souls. The deer. The snake. The great mountains and the rivers. The eagle and the smallest of stones. All are made of the same things. All have life, if only you know how to feel it. My dolls are made of the things of the earth, of the animals and the plants, of air and fire and water. All these things are within the dolls, given by Ometéotl. This is why the dolls have life. Yet the true life-spark, that which makes us move, makes children grow, the sun to rise, the rain to fall, is missing. That life-spark is here." The old woman gently tapped her breasts. "Inside. It is our heart. How we feel. How we love. Or hate. These things, the things of the heart, make us different from the living water, or stone. And it is this

85

thing of the heart that kindles the life-spark in the dolls. But only if one believes. That is why the dolls are for children. For it is the innocence of the child that gives true belief, and so lights the fire of life in the doll. And for this life-spark, the greatest gift of heaven or earth, the gift of emotions, the doll will give to the child the one thing that child wishes for more than anything else in the world. This is the exchange. Do you understand these things?"

The woman nodded again, too overcome to speak.

"Now that I have prepared this doll for your girl-child, its life is for her, as long as it wears the tear-cloth and the hair. Tell your Juana to love this doll. To hold it and comfort it. And to believe. Most of all, to believe. For this, the doll will take the disease from the child and keep it inside itself, if that is what the child wishes for most. Tomorrow bring back the doll and I will cleanse it. Then the disease will be gone. But from then on the doll must live with the child, for the child has become mother to the doll, the true giver of life and the doll will die without her."

The trailer began to dim again, until only the one lamp above the stove flickered in near darkness. The young woman genuflected as she stood up.

"*Gracias*," she whispered, taking the doll. "*Gracias*."

Suddenly the old woman's face contorted and she threw her hands across her eyes.

"Ayee!" she cried. "Something evil has touched my baby."

Victoria froze, horrified by the implication of her holy words. "I . . . I did not do anything. I came with belief as I was told. I . . . I did not . . ."

The woman groaned. "It is not of you I speak. Go. Quickly. Take care of your child."

The young woman leaped out the door and ran from the trailer.

"Mary?" The Doll-Maker's huge belly spasmed. "What is wrong? Why do you reflect such pain?"

The old woman rolled out from the table and doubled over.

"Ayy! She strikes her! She strikes my baby!"

Hugging her massive stomach, she began to hyperventilate from the sudden painful jolt.

Her tumultuous wails echoed out across the trailer camp into the flat desert night, stinging the ears of her people.

"My baby! Most beautiful of all . . . born to anger! And pain! Ayee! Ayee!"

Chapter IV

Eventually Gretchen Foster did emerge from her room to apologize. After that, the rest of the week passed smoothly. The only thing that bothered Barbra was Gretchen's insatiable need to have her new doll accompany her everywhere. But since it obviously gave her comfort, Barbra saw no reason to object.

Even in class, Gretchen kept the doll within arm's reach in her open backpack by the side of her desk. Although she continued to remain acutely quiet and removed, participating only when absolutely necessary, she was no longer disruptive.

In her thirty years as a teacher, Mrs. Bixby had never seen a child willfully retain such alienation. Try as she might, she could find no safe passageway through the twisted maze the girl had erected around herself. Every trick she had ever learned, and she had accumulated quite a bundle over thirty years to draw children out of their shells, had been met by cold, blank stares and deaf ears. Her pride as a professional and her deep love for children forced Mrs. Bixby to reach deeper and deeper into her bag of tricks. But after a week, she was beginning to become concerned about the child's mental and emotional stability. She decided to give Gretchen one more week. If there was no improvement by then, she would have to call Mrs. Foster and suggest special counseling.

It seemed especially sad because the girl's twin, Mary, was so open and sweet, so charmingly gregarious. She had had no trouble fitting right in and making friends with almost everyone in class.

Although in appearance they were the mirror image of each other, Mrs. Bixby discovered their personalities were as opposite as night and day. It was a strange notion, but she couldn't help wondering if somehow the angry barbarism and the more sublime spirituality rooted in man's consciousness had been split between the twins, leaving Gretchen the sole possessor of the darker, more paranoid, hateful side of man, and Mary, the more loving, kind, caring side. She just hoped her oversimplified conclusion would be proven wrong. She could imagine nothing more pitifully sad than a child without the ability to love.

Barbra, too, had made quite an impression in her first week at work, not all for the good either. As an amused Michael Striker had told her on Friday, she had single-handedly turned the old mill upside down. She had wasted no time instigating the initial phases of her plan, in which Striker was proving himself an invaluable asset. He knew every aspect of the mill, every nook and cranny. His was not a general overview, but a sharp, critical assessment of the company from the bottom up. Within three days, he had helped Barbra shear away another ten percent of the work force and had canceled the graveyard shift entirely. Those not on hourly wages found themselves voluntarily agreeing to a fifteen percent cut in salary, effective immediately. Althoug.1 there was a lot of complaining behind closed doors, upper management knew their jobs were under an expert's scrutiny and when Old Man Hopkins voted, without the slightest hesitation, for the pay cut, they knew they had no choice but to follow suit or risk possible termination. A little healthy paranoia, Barbra discovered, really got the corporate juices flowing.

The most comforting aspect of the mill's five-day upheaval was the fact that Barbra was beginning to enjoy her role. She was doing what she was good at and proving herself as able as always, as tough and as shrewd as any man would have been in the same position.

But that was only part of the reason she found her work so engrossing. Although it was still difficult for her to admit, she was beginning to trust someone of the opposite sex again . . . Striker. At first, her only ally had been her secretary, Mrs. Booker. But twice that week, in the privacy of Barbra's office, Mrs. Booker had told her how fervently Mr. Striker had stood against the old order (Mr. Hopkins's special cronies in the mill) to argue in favor of her plan. If, at some point in their many conversations, he had tried to slip in the fact that he had such heated arguments with his superiors, she would have suspected he was just trying to score points with his new boss . . . her. A possibility she had considered often after the first time he had approached her with his offer of alliance. But he never mentioned it. Not once. That, more than anything, had started to break down her emotional defenses.

He had risked his position, his job, to stand against the power structure on her behalf. If nothing else, at least she was convinced he believed in her plan.

And maybe, just maybe, in her as well.

The odd thing was, she kept finding herself more concerned with how he felt about her as a person than as a business associate. This added dimension to their relationship frightened her, yet somewhere deep in the recesses of her heart, it was also becoming powerfully exciting.

As Michael Striker closed her office door and approached her desk Tuesday morning, Barbra was startled to find herself engrossed, not by the prospect of their business coup, but by his tight-muscled thighs and broad, slightly sloping shoulders. She couldn't help thinking that he moved with the certain grace and confidence of an experienced warrior, a samurai primed for victory. The titillations that fantasy suddenly produced caused her to tremble momentarily. She hadn't experienced that kind of stimulation for a long time. Longer than she wanted to admit, even to herself. Although her more logical, protective side tried to force the strange tingling away, the woman, so long denied in her, fought back.

"We haven't exactly been making any friends lately," Michael Striker stated with a quick, wry smile.

"I seem to remember it was you who came to me. I didn't single you out as an accomplice," Barbra said, trying to find something to do with her hands.

"True. But I had no idea it was going to be a rerun of the *Poseidon Adventure*. You've shaken the old boys up so much they're walking on the ceilings around here."

Barbra chuckled. They had traveled to Seattle yesterday to meet with representatives from both Tashito and Petterson Brothers. An agreement had been reached and respective lawyers were now drawing up the contracts. The Japanese knew how to haggle percentage points, but the final product was definitely beneficial to all concerned. In exchange for technology and a crew of English-speaking specialists to accompany the computer-robotics, on Tashito's payroll of course, Hopkins Mill now had a lucrative contract to sell lumber to Japan. Petterson Brothers were the sole heir to all shipping agreements. Everyone, at least on paper, would benefit.

"I'm surprised the Tashito people went along with it so easily," Striker said, paging through his notes. "Those Japs are tough businessmen."

"But they're trained to look to the future. Look at the long-term benefits, not just the quick profit. That's something we don't seem to be willing to do as much of here." Barbra leaned back in her chair. The normal Monday morning meeting had been switched to Tuesday at eleven-thirty. She had wanted most of this morning to go over the details with Striker before presenting the new agreements. Only a few minutes were left before the meeting.

"I was still a little shocked. They must be betting on Lexon's willingness to buy more mills if their technology turns a profit here."

"A profit here they've guaranteed, Michael. They know what they're doing. They've set it up so we can't fail. They're willing to buy as much lumber as we can produce, but only after their new technology is installed. Thus, they create a shining example of the wonder of their products so Lexon will be sure to buy more mills. We have a great contract for our lumber, but will the other mills? Tashito will end up profitably exporting their high-tech products, but the other mills, if Lexon buys them, will have to wait until the recession abates and housing construction increases here, to sell their lumber.''

Striker shook his head, intrigued. "And the Rising Sun profits while we increase our trade deficit. Clever little bastards.''

Barbra smiled and nodded. "It's not completely one-sided. They are betting on the fact that our economy will turn around in a year or two. If it doesn't, Hopkins Lumber will profit nicely, but Lexon won't throw away needed capital on other mills when there is no market. I'll see to that. Most mills are too far in the red to come up with the money to modernize on their own. Of course they'll still have us as a showcase, so they won't really lose either way. They'll just wait.''

"Damn,'' Michael said, duly impressed. Not just by the Japanese, but by the brilliant, strategical mind of the beautiful woman sitting across from him.

"So.'' Barbra clasped her hands across her chest. "I think you should present our lucrative new agreements to the meeting. Even the old hard-liners will have to see the logic in our plan.'' A faint smile flickered across her face. "Then maybe you'll make friends again.''

"I appreciate the thought. But I really think you should.'' Sitting forward, he leaned his thick forearms on her desk. His dark eyes met hers with an honesty she had now begun to trust. "It's your concept. I just embellished it. You should take the credit. It will make it easier for you to function once you've won over more supporters. Most of the men here are suspicious of you and your new ideas, but they'll have to admit you're right now. And that's what is important."

Barbra was pleasantly surprised by his statement. She had thought he would have jumped at her offer. But she had another reason for his presenting their case. And now she was sure it was the right decision. "I want to make you head of the entire transition. Put you in charge of plant modernization. I thought your presenting this today would help squelch any opposition to that."

Michael Striker fumbled for his words. "I . . . I really don't . . ."

"Yes, you do," Barbra assured him. "You're the only one I'd trust with that position."

Striker grinned like a little boy. Running a hand through his hair, he sighed, still overwhelmed. Suddenly his eyes lit up and he laughed.

"What's so funny?"

"I still think you should present this, Barbra. I really do. Hell, I've already impressed the boss . . . you. No need to impress them. Whatever you say I'm sure will be the law now in this mill. After all, you've just saved their asses. They may not want to admit it, but they'll know it's true after the meeting today."

Barbra Foster would have gladly accepted, even gloated a little, over a compliment like that from anyone else, but it didn't feel right coming from Striker. She did not want her relationship with this man to be one of a general to an aide, a boss to her right-hand man. She wanted Michael to feel he was working with her as an equal partner, not segregated by corporate hierarchy. It startled her to realize just how much she wanted that. Even more startling was the fact that, again, it had nothing to do with business.

Michael Striker arose and fidgeted with his tie. He was awed by this woman. Yet there had been times in the last week when he had felt a strange and wonderful touching between them, an awkward tugging in his belly when their eyes met, as if somehow this powerful, self-assured woman actually needed him, even drew strength from him.

Or was it just foolish hoping? he wondered, knowing how captivated he had been from the moment they had met.

"Perhaps, ah . . ." Michael loosened his tie nervously. "After the meeting, we could,"—he forced himself to blurt it out, even though he had been rebuked once already—"maybe go celebrate our victory over the John Wayne coalition of Hopkins Mill. Drink to bringing this old place out of the mentality of the fifties and into the eighties."

His loss of confidence, the shyness in his quick, almost apologetic offer, moved Barbra. Suddenly, she felt as nervous as a teenager being asked out for the junior prom. It's strictly an offer for a drink by a business associate, she reminded herself. Happens all the time. So why do I feel like tiny cars are running a Grand Prix circuit in my stomach?

"I think we should," she heard herself agree.

* * *

"Billy?" Becky Hopkins called, waving through the mob of children in the playground. Although not particularly tall, Billy was built as solid as a tugboat. He was the star running back on Canaan's Pee-Wee football team. His best friend, Jack, was the quarterback. But this time, when Becky called, Jack did not join his buddy when he dashed over.

Becky put on her most forlorn look, the one that always broke her father's heart and got her what she wanted when all else failed. "Billy, why isn't Jack talking to me anymore?"

Billy kicked at a moist tuft of long grass. "You know why."

"No I don't. He's ignored me since last Thursday. And you haven't said more than ten words to me, either." Her pretty face pouted in sly flirtation. "I thought we were, well . . . good friends."

Billy eyed her suspiciously.

"Why are you looking at me like that?" she prodded.

"You really don't know?"

"No."

"Jack's dad got laid off at the mill. He spent the weekend at my house 'cause his dad's so mad he's been drinkin' again."

"I'm sorry. I didn't know."

"Your father owns the mill, Becky."

"But it wasn't his fault. It was that Mrs. Foster. The twins' mother. She's the one that's laying people off. My father's been really upset, too. Ever since she started working, he's been grumpy. Will hardly talk at all, even to me."

"But he's the boss."

Becky tossed her hands up innocently. "He says she's the one that's doing it. Then he gets so mad he won't talk."

"Geez." Billy slowly shook his head, letting that sink in.

"You gotta tell Jack for me. It's not my father's fault." Glancing past him at the swings, she pointed accusingly. "It's her mother's."

Gretchen Foster rocked up and back on the swing, the doll tucked onto her small lap.

"Let's go talk to him," Billy suggested. They jogged over to their hurt friend and Becky began explaining.

Gretchen had seen Becky's finger shoot toward her and watched the threesome anxiously. At first, they seemed to be arguing, but suddenly they all glanced at her. She knew, whatever the problem was, she was somehow responsible. Gretchen clutched her doll tightly and watched them approach.

Closing her eyes, she quietly pleaded with the doll. "Make them go away. Please?" When she peeked up through her long blond lashes, she saw they were almost upon her.

"I'm telling you, she's bonkers. She still won't talk in class. All she does is whisper to that silly doll." Becky had been priming the boys on the way over to make sure Jack's anger was directed securely in the right place. Becky grabbed both boys' arms. They stopped a few yards from the swings and huddled around her.

"I know how to make her talk. Grab her doll. That'll really get her good," she told them. "Remember, Jack, it was her mother that did it."

* * *

97

"There," Mary finished, backing away. Little Janet's radiant smile beamed back at her from the mirror in the girls' room.

"It looks beautiful," Janet cooed.

Linda anxiously tugged Mary's elbow. "Do mine now."

Mary peered up at her tall friend. "You're gonna have to bend down."

The three girls giggled. That morning, Barbra had braided Mary's hair in two wide loops tied back behind her ears. Her friends had thought it was absolutely gorgeous and had made her promise to do the same thing for them during recess. Linda crouched down in front of the sink, swept her hair back over her shoulders, and waited.

"Yours is kinda short," Mary told her. "But I think I could make two little loops, if the braids hold." After parting her hair into two equal sections, Mary divided one section into three thick strands.

"My mom told Daddy she thought your mom was pretty neat for tackling those . . ." Janet pondered momentarily. "Those cigar-chompers at the mill. That's what she called them. Daddy told her some of the guys said your mom's the real boss now. They said Old Man Hopkins is always agreein' with what she says, no matter what."

Linda glanced back. "Janet's dad owns a tavern in town. He knows everything that goes on in Canaan," she explained.

"I can't braid your hair if you keep moving around," Mary warned.

"Sorry." Linda faced the mirror stiffly.

"Well, isn't that what you said your dad said, too?" Janet inquired. "He works there. He should know."

Linda sighed, looking at Mary's reflection. She had heard her parents talking about it last night and had been wondering if she should tell Mary. She decided she'd better, even though it might upset her.

"I'm kinda worried for you, Mary," she began.

Her concerned gaze caught Mary's eyes in the mirror.

"How come?"

"He said some of the guys that got canned Thursday were pretty upset. They were kinda, well . . ."

"Kinda what?" Mary prodded.

"Kinda calling your mother names and stuff."

Janet scowled at her crouched friend. Her father had mentioned that too, but she didn't think Mary should know. Now that the cat was out of the bag, as her mother always said, Janet decided to tell Mary what else her father had said.

"My dad said some of the guys were drinking a whole lot more than usual at the bar this weekend. He had a hard time closing Saturday. There was a fight."

"Really?" Mary was beginning to become frightened.

"Just drunk talk mostly. That's what Daddy said."

"Who got in a fight?" Linda asked. "You didn't tell me that."

"Anyone's dad I know?" Mary inquired, no longer braiding, merely squeezing the strands of hair between her little fingers.

Janet shrugged. She had gone this far, why not tell the rest. "One of the guys who started it was Jack Stranton's dad."

"You mean Becky's beau?" Linda asked sarcastically. No one laughed.

"Yup." Janet put a hand on Mary's shoulder. "It's no big deal, really. Dad says those guys are always bitchin' about something. It's not the first fight Jack's dad has gotten into."

"I think they're all jealous," Mary stated, finishing the first braid. "It's just boy talk. Like the way boys brag in school about being so strong, and dumb things like that. They're all jealous of us girls. Even grown-ups."

" 'Cause we get better grades. Mrs. Bixby said that," Janet agreed.

"Girls have always been smarter than boys," Linda injected.

Janet giggled. "A lot cleaner, too."

With that, they all broke out into raucous, side-splitting laughter. It seemed to cleanse them of their earlier apprehension.

As the two boys circled around behind her, Gretchen sat up straight in the swing and fixed her eyes on Becky, her senses keenly aware of any sudden movements around her. When she heard the gritty slap of a sneaker in the sand close to her left foot, she instantly twisted around to her right.

Jack Stranton was waiting.

His long arms flashed out. Before Gretchen could tighten her grip, the doll had been ripped from her lap. She flew off the swing, but Jack leaped back under the A-framed steel poles.

"Does the little baby want her doll?" he teased in a

high, nasal whine.

Gretchen's jaw locked. Her eyes narrowed with rage.

"She can't talk, Jack," Billy called from behind her. Gretchen spun around. "Ooooh. I think she's mad."

"OK. We're sorry," Jack pretended. "Here. You can have your doll back." He held it out. Gretchen cautiously stepped forward. Waiting until she almost had it, he jumped sideways and tossed it over her head to Billy.

Gretchen was frantic. She couldn't stand the thought of their grubby little mitts touching her beautiful doll. The doll she was beginning to feel was her salvation. The doll her daddy had sent to make everything better. A living creature whose strange powers she was starting to believe could finally rid her of her nemesis.

"Give her back," she snarled. They began tossing it back and forth like a bean bag. "Give her back!"

"She can talk," Jack snickered.

Becky Hopkins kept her distance, reveling in the cruel game. The twins' mother had made life simply unbearable at home and this girl had to pay. Seeing Gretchen's tortured look, the utter despair in her moist eyes, merely heightened Becky's pleasure.

"Can't you catch it?" Billy challenged, stepping around the swings. As Gretchen inched toward him, he began twirling the doll over his head like a lasso.

"Stop it," Gretchen screamed, dashing at him. He side-armed it through the swings. Her eyes misted with tears, Gretchen hurled herself toward her doll.

By the time she saw the swing, it was too late.

She tried to leap over it, but stumbled. The hard metal seat caught her leg and she flipped, head over heels, into the sand. The steel hook connecting the chair to the swing ripped through her pants and tore the flesh on her upper thigh.

Lying facedown in the wet sand, her leg still twisted about the chain, Gretchen began to scream.

When they saw the blood dribbling down her leg, the boys froze. "Here. Here's your doll." Jack quickly flipped it on the ground next to her, then glanced at Billy. They were going to get it for sure, now.

"Let's split," Billy yelled.

As they tore off across the playground, Becky Hopkins sauntered away in the opposite direction, as innocent as the day she was born.

"I've got two blue ribbons." Linda reached into her jacket pocket. Mary had just finished with the second braid. "Could you tie them up with these?"

"Sure."

Before Mary could pick them off Linda's outstretched hand, her whole body went rigid.

A terrifying scream pierced the air.

Linda bolted up from her crouched position and stared at Mary in bewilderment.

"What's the matter?" Janet asked, as shaken by it as her neighbor.

"Gretchen," Mary mumbled, clutching her thigh.

"What about her?" Linda grabbed her new friend nervously.

Mary fell toward the sink. "My leg. My leg."

"What . . . What'd you do?" Linda asked.

"I didn't do anything," Mary whimpered, her face twisted in agony. "It's Gretchen. She hurt . . . us. My leg feels like it's burning."

Janet's startled eyes met Linda's, searching for an explanation.

"You were just standing here." Janet anxiously clutched Mary's other arm. "What happened?"

Linda gasped and stepped back from the sink, a hand covering her gaping mouth.

"Look." She pointed at Mary's foot, horrified.

A dark line of blood had soaked through Mary's yellow sock and was dripping down the side of her sneaker onto the floor.

By twelve:fifteen Barbra was only halfway through her presentation. At first, there had been a barrage of questions. Could the Japanese be trusted? What, exactly, was in it for them? Why were they being so generous? Barbra had felt like she was being interrogated by a group of unskilled detectives, each feeding off the others' questions, trying to discover some minuscule discrepancy in her statements.

But after the first twenty minutes, even the hardliners had quietly resigned themselves to the facts at hand and decided to keep their misjudgments to themselves. More than one had been made to feel foolish by Barbra's quick, solidly documented retorts.

"We'll need to begin a retraining program immediately," Barbra continued, relishing the absolute silence, save for the sporadic fizz of a lit match, knowing it meant at least tacit approval.

When the tall, oak doors of the huge conference

room opened, all heads turned in unison. Mrs. Booker, Barbra's secretary, smiled apprehensively and hurried in.

"Mrs. Foster, you have a call."

"Tell them to call back. I'm in the middle of a meeting," Barbra ordered, annoyed by the unwarranted interruption.

Mrs. Booker eased around Mr. Hopkins's chair. "I think you'd better take it," she said, not comfortable with the spotlight she suddenly found herself in.

Barbra put down her report. "Who is it?" She could tell Mrs. Booker didn't want to answer in front of the others and that worried her. But unless it was truly a dire emergency, she saw no reason to stop the meeting.

"It's . . ." Mrs. Booker leaned closer and continued in a partial whisper. "It's your girls."

Barbra's stomach knotted. "What happened? Are they all right?"

"There was an accident at school. It's nothing serious, but the nurse did say for you to come right away."

"If you'll excuse me?" Barbra scanned the room. "Mr. Striker, why don't you finish for me? You know the layout as well as I do."

Barbra followed Mrs. Booker out of the room. As she was closing the doors, she heard, "Are we running a nursery school here or a mill, for God's sake."

Her cheeks flushed crimson. Of all the obnoxious . . .

"Gentlemen," Michael Striker barked, interrupting the off-handed flurry of laughter. "I'm sure we're all mature enough to ignore such macho bullshit and get back down to business."

Barbra slammed the massive doors, causing the majority of people in the meeting to snap off their seats.

You tell 'em, Michael, she thought to herself.

If she wasn't completely sure she could trust Michael before, she was now.

The school nurse, Pamela White, met Barbra in the hall. "Could we talk for a minute?"

"What happened? Are they . . ."

"They're fine, Mrs. Foster. It's nothing that serious. Gretchen tripped over a swing and cut herself. I've cleaned and bandaged it."

"But I was told both of them had . . ."

"That's what I'd like to talk to you about." The nurse quickly explained the details of Gretchen's accident. Seeing the anger building in Barbra, she finished with: "The boys have been sent to the principal and will be dealt with appropriately, I assure you."

"I certainly hope so. This wasn't the first time Gretchen was picked on by those boys." Barbra hitched the strap of her purse back up onto her shoulder.

"So I've heard," Pamela admitted. "It won't happen again, Mrs. Foster. Our principal, Mr. Blake, can be tough when he has to."

"So may I see my children now, please?" The apprehensive look on the nurse's face troubled Barbra. As of yet, nothing had been said about Mary. Before she could ask why, Pamela White began again.

"Your other daughter, Mary cut her leg, too. To be truthful, it's rather baffling. She was with two girls in the bathroom. They brought her to my office right after the teacher on playground duty had brought in Gretchen." She paused momentarily to catch Barbra's full attention. "Mrs. Foster, the twins' wounds are identical. What's even stranger is the girls with Mary said she didn't fall down or brush against anything sharp. They said she was just standing there when suddenly she screamed and called for her sister. As if somehow she knew her sister had been hurt. They both agreed there was no way Mary could have cut herself like that. And, although she cut her leg, her pants aren't torn. I can't imagine how she could have done it without ripping her pants, at least slightly. Has Mary cut herself recently on her upper thigh? Perhaps yesterday or the day before?"

"No." Barbra gripped her purse tightly. "I'm sure I would have known if she had."

The nurse crossed her arms, looked down the hall, then back at Barbra. "Mrs. Foster, have the twins . . ." How could she put it? "Has anything like this ever happened before?"

"Anything like what?" Barbra asked.

"Like having identical accidents of one kind of another?"

"What are you trying to suggest, Miss . . ."

"White." The nurse smiled awkwardly. "I was just wondering if this could be some kind of sympathetic reaction on Mary's part. There seems to be no logical way in which she could have cut herself like that. Unless she already had the cut and accidentally tore off the scab. But you said she didn't, so . . ."

"I'm sure there's a logical explanation, Miss White. May I see my girls now?" Barbra's chilly tone startled the nurse. She reluctantly concurred. Going over it one more time as they headed for her office, Pamela White had to admit her deduction did seem far-fetched, but after reviewing the puzzling circumstances again, she still couldn't find an alternative answer.

As soon as the nurse opened the door, Gretchen spotted her mother and started crying again. Only seconds before, she had been laughing with her sister because they were going to get to go home for the afternoon.

"It's all right, honey," Barbra soothed. "I'm here now."

Gretchen threw herself into her mother's arms.

Mary shook her head, appalled by the silly act. Her sister was just trying to get attention. "It doesn't hurt that much, Gretchen," she scoffed. "It hurt us a lot more that time when I needed stitches."

The nurse's face snapped toward Mary. "What did you say?"

Mary glanced at her mother, then looked down at the floor.

"Mary?" Pamela tried to get her attention. "Why did you say, 'us'?"

The little girl plopped down off the examining table and wrapped herself in her mother's skirt. "Can we go home now?"

The nurse realized she was not going to get an answer and eyed Barbra suspiciously. "I think you should get Gretchen a tetanus shot," she informed her. "The chain was rusty. To be on the safe side, maybe Mary should get a shot, too, I . . . I guess."

Pamela White leaned into the hall and watched them leave, Barbra carrying Gretchen in her arms, Mary clinging to her mother's skirt.

Something was definitely wrong here, Miss White decided.

The more she thought about it, the more it frightened her.

Something strange had happened between those twins.

Something out of the realm of normal occurrences. Something . . .

She couldn't shake the clammy feeling that crawled over her flesh like a damp, chilling ocean breeze.

. . . Unnatural.

Chapter V

"Since I'm sick, can I have the little TV in here?" Gretchen asked in a babylike whimper.

"You're not sick," Mary objected. "You just got a cut. Same as me."

Gretchen looked imploringly at her mother. "But it hurts when I walk."

Gretchen was playing it for all it was worth, but if she needed the extra reassurance that she was loved and cared for, Barbra thought a little spoiling wouldn't hurt. She couldn't remember the last time Gretchen had reached out to her like this and was actually enjoying doting on her. She hoped it might be the basis for a closer, more intimate relationship, a relationship unhampered by the anger the girl felt toward her for divorcing her father. She tucked the covers around Gretchen's shoulders as she nestled into bed.

"You walked easily enough from the playground to the nurse's office," Mary continued. "I don't see why you have to stay in bed now." Mary stood up proudly. "I don't."

"It never hurts you as much." Gretchen wallowed in

her mother's concerned gaze. "I always hurt more. I'm more sensitive."

Barbra tried not to smile. Sensitivity had never been one of Gretchen's strong points. But as far as coping with pain, Gretchen was telling the truth. She had always had an exaggerated reaction to the slightest scrape or bump. It was as if even the most minor pain was more than she could bear.

After returning with the portable television and plugging it in, Barbra sat on the corner of the bed and brushed a blond curl from her daughter's forehead.

The whole scene annoyed Mary, but she decided to hold her tongue. If her sister wanted to act like a big baby again, that was up to her. It certainly wasn't the first time Gretchen had harped on a small wound to get all the attention.

"So, do you want to tell me why those boys took your doll in the first place?" Barbra inquired.

"I think Becky put 'em up to it." Gretchen hitched the pillows against the headboard and sat up.

"Becky?" Barbra looked from one twin to the other.

"Becky Hopkins," Mary explained. "She's a real snot."

"Does her father . . ."

"Yup." Mary had anticipated the question. "He owns the mill."

"Why would she do that?"

Gretchen shook her head. "I dunno."

"I do." Mary hopped on the bed by Gretchen's feet.

"Watch it," Gretchen cried.

"I didn't touch your leg." Mary crawled up next to Gretchen and lay on her side, one cheek propped in an open palm. Gretchen scowled at the intrusion of her sanctuary. The last thing she wanted was to share her mother's pity with her twin.

"Why did she?" Barbra asked again.

Mary repeated what her friends had told her in the girls' room about the fight in the tavern.

"And Jack's dad was just laid off at the mill?" Barbra asked when she had finished.

Mary nodded. "Becky doesn't like us because you're the boss now and not her dad. That's what Linda's dad says the guys at the mill think. First Jack was mad at Becky and wouldn't talk to her. Then they were friends again. I think she blamed you for the layoff so she could get him to pick on Gretchen for her."

Barbra was confused as well as startled. "Some of the people at the mill said that?"

"Linda's dad said it," Mary added. "He said Mr. Hopkins always is agreeing with you. So you must be the boss."

"My God, you know more about what's going on down there than I do." Barbra pieced all the fragments together. The picture it created was both ridiculous and a little frightening. "In other words, the two boys, after Becky egged them on, picked on Gretchen because of . . . of me?"

Mary considered that. "Sort of. Yeah."

Barbra slapped her knees. "I had no idea what I did at work would somehow trickle down into the grade school and affect you two. It's . . . it's ludicrous."

Gretchen cocked her head. "What's that mean?"

"It means it's just plain weird, that's all." She

patted Gretchen's shoulder. "But it's all over now. The boys will be punished and I'm sure they'll leave you alone after this."

Gretchen raised her eyebrows apprehensively. "I hope so."

"They will. Don't worry, honey." Barbra caressed her cheek and the girl smiled.

Seeing how forlorn her mother looked, Mary said, "Janet's mother thinks you're really neat, Mom."

"Why's that?"

" 'Cause you really showed the"—Mary searched for the words—"The cigar-chompers. That's what Janet said she called them."

Barbra grinned. She wasn't sure exactly what that meant, but remembered using the same description herself. "'And you heard all this while you were in the girls' room?"

"Yup." Mary twisted a long strand of hair around her finger and chewed on it.

"Before or after you cut yourself?"

She had been waiting for her mother to ask that and dreaded it. "Before, I . . . I think."

Barbra noticed Mary eyeing her sister. "How exactly did you cut yourself?"

Mary fumbled with the corner of the blanket, struggling for an answer she didn't have.

"She didn't cut herself, Mommy," Gretchen interceded. "I did. Then she felt it, too. Just like always."

"Gretchen, you know that's not true," Barbra admonished.

"It is true," Gretchen pleaded. "I always feel it when Mary hurts herself. And she feels it when . . ." She stopped when she saw she was losing her mother's

112

sympathy. She had thought Barbra would have to believe her this time. There was proof. Mary's identical wound. Her mother's disappointed frown convinced her it wasn't that simple. She glanced at her sister for support. "You tell her, Mary. You know it's true. Tell her."

Mary bowed her head, uncomfortably aware that at some point she would have to respond.

"What confused the nurse the most was how you could have cut yourself and not ripped your pants," Barbra coaxed impatiently.

Mary felt the pressure build in the ensuing pause. She had thought about nothing else since her mother had driven them home. But everything was so mixed up. Nothing made sense. They had never shared a physical wound before, just the pain. So this couldn't be like all the other times. She didn't remember scraping herself, but maybe she had. How else could it have happened?

Mary slowly rocked herself. She had to come up with something. And now. "I cut myself on . . . on the toilet paper holder when I stood up in the stall after I went to the bathroom." Her eyes rose hopefully toward her mother's. "Before I pulled up my pants. Maybe I was so busy thinking about how to braid hair I didn't even notice. Then Janet bumped me on the leg and Linda saw the blood and that's when I yelled. 'Cause it scared me. I didn't remember cutting myself and . . . and . . ."

Barbra turned to Gretchen. "See? There was an explanation. It didn't just happen."

"She just made that up," Gretchen argued.

"I didn't make it up. I kind of remember bumping

into the metal holder, now that I think about it."

Gretchen stared across the room at her panda bear.

"Well, that clears that up," Barbra proclaimed, rising from the bed.

When Mary lies, Mommy believes her, Gretchen thought crossly. *I tell the truth and she gets upset. It's not fair. Mommy was being nice and now Mary has made her think I'm a big liar.* Gretchen's jaw locked. *She never believes me anyway. She always sides with Mary.*

"You can watch TV all afternoon if you want, Gretchen." Barbra hoped that would appease her.

"I want my doll," Gretchen stated sullenly.

"Where is it?" Barbra fluffed the pillows under Gretchen's head. "Honey, listen. It's not good for you to think that what you just said is true. Remember what the doctor said that time Mary needed stitches and you were crying because you said your arm hurt, too? He called it a sympathetic reaction. Because you're so close to your sister. It wasn't real pain. It just scared you seeing Mary hurt and crying like that. I realize Mary cut herself in the same place you did and that is very unusual. But it's only coincidence. As you get older, you'll realize life is full of strange coincidences. But don't try to make something more out of it. I know you both have vivid imaginations and like to think, because you're twins, you share everything. But reality is reality. You have to face that without always making up stories like this. You're old enough to know better, honey."

When Barbra tried to kiss her on the forehead, Gretchen turned away.

"My doll's in my backpack in the kitchen," she

said to the wall.

As soon as Barbra left the room, Gretchen glared at her twin. "Why did you lie?"

Mary eased off her sister's bed. "I didn't lie. It happened that way."

"I know it didn't. And you know it, too."

"Then how did I get cut? It never happened like that before. We've both always felt it when one of us gets hurt, but the one who didn't have the accident never showed the bruises or the cuts. It was always just feelings before."

"You lied just to make Mommy happy. You've been doing that for years. Ever since we went to the doctor."

"I did not. I cut myself in the stall. I must of. I just don't remember it exactly."

"I know you don't believe that." Gretchen yanked the covers up over her head. "You know what really happened," she said in hiding. "You're just scared to say it—because you're Mommy's little helper."

Mary leaned back against her own bed, wishing her mother would return soon. "If Mommy says it's not true, then it's not true. And that's all there is to it." Mary pulled a thick strand of hair over her curled upper lip and held it like a mustache. "Besides, I thought we agreed not to talk about it anymore. You saw how the nurse looked at us today. Same way the nurse at our old school did. And that doctor. And our teachers."

"And Mommy," Gretchen injected.

"And Daddy, too."

"He did not. He never . . ."

"He agreed with the doctor, Gretchen. Same as

Mom. They all said it was just our imaginations. You know it makes Mommy mad when we say it isn't."

Gretchen tugged an arm out from under the covers and pointed accusingly. "Then you do admit you were lying."

Mary recoiled as if it were a deadly serpent ready to strike.

"No, I wasn't," she said unconvincingly. "I wasn't."

Ignoring her sister's half-hearted plea, Gretchen raised the covers higher over her head, forming a small tentlike enclosure.

Mary's right about one thing, she decided. We never have shown the physical signs of the other's accidents, just shared the pain before.

So why was it different this time?

Gretchen slowly smiled in the half-darkness of her sanctuary, remembering how her sister had suddenly, for no apparent reason, doubled over with cramps and vomited immediately after she had punched her doll's belly in anger last week. She couldn't help wondering if Mary's unaccounted-for wound today was somehow related to that previous incident.

The more she pondered the dilemma, the more certain she was that her doll really did have something to do with the sudden change in their relationship.

If Mary had cramps, I should have felt them too. I always did before. But I didn't feel anything that time. Not even a twinge of nausea, let alone pain.

How could that be?

Why is everything changing now?

It must be the doll, she concluded. What else could it be?

116

Visions of the power she would hold over her twin if she could perfect such a change began to consume her malicious mind.

It has to be true, she cried in her mind.

It has to be.

It just has to be.

"You've kept me in suspense long enough," Barbra said. "How did the meeting turn out?"

Michael Striker uncorked the bottle of wine and poured them each a glass. "This is one of Washington's finest Chardonnets. They have a lot of wonderful wineries in this state. Not as big as California's, but they're growing. Fantastic quality. Here." He handed her a glass. "See for yourself."

Barbra tasted it impatiently. "I'm no connoisseur, but it seems good. Now, how did the . . ."

"Good?" Michael pretended insult. "Delicate. Full-bodied. Rich. But . . . good?"

"Good means it doesn't taste like metallic grape juice or old books." Barbra took another sip. "Anything in between is good. That's the extent of my knowledge. I'm really not much of a wine drinker. Now, to get back to my original question."

Michael delicately lifted the bottle and gazed at it mournfully. " 'Tis a shame to mar such ambrosia with the lips of an infidel, an unbeliever."

Barbra slapped her palm on the kitchen counter. "I'm not about to sing praises for the local vino until you tell me how the meeting went. I've been waiting all afternoon."

"Fair shepherdess." He bowed ceremoniously. "Thy

117

flock is with thee."

"They voted our plan in?"

"Not one wolf in sheep's clothing among them." He grinned.

"It was unanimous?"

"Aye, there's the rub."

"Michael!" She stomped her foot. "A twentieth-century answer, please."

"It was unanimous." Michael held out his glass for a toast. "Here's to our new contract. May it feed the hungry mouths of Canaan."

"Down with the John Wayne Coalition." Barbra winked.

Having discovered, through Mr. Hopkins's secretary, Meg, that Barbra wouldn't be returning to work, Michael had called to ask how her children were. When she questioned him about the meeting, he reminded her that she had agreed to meet him for a drink and was holding her to her word. "No drinkie. No talkie," he had joked in a bad Japanese accent. She explained to him that she couldn't leave the twins home alone, but he had been adamant—"no drinkie. No talkie"—and had invited himself and his wine over to her house. Little did he suspect, when he had called, Barbra was sitting by the phone getting up the nerve to invite him over anyway.

"So would you like to meet the twins?" Barbra asked as they strolled into the living room.

"I'd love to." Michael wanted to add—if they're half as pretty and smart as their mother, I'm sure I'll be totally captivated—but didn't. He couldn't help wondering why he was so damn shy around Barbra. He certainly wasn't with other women.

"They're in their room." Barbra led him down the hall and opened their door. Gretchen was still in bed, her doll tucked under the covers next to her. Mary was sitting on the floor, rearranging the furniture in her dollhouse.

"Gretchen? Mary? This is Mr. Striker. He works with me at the mill."

Mary beamed up at him. "Hi."

Gretchen grunted a faint hello.

"Boy, that's some house you have there." Michael knelt next to Mary and examined each room, then stood up. "So you girls got to play hookey this afternoon, huh?" He peeked over his shoulder at Barbra. "All three of you."

"We both cut ourselves," Mary explained. "But Gretchen's hurts more than mine."

"It does, huh?" He walked up to the bed. Mary watched him stretch his neck like a curious turtle to get Gretchen's attention. "She looks pretty sick all right," he said. "Skin's starting to discolor." He waved Mary to his side. "See that? That kind of a yellowish tinge? That's the first sign, you know."

Gretchen peered at him suspiciously, then checked the skin on her arm. "First sign of what?"

He lowered his eyes fatalistically. "Hookey-itis. It can be fatal. I've seen them go—" he snapped his fingers—"like that."

Having been taken in by the act as much as her sister had, Mary chortled.

Gretchen buried her head under the pillows. A muted voice said, "Very funny."

Mary tagged along as they headed back into the living room. When Michael sat on the corner of the sofa, she plopped right down next to him. Barbra retrieved the wine from the refrigerator, refreshed their glasses, then retired to the chair on Michael's right. Mary snuggled closer, grinning every time he glanced down at her.

"Looks like I've got competition." Barbra laughed. She began circling the rim of her wineglass with her forefinger. The glass squeaked and Barbra put it back on the end table.

Mary studied her mother's behavior curiously, then looked at Mr. Striker again. Shifting his weight, he crossed his legs, then uncrossed them.

"What do you mean, Mom?" she asked, hoping to break the strange mood suddenly affecting both grown-ups.

"Nothing, honey." Barbra composed herself. "Mary, we're going to be talking business. It'll really be boring. So why don't you go back to your room and play?"

"I'm not bored."

Barbra eyed her daughter. "But you will be."

The way she said it assured Mary it was time to leave. "OK. If you two want to be alone."

"It's not that. It's just that we have to . . ."

Barbra cut her explanation short. Spying Mary's teasing half-smile, her eyes narrowed in a playful reprimand.

"Sometimes grown-ups are pretty weird, huh?" Michael said as the girl circled around the sofa. Mary nodded dramatically on her way out, wondering what it was that made adults act like children sometimes.

"I've got cold shrimp in the refrigerator. Care for some?" Barbra inquired, pushing up out of her chair.

120

"Sounds great."

When she returned, she sat on the sofa next to him and put the plate of shelled shrimp on the coffee table.

It didn't take long before the business conversation waned and Michael began talking about his marriage to his high school sweetheart while still in the army. It had lasted less than two years and was the main reason he had started working in the mill after being in the service.

"Just a couple of kids playing house," he summarized.

"That was what . . . over ten years ago?" Barbra calculated, suddenly feeling a little old. "What about now? Who's the lucky lady?"

He looked at his glass pensively, like a fortune-teller consumed by a dark vision in his crystal ball. When he spoke, his voice was soft and contemplative, as if tempered by wounds not yet healed. Barbra recognized the tone and cadence. She had often spoken of her divorce in the same manner.

"I lived with a woman for three years. Up until four months ago." Michael sighed painfully. "I wanted to get married. She didn't. One day I came home from work and she was gone. A few weeks later she called from Frisco. She said she couldn't face the good-byes." His lips stretched into a weak smile as he faced Barbra. "To make a long story short, she dumped me."

"Foolish wench." Barbra tried not to look pleased.

"Life can make fools of us all sometimes." He swept his glass up and extended it toward Barbra. "To the fools."

Barbra understood the feeling well. Rather than let the conversation die, she started to talk about the slow deterioration of her twenty-year marriage. She wanted him to know she understood. But more than that, she wanted him to understand her, too. When she had finished, she checked her watch.

"Must be getting over it," she concluded. "That only took ten minutes." She gazed into the clear brown eyes that had been watching her so intently. The accompanying silence quickly became embarrassing.

"Michael? Do you . . ." She tugged the hem of her skirt back over her knees. "Do you think I'm"—exhaling loudly—"I'm too cold and businesslike?" She erased that with a wave of her hand. "I mean, does it make me . . . unfeminine?"

He put down the shrimp he was about to eat. "I think your strength, your intelligence, your corporate savvy, the way you told off Old Man Hopkins, all enhance your appeal. But more than that, you've got a body men go to war over." There, he thought. I'm not that shy.

"But it ruined my marriage."

Michael's face lit up teasingly. "Your body?"

"No." Their laughter came as a relief. "My corporate savvy, as you put it."

"O-oh," he warned.

It caught her off guard and she drew back. "What?"

"You're doing the same thing I did. Blaming yourself for someone else's prejudices. You're a fantastic businesswoman. It's part of you. An integral part. If someone doesn't like it, they're refusing to see

122

you as a whole person. That's their fault. Not yours. Personally, I think your ex-husband was nuts."

Barbra touched his hand momentarily. "That's nice of you to say."

"It's true."

Suddenly they were both at a loss for words. Barbra arose and tucked in her blouse. Michael watched her breasts push against the thin material.

"I'd better get on my way," he said.

She walked him to the door.

"There's something else I'd like to ask you." She opened the front door slowly. The lamp at the end of the walkway glittered fuzzily through the light rain. Michael hesitated, enjoying the closeness of their bodies in the doorway. The clean fresh scent of her hair reminded him of a wet spring morning. "Did you tell anyone about what happened that day in the my office with Mr. Hopkins?"

"Of course I didn't." He took her shoulders. "Don't you trust me?"

"Surprisingly I guess I do." She quickly explained what Janet had told Mary about the rumors in the mill, to let him know why she had asked. "I just can't believe what happens at work could affect my children. Small town gossip sure gets around."

"Anyone with half a brain could tell you are the boss now, Barbra. You can see it in Old Man Hopkins. He isn't the same old bastard anymore. I really didn't utter a word, though."

Something in her eyes made him want to draw her to him and hold her. Instead, he traced her jawline with the tip of his finger.

"Mom, is that man gone yet?" Gretchen yelled

from her room. "I'm starved."

His hand fell back to his side. "I'll see you at work."

Smiling that little boy smile again, the one that had touched her heart the first day they had met, he stepped out into the rain.

Before Barbra had time to react, Mary had slammed her flat palm against the cards piled on the floor between them.

"Got ya again." She giggled.

They were playing Slap Jack.

"You have to keep your hand back," Barbra insisted. "You slap every card I throw."

"OK." Mary arched back. "What if we both keep our hands on our knee. That'd be fair."

"Then how do I flip the cards?"

Mary considered that. "Only the one not dealing has to."

Gretchen had been listening to Mary's squeals of delight for the last half hour. They were driving her crazy.

"Mommy?" she cried. "Come shut the door. Mary's making too much noise."

Barbra uncrossed her legs and stood up. "No looking at the cards," she warned.

Mary frowned. "She can close the door herself. She's not a cripple."

"I know, honey." Barbra patted the top of her head. "But we'll let her have her way just for today. OK?"

"Geez, we already brought her dinner in bed," Mary complained. "We're not her maids."

Barbra chuckled. "Wait till you become a mother. Then tell me about not being a maid."

Even with the door closed, Gretchen could still hear her sister's victory shouts. She yanked one of the pillows out from underneath her and wrapped it around her ears. It didn't help.

"You can't stand it either, can you?" She kicked off her covers and took one of the doll's short, stubby hands in hers. "Want me to tell you a story? Then we won't have to listen to,"—she tossed her thumb toward the door—"*that* anymore." Gretchen carefully fluffed out the ruffles on the doll's yellow dress. "Mary doesn't like this story, but Daddy used to tell it to us all the time. I know it all by heart. It's a true story." The doll's huge dark eyes, sunk behind the short sculptured nose, stared at her blankly. Gretchen grinned and pinched its cheek. "I'll pretend I'm Daddy. I'll be me, too, of course. You'll be Mary." Gretchen petted its hair sympathetically. "That's who you are now, you know. You're my sister, Mary. My twin. Daddy sent you to be my sister. He hates Mary and Mommy just like me."

Gretchen tucked in her chin and deepened her voice. "Now I'm Daddy."

Glancing up and to her right, she said, "Tell us about our being born, Daddy."

She pursed her lips and looked down, her voice deep again. "You two were certainly a surprise. Even Dr. Peterson didn't know Mommy was going to have twins. Shocked the heck out of him. He said he never heard two separate heartbeats and Mommy wasn't exceptionally big so it just didn't occur to him she could be carrying twins. To this day, he still talks

125

about it. But if you think he was surprised, you should have seen the look on my face."

Gretchen turned her head. "Who came first, Daddy? Who's the oldest?"

Pouting again, she said, "You were the first born, Gretchen. You took quite a while, though. Mommy was almost thirty and it wasn't an easy delivery."

"How come, Daddy?"

"Well." Gretchen clapped her hands on her knees the way her father always did. "The doctor called it: Para . . . bi . . . osis Syndrome. He said it was probably the reason he was never aware Mommy was going to have twins. Gretchen, you were born much bigger than Mary because you got most of Mommy's nourishment while you both were growing in her tummy. Poor little Mary wasn't getting fed well at all, I'm afraid."

" 'Cause I was dominant, right?"

"That's right, Gretchen. You sure were healthy and full of the devil. When the doctor tried to slap your behind, you gave him such a kick, he almost dropped you."

Gretchen twisted the doll's head toward her. "What about me, Daddy?"

She tucked in her chin again. "Well, I guess things didn't look too good there in the beginning."

Gretchen let go of the doll. "You almost died, Mary. Right, Daddy?"

"That's right. You were born anemic. Very sickly. Had to have a transfusion to save your life. That means you needed blood. It was touch and go for awhile. Dr. Peterson said he'd never seen a stranger case in his whole career. Although you're the same size now, when you were born you were barely half your sister's size."

Gretchen picked up the doll and set it in her lap. She was no longer pretending to be her father. The story was over. Her little fingers curled tightly around her doll's short arms. Tilting her head, her big blue eyes suddenly seemed as blank as the doll's.

When she spoke again, her voice trembled. "You weren't supposed to be born, Mary." The pretty curve of her mouth hardened. "It was just supposed to be me." Her hands dug into the doll's soft arms. "I was stronger and better fed inside Mommy because she didn't want you. But you came anyway. And you stole part of my life. You should have died, but you didn't. I wasn't supposed to have a twin. Even the doctor thought that."

Mary walked into the room. "What are you doing?"

"You weren't supposed to live," Gretchen hissed, holding the doll at arm's length. She slowly began to twist the doll's wrist in opposite directions, as if wringing out a wet towel. Her mouth cracked into a bestial sneer.

Suddenly the muscles in Mary's shoulders cramped into knots. The pain literally threw her back against the frame of the doorway.

"What's going on?" Barbra asked, coming to investigate.

Her mother's voice shook Gretchen from her trance. She tossed the doll on the floor.

Mary's agony ceased abruptly. "I got a cramp in both arms suddenly," she said.

Barbra glanced at Gretchen. "You didn't hurt your

sister again, did you?"

"No," Gretchen denied. "How could I? I'm in bed."

Barbra gently lifted Mary's chin. "You sure you're all right? You look awfully pale."

"Gretchen didn't hurt me," she admitted. "She was playing with her doll when I came in. Then I suddenly got cramps." She crossed her arms and rubbed both shoulders.

"It's almost bedtime. How would you both like some chocolate chip cookies and milk first?" Barbra asked, wishing she hadn't accused Gretchen like that.

"Will you bring me mine in bed?" Gretchen asked, snuggling against the pillows.

Barbra said she would and Mary trailed her into the kitchen.

Once alone, Gretchen quickly snatched her doll off the floor. "You did that, didn't you?"

The doll almost seemed to smile.

"You did do it." Gretchen grinned. "It was you that made Mary cut herself, the same as me, wasn't it? And you gave her cramps because I hit you."

Then it dawned on her. Her face quivered with triumph as she glanced out the door, listening for footsteps.

"If that's true"—the possibilities danced in her mind—"could you make her hurt for both of us? Even when I have the accident? Then I'd never hurt again."

She bit her lower lip excitedly and hugged the doll against her cheek. "If you can hurt Mary and not hurt me, you could do that, too, couldn't you? Then I . . . I could punish her for what she did to me. What she stole from me. I could do anything I wanted to her, without ever hurting myself."

She laid the doll on a pillow as if it were a golden crown or a hallowed charm to be worshipped.

"Oh, please," she pleaded eagerly. "Help me do that. I wish it more than anything in the world. I know you're alive, that you are my one true sister. I know you can help me. Please?"

Slowly she smoothed back the braided lock of Mary's hair entwined in the doll's.

"Make my wish come true, Mary. Oh, please make it come true."

"Mi bebé," the Doll-Maker moaned. The pale green light of the moon sketched the terrible agony on her wide trembling face. "My Mary . . . is sick. Sick with hate, the fury of an evil one. A child of darkness has taken my baby's loving soul and soiled it with cries of vengeance!"

Like a tidal wave rising up out of the ocean toward an unsuspecting vessel, the huge old woman slid off the small, vinyl-covered bench, her big fists pounding her skull in torment.

"It is not fair," she cried in the stillness of the trailer. "My best. My most lovely. And strongest of all. She could have given more love and warmth than all my other babies combined."

Again, she sensed the sudden sharp, twisting pain. The vision of the doll's arms being twisted, tortured to purposely hurt an innocent child, exploded in her mind.

All her dolls touched her at times, caressed her

great soul with the cherished warmth of their child-mothers during the times of second birth, when the child's emotional power, its love and special needs filled each new doll with life.

But never this! Her consciousness screamed.

Never with hate and loathing!

My doll's powers were not made for that!

"Ayee!" she howled.

Sinking down onto her knees, the woman prayed to Ometéotl to take the life-power, the wish-giving away from the most precious of all her creations.

But the evil one, the blond child whose face haunted her dreams, tearing apart her heart like a meat grinder, was too strong.

She knew, then, that the child's life-force had already entered the doll, was growing inside it like a killing vine.

And she could do nothing to stop it.

It was the child-mother's doll now.

Not hers.

And, like all her creations, the doll would fulfill the wishes of her life-giver.

For that was her duty, her promise to the child-mother for the gift of life.

Falling flat against the floor, her face pressed against the worn red rug, the Doll-Maker wept in disgrace.

Not for this! her soul cried out.

My dolls were not made for such evil as this!

Chapter VI

"Mom told you they wouldn't bother us anymore," Mary stated, hopping off the school bus. The damp winter wind lapped its chilly tongue across her face. She zipped her parka up to her chin.

The other children on Highline Road ran past them excitedly. It was Friday and the whole glorious weekend spread out before them like a great feast. A couple of their classmates waved, then rushed up the slow-curving hill toward their houses.

"I could see them watching me all week," Gretchen confessed. "They're up to something."

"But they kept their distance." Mary tugged her blue stocking cap down over her ears. "They don't want to have to stay after school all next week too." Mary looked at her sister with an air of authority. "Quit worrying. They've learned their lesson. Even Becky stays away from them now."

"She's still scared I might blame her, too." Setting her hands behind her, she jerked her pack up higher on her back. "And maybe I should. It would serve her right."

"It's too late now, Gretchen. Why don't you just let

it go and relax." As they neared the entrance to their driveway, Mary stopped and looped her arm through Gretchen's. "You've been nice to Mom all week. You're not going to get mad about tonight, are you? Mom's really looking forward to it."

Gretchen stared at her sister sullenly. "What'd she invite that man over again for, anyway. I don't like him. He made fun of me before."

"Gretchen, you promised Mom you'd be good about it. And he didn't make fun of you, he just made a joke. There's a difference. I don't know why you can't see that."

Ripping her arm free, Gretchen dashed up the driveway. "So?" she called back arrogantly.

Mary chased after her. "So Mommy likes him. Don't be a nerd. Don't wreck it."

"What do you mean—likes him?" When she spotted their mother's car in the garage, she halted. "She must have come home early today." Her button nose wrinkled with disdain. "To make herself all pretty."

Circling in front of her twin, Mary said, "What's wrong with that? Remember what she told us yesterday about men and women and being divorced and maybe having a boyfriend someday?"

"She doesn't need a boyfriend. She has Daddy," Gretchen insisted adamantly.

"She *had* Daddy, Gretchen. That's not the same anymore. She's lonely. You should understand that."

"She has us. Why is she lonely?"

Mary shook her head. "Didn't you listen to anything she said? It's a different kind of lonely. Men and women lonely. Not children lonely."

Pushing past her sister, Gretchen opened the front

door. Mary watched her disappear inside and sighed. She won't even try to understand, she thought. Mommy's been happier this week than she's been in months, but Gretchen doesn't care. She's gonna do something weird. I can just tell she's getting ready to have one of her little tantrums again.

Mary hurried into the house. Spying Gretchen outside her mother's bathroom, she shucked her boots, coat, and hat and quickly joined her. Somehow I've got to stop her, she decided, sadly remembering how many times she had said that and failed.

Barbra smiled down at her daughters as she pinned the last big roller in her hair.

"Why are you doing your hair again?" Gretchen asked, her question tainted with disgust. "You did that this morning."

"For our guest, honey." Barbra was too engrossed with her task to notice the antagonistic slur in Gretchen's tone.

"*Your* guest," Gretchen corrected.

She noticed it then. "OK, *my* guest."

"Mine, too," Mary injected.

"See?" Barbra nodded at Mary, but kept an uncertain watch on Gretchen. The little girl's jaw locked. Dropping her comb, Barbra turned to face her squarely, her hands on her hips. "I expect you to be polite and respectful, if nothing else, Gretchen."

Without the slightest hint of agreement, Gretchen spun around and stomped to her room. Barbra looked into the mirror apprehensively, praying the evening would go smoothly. To insure that, she decided to have another talk with Gretchen. She couldn't ask her to like Michael Striker. Hopefully that would come in

133

time. All she wanted, for now, was a modicum of understanding and a little tolerance. It didn't seem like much to ask. But with Gretchen, who could tell?

The dinner actually turned out better than Barbra had hoped. She had fed the twins before Michael arrived, then set the good silver and crystal in a beautiful table for two in the dining room. The meal was superb. Fresh Dungeness crab for an appetizer, accompanied by a cold bottle of Chablis from Italy. A very good buy for the price, Michael had said. The entreé was even better. Glazed cornish game hens, asparagus with a light cream sauce, and a salad, plus an expensive French Chardonnet. For dessert, Michael had brought a small bottle of B. and B.

The gentle patter of rain on the roof, the tall white candles flickering sensuously, soft classical music in the background, the lingering sweetness of the liqueur on her tongue, made Barbra feel absolutely heavenly. Everything was perfect, especially Michael Striker. He made her feel like the most beautiful, alluring woman in the world, a precious gem so magnificent he just couldn't take his eyes away.

When he offered her a second glass of B. and B., the tape ended and she heard the television in the living room. She was startled to discover it was almost eleven.

"I'd better send the twins off to bed." Rising from her chair was like waking up from a dream. Feeling light-headed, she said, "Maybe I should skip that second snifter of B. and B. and make some coffee."

Michael's eyes danced in the candlelight. "Did I tell you you looked ravishing?"

"Twice. But don't let that stop you."

Barbra paused before his chair, watching him drink in every inch of her without embarrassment. She was glad she had worn the pink gown without pinning its plunging neckline to accommodate a bra. She wanted to excite him. Needed to excite him. She had forgotten what it was like to be caressed by a man's gaze. It reawakened something inside her with an aching she could barely contain. Inhaling deeply, she walked out.

"If I was a sculptor, I'd kill to have you as my model," he called after her, watching her firm buttocks tighten and bob against the soft material like a fine, long-legged race horse moving into the gate.

"Damn," he muttered under his breath as he rose to follow her.

"Let's get ready for bed now," Barbra said, sitting sidesaddle on the arm of the big chair Gretchen was curled up in.

"Do we have to?" Mary asked.

"It's eleven o'clock."

"Can't we stay up another half hour?" Gretchen pleaded. "There's no school tomorrow."

Barbra smiled. "You've still got the other TV in your room. If you hurry, you can watch that for a while. OK?"

Mary jumped off the sofa and ran down the hall. "Come on, Gretchen. There's gonna be a scary show on."

Gretchen tucked herself deeper into the chair. "I want to watch TV in here. I don't want to watch the one in our bedroom. It's too small."

Barbra ruffled her daughter's hair. "You've been real good all evening, honey. And I'm grateful. But we're going to have coffee in here and listen to the stereo. So I'd really appreciate it if you . . ."

Gretchen bolted off the chair and sat down on the floor in front of the television. "Why can't I stay out here with you? I'll keep the TV way down."

Michael chuckled, remembering how he and his brother used to fight for every extra minute. He squatted next to Gretchen. "It's tough being a kid, isn't it?"

Gretchen glanced at him resentfully. "Daddy let me stay up late sometimes."

"I hated having to go to bed too," he said. "My brother and I always wanted to watch late night wrestling on Saturdays."

Gretchen leaned as far away from him as she could.

"What is it? My breath?" Michael asked. She didn't try to hide her disdain as she rolled onto her stomach to avoid him.

"Can't even get a little smile out of you," he said, patting her leg.

"Don't touch me," she cried, leaping to her feet. "You're not my daddy. You shouldn't be here."

Before Barbra could grab her, she had run out of the room.

Michael shrugged apologetically. "I'm sorry."

"It's not your fault," she assured him. "I'll go tuck them in."

A few minutes later, they were sitting on the sofa drinking coffee. The electric mood of the evening had dimmed, but the quiet, warm sense of shared intimacy remained.

Not wanting to dwell on the subject, Barbra briefly tried to explain Gretchen's outburst. She told him how close she and her father were and how hard

Gretchen had always been to handle.

"I think he actually relishes the fact that Gretchen has well . . . problems. He sees her as living proof of my inadequacies. Maybe that evens the score in his book."

"How's that?" Michael rested his arm across the top of the sofa behind her.

Barbra leaned back, her cheek against his wrist. "It's not worth explaining. It's history now."

"They say history repeats itself."

She lifted her head. "I don't think I could stand that."

There was something terribly vulnerable in the way she looked at him then. It made his heart skip a beat. His throat tightened as he drew her to him. She felt a sudden trembling in his touch as she raised her lips to meet his. His strong hand flattened against the small of her back and she arched, pressing against him with an urgency that took her breath away.

After the slow, delicate kiss, she said, "How old are you?"

The question seemed ill-timed until he thought about it. "Thirty-four. Why?"

"I'll be forty in three months."

Bending down, Michael pointed at the top of his skull. "See that. Right there. It's starting to thin. In a couple of years, I'll be as bald as my dad. Then people will look at us and think I'm the eldest." He grinned. "We'd be a perfect match."

"But . . ."

"But? But?" he balked, doing a comic imitation of Groucho Marx while turning her shoulders to examine her rump. "With a butt like that I'd marry six-hundred-year-old Methuselah, even if he was the wrong gender."

"It's about time you got up," Gretchen said when her mother sauntered into the kitchen. She was kneeling on her chair at the breakfast table. Her doll stood next to her on Mary's chair. Two hands of cards were spread on the table. The rest of the deck was stacked between them. New Wave music blared from her portable radio on the counter.

Barbra turned down the volume. "I can't take chain-saw rock this early in the morning."

Gretchen huffed. "Give me all your sixes," she said, scooping two cards from the doll's hand.

"Playing Go-Fish?" Barbra asked. Gretchen nodded. "A little one-sided, don't you think?"

Gretchen jerked her thumb across the table, too engrossed in her hand to look up. "She won the last two games."

Barbra chuckled while she stretched. "Where's Mary?"

"Playing cards with me."

Barbra gazed lazily out the triangled panes of glass in the upper half of the back door. "The other Mary."

"Oh." Gretchen put down her cards. "She went outside. I think she's playing with Nancy and some other kids."

Barbra opened the door and breathed the cold, damp winter air. The fog was so dense she could barely discern the dark shadows of the trees beyond the small lawn.

"Looks like Chicken Little's prophecy has finally

come true," she said, closing the door. "The sky has fallen."

After warming up last night's coffee, she joined her daughter at the table. Barbra always arose early on the weekends to be with the kids, but today she had slept in. The bed had seemed especially warm and cozy this morning and she had enjoyed lingering there, the memories of last night as her sole companion. She felt as if a light had been switched on inside her and was beaming out through every pore in her skin like the constellation globe she had loved as a girl. She used to spend hours alone in her room with the stars of the northern hemisphere twinkling on the ceiling.

"I think you should apologize to Michael the next time you see him," Barbra said suddenly.

Gretchen tossed her last three cards on the table. "She won again."

Barbra gripped her daughter's wrist firmly enough to convince her she was serious. "Did you hear me?"

"Yeah." Gretchen scooped the entire pile of cards up. "Does that mean he's gonna come over again?"

"I hope so, yes." Barbra's grip turned into a soft caress. "And I wish you'd accept that."

Gretchen stared at her mother. "Why?"

"Because it means a lot to me. Isn't that enough?"

"I guess. But . . ." Gretchen picked out the cards in the deck that were upside down and reversed them.

"But what?"

She tucked her elbows in against her ribs to keep her mother from touching her again. "But what about Daddy?"

Barbra warmed her hands around the coffee cup.

"Daddy and I are never going to get back together. It's over. For good. Forever. Can you understand that? We've gone over it often enough."

Gretchen sucked her lower lip between her teeth and looked out the window. A tear rolled down the side of her nose.

"Gretchen, I have to have my own life. I'm starting over. I need your cooperation. It isn't easy. For either of us. But someday a man might come into my life that I'll want to marry again. Someone I'll love. And who loves me. And who will love you, too. Even if that never happens, there are still going to be men in my life." Barbra smiled. "I hope. And you're going to have to accept that. Just like Mary has."

Gretchen slumped forward and rested her forehead on the edge of the table. Her thighs tightened around her little fists and the cards began to spill onto the floor as she wept.

"I caught her. Nancy's It now," one of the neighborhood girls announced. Shadows flickered through the mist as the children playing Hide-and-Seek returned to the starting tree where the horse trail met the cul-de-sac. They circled around Nancy.

"This fog makes it easy to hide," the youngest of the group commented.

"I got lost trying to get back here," another said.

"Let's say you only have to count to fifty. Not a hundred," Mary suggested. "Maybe we should have smaller boundaries, too."

They all agreed and quickly mapped out a new territory. Part of the woods was still included, but only to the fence where Nancy's parents kept their horses.

Leaning against the old Adler tree, Nancy covered her face and started counting. Like an exploding shrapnel, five children raced off in different directions. As Mary ran up the horse trail, she didn't see the two ghostly figures on bicycles watching from the deer path that connected Highline with Clove Road.

"That's her all right," Jack said, squinting through the fog.

"How can you tell?" Billy asked, resting his bike on its kickstand. "They both look alike."

Jack got off his bike, too. "It doesn't really matter, anyway. But I'm sure it's Gretchen."

Billy straddled his front tire and straightened out the handlebars. "Maybe we should just forget it. If I get in any more trouble, Dad's gonna ground me for sure."

"Ground you? Big fucking deal! At least your old man doesn't knock you around."

Billy peeked at Jack's eye. The swelling was almost gone, but it was still discolored.

Jack turned away. "We're only gonna pop her with a couple of mud balls. She'll never even see who did it. Not in this fog." He punched his friend's arm. "We won't get caught. Why worry about it? Don't you want to even the score for having to stay after school all week?"

"Sure. But . . ."

"Then let's go. We'll leave our bikes here. We can tear back to our road in two minutes. No one will ever know. Come on. We'd better hurry or we'll lose her."

Mary perused the small open field bordering the long white fence. The fog wasn't as thick in the higher

141

ground, but she still couldn't see the entire perimeter of the clearing.

She started to push aside a wet branch but suddenly clung to it. Someone was coming. She could hear the sound of boots gooshing in the mud somewhere behind her.

Frantically she searched the immediate vicinity. Over there. A big rock. As big as a car. Carefully avoiding the puddles, she zigzagged along the edge of the field until she was safely behind it, her back to the woods.

"Did you see where she went?" Jack asked. "I think she heard us."

"She's over there. See that boulder?"

Jack wiped the moisture from the fog off his forehead. "We could cut around through those trees and get behind her. It's perfect. After we pop her, we'll tear-ass along the fence. It'll be easy running and it goes almost all the way back up to our bikes."

Crouching like Indians, they began stalking their prey, carefully eluding the thick clumps of blackberry vines and their sharp thorns.

"See her?" Billy pointed between two fir trees.

Jack stretched to look over his head. "Yeah," he whispered. They bent into a huddle. "We'll move up, real slow, to that fallen tree. We can't miss from there."

"Should we make the mud balls here? It's a good spot." Billy sunk his hands into a puddle and excavated a slimy chunk of moist earth.

"OK." Jack waited until Billy was busy packing before he took the chestnut-sized stone out of his pocket and crusted it with mud.

142

"You ready?" Billy asked.

Jack nodded and led the way to the moss-covered log less than ten yards from the boulder.

Mary scanned the trees where the horse trail crossed into the clearing. She hadn't played Hide-and-Seek since she was at camp two summers ago and had been surprised when Nancy suggested it. She had thought they were a little old for the game and now decided she was right. It was really boring, just squatting there, waiting and watching. Besides, it was getting colder and the fog was turning into rain.

Might as well head back, she surmised. No one will find me here, anyway. Maybe Mommy's finally up and we could make pancakes.

Something brittle snapped to her left and she stood up to investigate.

All she saw was a streaking brown flash just before the two mud balls struck her. One thudded against her ribs. The other splattered above her right eye.

She lunged back against the cold, wet rock and covered her face. Everything was spinning. A wave of pain overwhelmed her sense of balance and her knees buckled.

Something hot streamed down between her fingers and over her right eye. Drawing her hands away, she saw all the blood and started screaming for her mother.

"You do understand, now, don't you?" Barbra asked, after Gretchen stopped crying.

"I guess so." Gretchen lied, wishing her mother would just go away and leave her alone with her sorrow.

"That's my girl." Barbra rubbed her daughter's back. "You know you're being real good about this. I'm really impressed."

Gretchen pretended to smile as she wiped the tears from her cheeks. "I'd better pick the cards up off the floor."

"I'll help." Barbra pushed her chair back as Gretchen descended under the table.

A horrifying cry pierced the air, followed by a heavy thump.

Barbra dropped to her knees. Gretchen was lying facedown on the linoleum, clutching her head.

"Gretchen? What is it?" Barbra crawled up next to her.

"My eye!" the girl howled. "My eye!"

Barbra gently turned her over.

"Oh, my God!" she gasped, dragging Gretchen out from under the table.

Blood was bubbling out of a two-inch gash above Gretchen's right eye, soaking her tangled blond hair. A line of it led back to a small puddle between the scattered cards where her head had been.

Barbra grabbed a clean towel from the drawer and pressed it against Gretchen's forehead. The girl was choked with fright. Her quick breaths heaved erratically. "I'm going to get our coats, honey. Just hold that against your head and lay still. I'll be back in one second and we'll drive to the doctor's."

As soon as Barbra arose, the kitchen door flew open. Two girls helped Mary inside, each holding her under an arm.

"Mommy?" Mary moaned weakly. Her little body

shook like a torn sail in a storm. Blood covered her shirt, face, and arms.

Barbra shuddered when she saw the awful-looking wound on her forehead, just above the . . .

Her eyes darted down at Gretchen, then back at Mary.

. . . the right eye.

Exactly like Gretchen's.

Exactly!

Barbra hugged herself to keep from shaking and stared out the window of the doctor's office. Past the well-trimmed row of shrubs, the muddy Snohomish River churned around a shallow, rock-strewn bend. Its bubbling currents reminded her of those horrible army ants on the march.

Hearing the slight metallic click of the door, she turned. Her fingers dug into her shoulders.

"Please sit down, Mrs. Foster." Dr. Bernstein drew a chair to his desk.

"I'd just as . . . as soon stand, thank you," she stammered. Her face was drawn taut. Air fluttered into her lungs in short machine gun bursts.

The doctor remained standing, too. Barbra watched his long skinny fingers flex on the surface of his desk like water-spiders.

"An unusual case," he said, a false smile emphasizing the absurdity of his understatement. Barbra searched his face as the smile dimmed. The nervous tick in her left eye stopped when another chill rushed up her spine. She hadn't been able to stop shivering since she had left the house.

"Will they be scarred?" she asked bluntly.

"Not noticeably. No," he reassured her, half-sitting on the corner of his desk. "I made the stitches as small and as tight as I could. In a year or so, you'll need a magnifying glass to find the cuts."

When he asked her to tell him exactly what happened to Gretchen in the kitchen, he tried not to sound over-anxious. She explained the events leading up to the accident.

"She must have slipped on the cards, I guess. Next thing I knew, she was lying on the floor, screaming."

"It's hard to believe a child could fall onto a flat surface and cut herself like that." He noticed her jaws bulge slightly just below the ears. "A bump, perhaps. A little swelling. Maybe a scrape. But not a gash that needed ten stitches. Was there anything sharp on the floor? A sliver of glass, perhaps?"

Barbra had mopped the kitchen floor yesterday. "No. I'm sure there wasn't."

"Mrs. Foster, Gretchen swears her wound was caused by Mary's accident. Why do you think she would say that?"

"I don't know." Barbra looked back out at the river. She could feel the doctor scrutinizing her. Nervous spasms rippled up her back. She hunched her shoulders to keep from shivering again.

"This is the second time in a week you've brought the twins in. When I gave them tetanus shots, I examined their legs. The cuts were as identical as the wounds are on their foreheads. And both times, only one of them had had an accident that could account for such a wound. Don't you find that at least curious?"

146

Her eyes flashed at him defiantly. Then her whole body seemed to go limp. She stumbled past him and slumped into the chair. Fighting to keep back the flood of tears now welling in her throat, she stared at the rug and desperately searched her mind for an answer.

But there was none.

Unless . . .

She felt the doctor's hand on her shoulder. "I heard her fall," she uttered somberly. "She hit the floor pretty hard."

Her neck muscles twitched against his hand. "Do you really believe that could account for it?" he asked.

Suddenly something broke inside and she could no longer hold it in. "Since they were little, they've always acted as if they felt each other's pain. When one was sick, the other was sick. When one fell and hurt herself, the other always cried, too. Our family doctor thought it might be some kind of sympathetic reaction. Because they were twins. He said it was probably all in their minds, an imaginary game they would eventually grow out of. But I'm not sure anymore. Maybe it really is true. Maybe they really do share each other's pain. And now even the wounds themselves."

Barbra closed her eyes tightly. Her mind shuttered between denial and the sudden, terrifying reality of acceptance. It couldn't be true, she told herself.

But what other explanation was there?

That something unnatural was festering inside her daughters? That some unholy disease was causing their minds to crumble?

Barbra peered up at the doctor through a blurry

screen of tears. "Wounds don't just appear out of nowhere, Doctor. My babies aren't crazy, you know. They didn't just make this all up. Gretchen's cut proves that."

Dr. Bernstein dreaded what he had to say next. He tried to think of an easy way to put it, but couldn't.

"It may be a bizarre set of coincidences, Mrs. Foster. I can't say for sure. As far as wounds appearing out of nowhere, there are many documented cases of just such occurrences. I saw a case like that when I was an intern. A woman in the psych ward thought she was being attacked by the devil. She was in restraints, yet deep scratches kept appearing all over her body. I'm not saying the same type of thing is happening to your twins, but . . ." The horror on Barbra's face almost stopped him from going on. "But I do strongly recommend you take the twins to see a psychiatrist."

The last vestige of Barbra's courage flowed from her body like a dark wave on the cold sand being sucked back to sea.

Dr. Bernstein reached across his desk for a pad of paper. "I can give you the name of someone in Brownsville. He's very capable."

"What exactly are you trying to say?" Barbra arose from the chair, welcoming the strength that came with the sudden surge of anger. "That somehow my children mentally willed their physical wounds on themselves?" The strain on her face hardened in defense of her offspring. "That they're as crazy as that . . . that woman?"

"Not at all, Mrs. Foster. Please . . ." He extended the paper. "Try to look at it as a precautionary measure. A form of insurance."

"Insurance?" Barbra spat out, snapping the paper from him.

"Yes, insurance," he stated frankly. "Whatever the reason for these events, whether it is psychosomatic or not, I think a qualified psychiatrist should be consulted. The mind is a powerful thing. We've only just begun to understand it. What happens if one of the twins has a more serious accident next time? Have you ever thought of that? If it is true that somehow they do physically feel each other's pain, now that they exhibit the wounds as well, it could endanger the other's life if one was critically hurt. Consider the possibility at least, Mrs. Foster. I know it sounds farfetched, but as long as the slightest possibility of that happening exists, I think it's worth a thorough investigation. By a professional. And neither of us are qualified to do that."

He pointed at the paper in her clenched fist. "But he is."

Chapter VII

Like two war orphans, the twins bivouacked on either end of the long sofa, blankets wrapped around them like cocoons, the identical, square white patches above their right eyes yellowing around the dried, rust-colored blood. Barbra had given each of them half a Valium and they were calmer now, grateful the frightening ordeal at the clinic was over and happy to have been rewarded with heaping bowls of ice cream. Yet neither could sleep, knowing that the worst ordeal was yet to come . . . their mother's interrogation.

After retrieving their empty bowls and putting them in the sink, Barbra started pacing the kitchen again. The twins looked at each other pensively. When Barbra sat between them, Gretchen pulled in her legs and pretended to be engrossed in the movie on TV.

Sensing the sudden increase in tension the way small fish feel the watery vibration of an approaching predator, Mary put her book on the floor and sat up to wait for the inevitable.

For a long time, the only sound was the popping of six-guns and the clip-clopping of horses in the old black and white western.

Suddenly Barbra bolted from the sofa and turned off the set. Turning, she glanced from one twin to the other, as if deciding who to address first. She chose Gretchen.

"I want you to tell me the truth." Her eyebrows raised in emphasis. "How, exactly, did you cut yourself today? Don't look at Mary. I'm not asking her. I'm asking you."

Gretchen pulled her knees up against her chest and wrapped her arms around them. "Are you mad at me? 'Cause of what I told the doctor?"

"I'm not mad. I just want the truth. It's very important, Gretchen. To all of us." Sitting back down between them, she met Gretchen's questioning gaze with a look that was threatening but not malicious.

Gretchen tugged her legs closer and rested her chin on her knees, not daring to take her eyes from her mother's. "I fell."

"Why?"

Gretchen stared, puzzled. "What do you mean—why?"

"Why did you fall? Did you slide on the cards? Or did something else cause you to fall?"

"I don't know. I felt a pain in my head. I got dizzy and I fell. That's all."

"You felt the pain first? Before you fell?"

"I guess so."

"Don't guess. I'm not going to be angry, Gretchen. I promise. Just tell me exactly what happened."

"Why're you picking on me? I didn't do anything."

"I never said you did."

"You won't believe me." Gretchen hooked her

fingers around her bare toes and pouted. Her mother sure sounded mad to her. "You never believe me."

Barbra felt like a magistrate during the Spanish Inquisition. But if her questions frightened the girls, she had to know why. Especially since they frightened her even more. "I'll believe the truth, Gretchen. Go on."

"I was picking up the cards. Then I felt like I got hit on the head by something and everything was spinning and I fell on my face." Gretchen peeked up at her mother to monitor her reaction.

"What caused that first pain, Gretchen?" The girl tried to look around at her sister, but Barbra blocked her view. "Just tell me, Gretchen. Don't worry about Mary."

Gretchen drew a deep breath and blurted it out. "Mary caused it. When she got smacked in the head out in the woods."

The muscles between Barbra's shoulder blades bunched into a knot. She forced herself to remain calm and turned toward Mary. "Is that how it happened to you in the girls' room on Monday?"

Mary avoided direct eye contact and shrugged.

"Mary, I want an answer."

She pulled at a button on the back cushion of the sofa. Barbra brushed her hand down and waited.

"I cut myself in the stall," she said innocuously. "Like I told you before."

"You don't sound like you believe it." Barbra took her hand. "Is that the truth? The honest to God truth?" She was trying to be more gentle.

Mary pinched the inside of her lower lip between her teeth and shook her head no. There was no use lying anymore, not even to herself. "As soon as my leg stung, I knew Gretchen had been hurt. Like Gretchen felt it when I got hit today. We always feel it." Mary threw herself toward her mother and started crying. "I know you don't believe it. You've never believed it. No one has." Her chest heaved against Barbra's ribs. "I wanted it not to be true. I tried to know it wasn't. Just like you told us to. I tried, Mommy. But it is true. It's always been true." Her tear-streaked face lifted in a mixture of confusion and horror. "But now it's all different. We only felt it before, but . . ." She choked on her words. "Now there's gashes and blood and it scares me something awful. I don't know why it's all different now, but it is." Her little fingers dug into Barbra's side. "Something's happening to us, Mommy. Something terrible."

Barbra hugged Mary with one arm and reached out to her sister with the other. Gretchen let herself be drawn into her mother's embrace.

Resting her cheek up against Barbra's soft breast, Gretchen listened with pleasure as her sister wept.

"Don't cry, honey," Barbra soothed. "I believe you now. I do. I really do."

What else could it be? Barbra asked herself, startled to realize she meant what she had just said.

It has to be true, she told herself, terrified of the alternative.

My babies aren't crazy. They're not.

It must be true.

The left corner of Gretchen's upper lip curled into a malevolent but hidden, sneer.

You've hurt me for the last time, she told herself, glowering at her sobbing twin.

You won't hurt me again . . .
Not after tonight.

Barbra Foster felt herself teetering on the edge of emotional exhaustion. Nothing made sense anymore. Like their family doctor in San Diego, she had thought the strange bond between her children would eventually disappear once they had finally stopped believing in it. For ten years, she had been trying to convince herself that their shared pain was just some kind of innocent, childish game, but not anymore.

Barbra lay back in her bed, the afternoon light hidden behind drawn curtains, and tried to construct a logical scenario. One that made sense. Her mind fluttered like a strobe light as nightmarish images of her children, torn and bloody and screaming for their Mommy, flickered grotesquely behind the lids of her closed eyes.

Her stomach wrenched and she snapped her eyes open, tightening her throat to keep from being sick. The semidarkness of her room was no longer comforting and she opened the drapes.

Gray light flooded the room like a ghostly mist.

You know when they are lying and when they're not, a voice inside her said. You asked for the truth and they gave it to you.

Barbra slid open the window and tried to clear her mind in the cold winter air.

They weren't lying. She knew that now.

In some unexplainable way, her twins had been melded together beyond the scope of any normal human bonding, as if some kind of ethereal umbilical cord had been fused between them since birth.

The cold finality of that conclusion struck her with such force it felt like sharp icicles being jammed in between her ribs.

Fumbling in her purse, Barbra extracted the paper Dr. Bernstein had given her and stared at the name of the psychiatrist. A trembling erupted deep from within her belly and racked her limbs. She tossed the crumpled paper onto the table by the bed and shook her head violently, as if trying to exorcise a demon that had suddenly possessed her.

They're not crazy, she screamed in her heart.

And I'll prove it.

Barbra fell across the bed. Rolling onto her side, her eyes riveted to the phone.

She had no choice and she knew it.

There was only one way to prove her children were telling the truth.

A chilling breeze swept through the open window.

Inching across the blanket, her hand slowly quivered toward the badly wrinkled paper.

As soon as he hung up the phone, Michael Striker ran to his car. The frightening urgency in Barbra's voice sent him speeding through town at seventy miles an hour. Screeching around the turn onto Highline Road, the back end of his silver 280Z fishtailed, then caught the gravel as he floored it up the hill.

Barbra saw the headlights flash across the kitchen window. When she heard the short squeal of rubber, she rushed to the front door.

"Barbra, what the . . ."

155

She put a finger to his lips.

"The kids are in bed," she whispered. "Let's go in the kitchen."

They sat at the breakfast table and Barbra brought over a pot of tea.

"It's only seven-thirty," he said softly. "Why are they in bed?"

"Would you like a drink instead?" she asked.

"Tea's fine."

He noted the way the top of the pot kept clanking as she poured them each a cup. For the first time in months, he wished he had a cigarette.

Barbra had pinned her disheveled hair into a bun right after calling Michael. It now dangled down the back of her neck like a question mark. When she sat down, she moved like an old woman brittle with arthritis.

Pushing back a loose strand of hair, she said, "I must look terrible," and fumbled to repin the bun.

It was the first time he had seen her look older than her years.

"You look fine. Don't worry about it." Michael took her icy hand and rubbed it between his. "Now tell me what's wrong."

Barbra stared at her tea as if she were reading the leaves in the bottom of the cup. Michael waited. She pushed out of her chair and opened a cupboard next to the stove.

"The hell with tea," she said. "I'm going to have Scotch. Sure you wouldn't rather have a drink?"

"No thanks."

As she mixed it with water from the tap, she spied the open bottle of Valiums above the sink. Her doctor had prescribed them to her a few days after she had kicked Matt out. She was having problems sleeping and had taken them for a week before deciding they were a crutch she didn't need. Keeping her back to the table, she shook out two pills.

Tonight she needed a crutch.

By the time Barbra had finished describing what had happened to the twins and what the doctor had recommended, she was on her second drink.

"They didn't feel good, so I gave them a little soup and put them to bed at seven." Barbra's limbs began to loosen. She felt rubbery and her skin tingled. It was a welcome relief from the heavy rock hardness that had been weighing her down all afternoon. Soft-rushing waves washed through her body like silky clouds, cushioning the sharp, jabbing realities that still tortured her heart and mind.

"So what are you going to do?" Michael watched Barbra's head bob slightly as she stirred her drink. He had seen her take the pills, but didn't think it was his place to mention it. "Are you all right?"

His worried expression touched her. "I took two Valium. They work fast on an empty stomach."

"Want me to make you a sandwich or something? Is there any of that soup left?"

She stopped him from getting up. "I don't think I could keep it down."

He gently kneaded her forearm and smiled. What she had told him about the twins shocked him considerably. They seemed like such normal kids. But at this point, he was more concerned about Barbra. It wasn't hard to imagine how deeply this was affecting her.

"And you called the psychiatrist?" he asked cautiously.

"They have an appointment on Wednesday." Her head sagged forward in defeat, like someone who had just been convicted of a terrible atrocity in court. "I know what he's going to say." Her fingers tightened around the glass until the knuckles whitened. "He's going to blame me. Just like Matt will. He's going to say the girls are insecure and . . . and don't feel loved. So they developed this strange illusion to compensate for it." Barbra slowly shook her bowed head. "But it's not true. I'm going to ask him to test the twins, first thing. Put them in different rooms and then see if they can feel what the other feels." She peered up at Michael, the growing pain etched in her swollen eyes. "Then he'll know it's true, too!" She sniffed loudly, fighting back the tears of guilt. "God, what am I saying? It sounds so absurd."

Michael quickly slid his chair next to hers. Barbra let herself cry in the warmth of his embrace until there was no crying left.

"You know, I believe they could be telling the truth, too," he stated quietly.

Barbra rested her forehead against his neck. She felt drained and empty. The Scotch and the Valium no longer cushioned her fear. She was beginning to feel nauseous when his last statement finally registered. She twitched in his arms and looked up.

"What do you mean? You actually think it's possible they . . ."

"Anything's possible. I had a friend in the army who was an identical twin. We were stationed in Germany for a year. When we were on leave, getting drunk like only soldiers of eighteen trying to be men can, he told me something that I've never forgotten. He was fourteen at the time. His brother was at home, out in the fields of Iowa planting corn. My buddy was playing baseball with his eighth-grade team. He was going to bat when suddenly he had this, well, vision. He swore to me he actually heard his brother scream to him. He said he had this mental picture of his brother pinned under the wheel of their overturned tractor. It scared him so much he ran to his friend's house and called his parents. His dad went out to the field to check just because he sounded so hysterical on the phone. He found his son pinned just like my buddy had described. If he hadn't gone out there when he did, his brother might have died. The tractor was sinking in the mud and would have crushed him. After my buddy told me this, he started bawling like a little kid. I've never doubted it was true."

Barbra held him even tighter, as if she were trying to draw out his strength through osmosis. Mascara smudged her cheeks as she wiped away her tears, grateful for his understanding and the sense of calm she felt in his powerful limbs.

"Do you really believe it could be true?" she asked weakly. "That it isn't my fault somehow? That they're not . . . unbalanced?"

"Stop it," he whispered. "It's not your fault. Quit trying to blame yourself."

After checking to make sure her sister was sound asleep, Gretchen tiptoed out of their room. She was relieved to discover the door to the basement, across from the hall closet, was still slightly ajar. She had opened it just before trotting off to bed. Tucking her doll under her arm, she carefully squeezed through. A dim crack of light filtered down the stairs. Steadying herself against the wall, she descended into the blackness below.

One of the stairs creaked. Pulling herself back, she edged her toes across the wood until they touched the opposite wall, then slowly lowered her weight onto her heel.

She could still hear her mother and that awful man talking in the kitchen as she felt her way to the furnace room. Like a safe-cracker, she gently turned the doorknob and pushed her shoulder against the wood. It slid open without a sound.

Once inside, she searched the dusty cement floor until she found the flashlight she had hidden there. She clicked it on and sat the doll up onto one of the stacks of empty boxes left over from moving. Turning over the two boxes next to it, she braced the flashlight between them so it spotlighted the doll's head. The sharp contrast of light and shadow cut its face in an obscene profile. The illuminated half glowed a yellowish-pink. Its one visible eye seemed to enlarge as Gretchen crawled closer.

Like a lantern beckoning at the end of a long black tunnel, she felt herself being drawn into it. The longer Gretchen concentrated, the more it seemed to pulsate and grow. Soon it was the only thing she saw. One shimmering red light in a sea of darkness.

"She hurt me again," Gretchen whispered hypnotically.

Her body slowly began to sway to the rhythm now

160

beating inside her skull like drums inside a huge empty temple.

"Look."

Her fingernails curled under the tape on her forehead and peeled away the bandage.

"Remember your promise."

Gretchen's spine arched as if she were being tied back against a sacrificial pole, but her eyes never left the doll's. Like a cobra, mesmerized by the swaying of a flute, she kept rocking in a smooth circular motion.

"Take the hurt from me."

The doll's other eye began to glow in the shadows until both became one huge, firey pit.

"So I will never hurt again."

Leaning into the light, the bandage dangled open. Black stitches sparkled above the line of dried blood.

"Make us sisters."

Her hand crawled up to the pocket of her nightgown like a tarantula. Feeling the cold steel, she smiled.

"What she stole from me, I now give to you."

The razor blade exploded in blue light as it moved up toward her glistening stitches.

"Forever."

Barbra's eyelids felt like they were made of lead. Every unkind word, every angry quarrel, every punishment, every self-centered decision Barbra could remember making since she had given birth to the twins had been repeated tonight. Michael picked each little incident apart to show her she was not the cruel, heartless mother she imagined herself to be. Nothing she had done was so abhorrent it could have triggered such abnormal reactions in her children.

He cupped her chin like a crystal brandy snifter and kissed her softly. "I'm no shrink, but from everything you've told me, I really don't think their problem comes from any lack of love. You're a fine mother. Except for the divorce, they've had a damn good childhood so far. Better than most, I'd say. There's been a little sibling rivalry, a little jealousy of their parents' attention, but that's normal."

To his relief, he could see Barbra was finally putting an end to her self-abnegations.

"So that leaves us with only one alternative," he concluded. "That they are telling the truth and it isn't psychological at all. It could simply be an act of nature, of God. Something beyond medical science's rather limited repertoire. There are many things science can't explain and this could be one of them. It's the only logical explanation left, really."

Barbra tipped too far back in her chair and had to grab the counter for balance. "You're right," she mumbled. "It is the only explanation. I'm not such a bad mom, am I?"

Michael helped steady her as she arose. "Not at all. You're a wonderful mother. If you were as cruel or as selfish as you were trying to make yourself out to be, you wouldn't be going through all this. You wouldn't care. But you do. You care as much as any mother would. Now let it go. You're beating yourself to death for no reason. OK?"

Barbra nodded, gratefully accepting his verdict.

Bracing her by the elbow, Michael led her down the hall. She stopped in the doorway to her bedroom and turned dizzily. "Michael, I'm really sorry about this. The Valium and the booze hit me like a ton of bricks. I feel like a stupid sot." Suddenly she chuckled. "Just like my ex-husband."

Michael caught her before she fell back against the wall. He was glad she could joke about it now, even if she couldn't stand up.

"I doubt it's all the drug's fault. You've been through a tough day, to put it mildly. Actually, I'm surprised you're holding up as well as you are."

"I'm not holding myself up at all." She grinned, bleary-eyed. "You are."

He was suddenly aware of his close proximity to her bed.

"Well, I suppose I should get going."

She rested against his chest. "Don't go. I don't want to be alone."

Michael swept her up and carried her to her bed. After helping her off with her jeans, he tucked her in like a little girl. "I'll be in the living room. In case you wake up in the middle of the night and need something. The big sofa looks comfortable enough."

Barbra tried to prop herself up long enough to kiss him, but everything started whirling so badly she had to drop back onto the pillows.

"Thank you, Michael," she mumbled. "For everything. You are one sweet, handsome, wonderful . . ."

Before she could finish, she was asleep.

The razor blade sliced across Gretchen's wound, snapping the stitches one by one. A line of blood trickled around her right eye and broke into two streams along the contours of her cheek.

"For you," she chanted. "To make you mine."

She bent forward until the torn, raw scar touched the doll's lips.

"Drink."

Reaching behind the doll's head, she pressed its mouth hard against her open wound.

The streams of blood running down her face thinned.

Then they stopped completely.

"Let me grow within you."

The girl's insides shuddered, as if the evil burning through her veins was now pouring into the doll.

"We are twins."

Suddenly she went completely rigid. Her pupils quivered erratically, then turned up into her lids. Only the whiteness of her retinas glowed in the light.

"Drink her life-blood, too. The blood of my twin. Your blood now. For you are my only twin."

From her pocket, Gretchen lifted the towel her mother had used to stem her sister's flow of blood on their way to the doctor's and wrapped it around the doll like a sacrificial robe.

"Now we are one. The three of us. But soon there will be only two."

Chapter VIII

The early morning storm battered the mountains. Gale-force winds bent the trees like wheat. Tall, century-old centennials fell to the earth to continue the reincarnate processes of the forest. With the fury of shotgun blasts, the rain pelted the mountains. Barbra awoke from a restless sleep to the sound of hail, like marbles, pummeling the roof. Her teeth felt like dry stubs of chalk, her tongue a dusty eraser. Raising her head from the pillow was a major catastrophe.

"Oh, Jesus," she muttered, closing her eyes and arching her brows. Pieces of yesterday filtered into her mind like broken glass. She massaged her temples as she fitted them into place. With slow deliberation, she staggered into the bathroom and began her own rejuvenating process with a long, hot shower.

"Michael?" She kissed his ear.

"Good morning," he said, then noticed it was still dark outside. "I guess." He swung his legs onto the floor and brushed back his hair. "How do you feel?"

"Not that bad."

"What time is it?"

"A little after seven." She sat down next to him. "You helped me more than I can tell you last night. I was pretty shaky and you were wonderful. I shouldn't have burdened you like I did. You must have heard every petty little thing I don't like about myself. I hope you don't think I'm awful."

"Just the opposite." He patted her thigh where the robe had opened. "Are you going to be all right today?"

"I'll make it. I think we cleansed my battered soul last night. I'm more comfortable with what I have to do, at least. That's a good step in the right direction." She slipped her fingers under the hand on her leg.

"And the guilt?"

"If you still like me, I guess I'll just have to take your word on it."

He winked in a theatrical parody of seduction. "More than you know."

A surge of gratitude and affection swept over her like a hot summer breeze. "You're really too good to be true, you know that?" The urge to lead him to her bed, to feel him naked and wanting, to lose herself in his touch, his hardness, his warmth, was almost uncontrollable.

But it wasn't time. Not yet.

She liked him more than any man she had known in years and he certainly did arouse her sexually, but that wasn't enough. In her old-fashioned way, she still believed love came before sex, not after.

"Do you want some coffee?" she asked, wondering if it showed somehow, her wanting him so much.

"You wouldn't have an extra toothbrush?" He stood up and attempted to straighten out the wrinkles embedded in his clothes.

"Use the blue one hanging by the mirror in the hall bathroom." She watched him amble down the hall and touched the spot on her thigh where his hand had been. It's been a long time, she thought, titillated by the prickling volts that raced up between her legs. Too long.

She heard the twins stirring and saw Gretchen make her way toward the bathroom, rubbing the sleep from her eyes.

"Don't go in there," she warned.

Gretchen glanced at her quizzically. "Why?"

"Michael's in there."

"What's he still doing here?"

"He slept on the sofa," Barbra answered quickly. "It was late."

"Oh."

Barbra had expected more than a simple Oh. Mary walked up next to her sister.

"He's in the bathroom," Gretchen told her and disappeared back into their room.

"Who?" Mary asked.

"Michael." Barbra pointed at the sofa. "He slept out here."

Speaking of guilt, she thought, amused.

Mary hurried to her mother.

"I don't feel good," she moaned. "My head hurts worse than it did yesterday. And I feel all dizzy."

Gretchen peeked out the doorway and smiled as Barbra felt her sister's forehead. Skipping across the room, she reached down under her bed. After making sure no one was coming, she exhumed the nightgown and the towel she had discarded there last night. Both were covered with dried blood. She stuffed them into her pillowcase and reminded herself to throw them away later. Then she dressed the doll in one of her twin's old T-shirts. When she heard the bathroom door open, she raced across the hall.

After locking the door, she examined the doll thoroughly. There wasn't a speck of blood on it anywhere. She looked in the mirror and felt the bandage on her forehead. It didn't hurt at all, not even when she pressed on it.

Her stomach churned with anticipation and wonder as she glanced at the doll, then back at the mirror.

The tape, on one side of the bandage, was loose and she peeled it open. What she saw caused her to giggle with delight.

There was no trace of a wound above her right eye.

After retaping the bandage, she unlocked the door and trotted into the living room. Mary was curled up on the sofa, holding her head.

Barbra brought her some apple juice and an aspirin. "Take this, honey. It'll help."

Mary winced as she sat up.

"Don't you feel good?" Gretchen inquired, ruffling her twin's hair. It took all her will power not to burst out laughing at Mary's doleful expression.

"I'd better get going," Michael said, putting on his shoes.

Barbra took the empty glass from Mary. "You sure you don't want to stay for breakfast?"

"Thanks, but I'd better go."

As Barbra walked him to the back door in the

kitchen, she tried to think of the appropriate words to thank him. There were none. "Can I buy you lunch tomorrow?"

"I'd like that."

They stepped outside under the protection of the short overhang. The storm was still raging through the valley as the first gray light of day emerged in the east. The hail had stopped, but it was pouring rain. A gust of wind blew one side of Barbra's robe open almost to the waist, revealing the supple whiteness of her hip.

"I can never thank you enough," she said, stooped over, clutching her robe closed.

Michael couldn't help thinking how much he suddenly liked these winter storms.

Having put it off all morning Barbra finally decided to call Matt. She knew she should have called yesterday, but she just couldn't face it then. At least she felt stronger today, a little more sure of herself.

Maybe the whole thing was inevitable, she thought, remembering the conversation they had had with their doctor in San Diego about the twins. She doubted Matt would agree they should see a psychiatrist. They had discussed that with the doctor, too. Matt had seen no reason for one at that point and neither had she. It was one of the few things they had agreed on in the last two years.

But they had been wrong.

Now there was no choice. Arguing about it would be academic, she thought. And foolishly dangerous.

Only one thing mattered now.

The children.

The rest was ego. Stupid, insecure adult ego.

The call went exactly like she had thought it would. The only thing that surprised her was how calmly she could listen to his insulting insinuations. Last night's vigil had done her more good than she had thought. If they had talked yesterday, she probably would have been screaming back accusations of her own, but she saw no reason for it anymore. She didn't really care if he believed their old family doctor and not the children. She did, and that's all that counted.

When he had finally run out of things to blame on her, she said, "They need professional help, Matt. At least until we're sure what's causing it. The rest is bullshit," and hung up.

As she strutted back into the living room, she suddenly felt like a surgeon had skillfully cut away a tumor that had been festering inside her for years and had just given her a clean bill of health. She was finally free of him now. He couldn't hurt her anymore.

Barbra crouched beside the sofa. "Is the headache any better?"

"A little," Mary answered, wishing it was.

Gretchen looked back from her prone position on the floor in front of the TV as Barbra turned toward her. "And how do you feel, honey?"

"I'm all right," Gretchen stated.

Barbra arose stiffly, still feeling the effects of last night.

"Mom?" Mary called.

"What, honey?"

"When do we get our stitches out?"

"In a few days. Maybe a week. The doctor will decide on Thursday."

Gretchen jumped up off the floor. "Do we have to?"

"It's not going to hurt," Barbra reassured her. "Don't worry."

"I don't care if it hurts," Gretchen argued. "I don't want to. I don't like him."

Barbra leaned the vacuum against the closet door. "It's really a simple procedure, honey. I swear it won't hurt a bit."

Gretchen stamped her foot. "I don't want to go. I'll . . . I'll do it myself. I can take 'em out as good as he can."

Barbra smiled. "I don't think that's a good idea. We'll let the doctor do it, OK?"

"No!" Gretchen cried, kicking the chair by the TV. "I don't want to go."

"What is the matter, Gretchen?" Barbra queried, perplexed by the sudden outburst.

"I won't go," she snarled, punching her fists against her hips. "And you can't make me."

With that, she ran to her room and slammed the door.

Barbra looked down the hall, then at Mary, totally baffled. "What was that all about?"

"I don't know."

Barbra didn't have the energy or the will to argue with Gretchen today and decided to let it run its own course. If it was still a problem on Thursday, she would deal with it then.

The rain never let up all day. Barbra began to understand why this region had the highest suicide rate in the country. A few weeks of this and anyone would go stir crazy, she thought. After cleaning the entire house by midafternoon, she had tried to relax with a good book, but couldn't sit still long enough to enjoy it. She needed to stay busy, to keep her mind occupied, so she decided to prepare some new figures for Monday's meeting. At first, she had a hard time concentrating, but soon she was pumping out estimates like a computer. Work had always been a good therapeutic tool for her, even in college. It put things in perspective and helped draw her out of herself. When she felt confused or trapped, she could work the way others might use meditation or self-hypnosis.

"What are you doin'?" Gretchen asked, stretching up on her toes to see over her mother's shoulder.

Barbra swiveled around in the chair. "Making some estimates for the mill."

"It looks boring."

"The figures, by themselves, are boring. But when you know what they represent, in terms of cost and labor and profit, they can become rather interesting." She smiled. "Especially if you have a piece of the action, so to speak."

Gretchen looked at her doll and rolled her eyes. "Mary thinks it's boring, too."

"Your sister or the doll?" Barbra asked, putting down her pen.

"She's not a doll," Gretchen insisted. "I adopted her. She's my sister."

"It certainly gets complicated when you have two sisters with the same name." Barbra could tell Gretchen didn't see the humor in that. "You really like that doll." She held up her hands before Gretchen could voice an objection. "I mean, your new sister, don't you?"

"She's my best friend." Gretchen kissed its pudgy nose. "And she'll do anything to make me happy."

"I'm glad, honey. But do you think it's a good idea to keep taking her to school every day? School is for learning, not for playing."

"I have to, Mommy." Gretchen suddenly looked very serious. "She doesn't like being alone. She gets scared when she's not with me."

Barbra wondered if it really wasn't the other way around. "It's nice of you to be such a good friend to her, but don't you think you should make other friends, too?"

Gretchen tilted her head. "Why?"

"Because people need friends. You need friends. Real friends. Not just pretend friends."

"She is real, Mommy." Gretchen started out of the room, then turned. "And she doesn't like the kids at school. They're not worth making friends with. They always make fun of her."

Then she was gone.

Barbra stared sadly at the blurred reflection of the empty doorway in the black, rain-washed window above her desk. When she tried to resume her computations, she found her heart was no longer in it.

After checking to make sure Mary was still asleep on the sofa, Gretchen quietly entered the kitchen. She leaned the doll against the toaster next to the stove and turned the front burner on high. While she waited for it to get hot, she pulled the toaster out from the wall until the doll was sitting on the edge of the counter beside her, at eye level.

Silently she began to mouth the words "Remember your duty" over and over again like a faithful nun repeating "Hail Mary's" in the hope of obtaining religious bliss.

With fingers splayed, she began to lower them toward the glowing burner. Six inches above the stove, she began to feel the heat. Without removing her hand, she stretched back to look at the sofa. Mary must still be asleep, she concluded.

Concentrating on the doll, she began to hum. Soon, strange foreign words were rolling off her tongue.

Words of the Nahuas.

Aztec words.

She no longer felt the heat as her hand descended toward the burner.

Mary awoke with a start, yanked her left hand out from under the afghan, and shook it vigorously. She thought it was asleep, but it wasn't numb or prickly. It felt more like it was wrapped in an electric blanket.

And it was getting hotter.

"Gretchen?" she called. "What are you doing? Gretchen?" She leaped off the sofa and hurried down the hall. "Gretchen?"

Her hand was no longer just hot. It was burning.

"Gretchen, answer me!"

The sharp apprehension in her daughter's voice startled Barbra. She got up from her desk in time to see Mary running through the living room, waving her hand.

It felt like it was buried in a bed of coals.

"Stop it!" Mary howled, stumbling into the kitchen, one hand jammed in between her legs. "Gretchen, please!"

174

Her sister smiled at her calmly.

The pain was so unbearable Mary couldn't move, couldn't think. Writhing in torment, she threw her head back and screamed, then crumpled to the floor.

Gretchen's hand reflected the orange glow of the burner as she lowered it still further.

Barbra tripped over Mary's squirming body as she spun around the corner into the kitchen.

"Gretchen, move your hand!" she cried, fighting to untangle herself.

The little girl's dull, heavy-lidded eyes turned blindly toward the doorway.

"Stop her!" Mary howled.

Barbra leaped toward the stove and yanked Gretchen away.

"What the hell were you doing?" She shook her daughter roughly. "Trying to burn yourself?"

Gretchen grinned. "I didn't burn myself." She extended her hand. "Look."

Barbra examined it quickly. It wasn't even warm, let alone blistered.

Gretchen swayed back drunkenly and reached for her doll.

"Mommy?" a small voice called from the floor. Barbra helped Mary to her feet. "My hand, Mommy. It hurts. It's all red and there's bubbles."

Barbra stared at the burns, stunned. It should have been Gretchen's hand. She led her to the sink and turned the faucet on cold. "Just hold it there, honey. The water will make it feel better."

Cradling her doll against her cheek, her head nodding like an old wino's, Gretchen kept smiling at her mother.

"You did that on purpose, didn't you?" Bårbra yanked Gretchen toward her and squeezed her arm until it hurt. "Didn't you?"

Gretchen stared at her mother coldly. "Let go of me," she demanded.

"Don't tell me what to do," Barbra warned angrily. "I want answers and I want them now. Why were you trying to burn your sister? You knew you'd burn her, didn't you? I don't know how or why, but you did it on purpose." She shook her again. "You'd better start talking and talking fast, or I'll . . ."

The little girl's face hardened into granite. "I did it 'cause I felt like it."

Totally repulsed, Barbra shoved her back against the counter and slapped her as hard as she could.

Gretchen sneered at her tauntingly.

Barbra was about to slap that look off her face when the bandage on her forehead dangled open.

There was no wound.

No stitches.

Nothing.

Gretchen felt her forehead. Realizing her mother had slapped open the bandage, she started to slide along the counter toward the living room.

"How . . ." Barbra let her arm fall to her side and looked at her daughter as if she were some hideous demon.

Gretchen bolted out of the kitchen.

By the time Barbra reached the bedroom door, she had locked it.

"You open this door!" Barbra threatened. "Now!" She twisted the knob furiously, then stepped back and kicked it. "Open this damn thing or I'll bust it in!"

Gretchen backed away from the door as Barbra's fists pounded it unmercifully. After each whack, Gretchen winced as if struck by the shock waves. Finding herself pinned against the windowsill on the opposite side of the room, she hugged her doll, petrified. Keeping a terrified watch on the locked door, she searched behind her for the latch.

The pounding stopped.

Gretchen sucked in her breath. All she could hear was the rapid drumming of her heart.

She was trapped.

Pushing the window open, she frantically perused the darkness for her salvation.

"Daddy?" she whimpered, scanning the perimeter of the woods. "Help me. Please, Daddy. Please!"

The Doll-Maker had sensed the final phase of her doll's transition, the last exchange for her debt of life, the sacred wish-fulfillment, late last night. It was like a mother's intuition, a feeling for her distant child's welfare, her well-being, but much more powerful. Usually the time of wish-fulfillment filled her with a glowing warmth, a sense of love radiating within her great belly like that sense of change a woman feels when first pregnant.

But this time it filled her with dread.

She had not left her trailer since the terrible feeling began. The women from the factory had come to her trailer in the morning to escort her to work as they always did, but she would not unlock the door.

When the sun had set and the lights of the factory glittered in the desert night, she finally arose from her place of meditation.

Again, she had felt a cry of agony touch the shadowy recesses of her soul.

But it was not her baby, her doll, that had suddenly chilled her old bones, as if the cold winter winds of the mountains had seeped through her skin.

It was another child who cried out. A child of flesh and blood whose innocence had been struck by the wish-fulfillment of her doll, struck by that perverse side of humanity which had given her most precious doll life . . . hatred.

But how? she wondered.

How could another child, a child not a part of the doll, touch me like this?

What connection does this child of innocence, who calls to my soul, have with the wicked one, the child of evil?

What is this strange bonding that holds one human child to another?

And why is my baby, my doll, the catalyst? How can it touch two children at once, when only one is her life-giver, her child-mother?

Reeling in confusion, the huge woman stumbled out of the trailer and entered the factory. Ignoring the concerned gazes and quick, nervous greetings, she hurried into the main office and locked the door.

Gloria, the president's secretary, arose from her desk in respect.

"*Cómo está usted*, Doll-maker? Are you sick today? Your people have been worried because you did not come to work."

"*Sí*, I am sick," the old woman signed, slumping into the big leather chair. "Sick with grief."

"Why? What is wrong?" the secretary asked, frightened by the forlorn, downturned gaze of the Doll-Maker.

The old woman brushed the questions away as if swatting a mosquito. "Tell Mr. President, Senior Rodriguez, that I can make no more dolls."

"But why? You are *el lider*. If you do not make the dolls, the others will stop too. The whole factory will shut down. You can not just . . ."

The sudden, stern stare stopped Gloria from going on. It was not her place to raise her voice to the Doll-Maker, or to question the ways of the holy woman.

To make amends, she asked, "Should I call Mr. Rodriguez? If it is your request, he will drive here immediately."

"Yes. Call him. I need to know where the last group of dolls were sent. Ask him to call the store and tell them I am coming. And that I must see the sales slips for my dolls. It is only a two-hour drive to San Diego. I can be there before they close tonight. If he will do that, I will tell my people to continue making the dolls."

Although curious, Gloria knew better than to ask why. "I'm sure Mr. Rodriguez will do as you request."

"*Es bueno.*" The Doll-Maker got up out of the chair and unlocked the door. "I will prepare for the journey. When you have spoken with him, come to my trailer." Halfway out the door, the old woman turned. "And hurry. There is no time to waste."

"I know it sounds crazy," Barbra explained. "But I saw it with my own eyes. There was no cut. And when

179

I pulled her hand from the burner, it wasn't even red. It . . . it was actually cold."

Dr. Bernstein finished examining Mary's hand and opened his medical bag. "It's going to hurt for a while," he told the girl. "But it's not serious. I've got medication that will take away the sting." He spread the cream gently over her blistered fingers. "Feels cool, doesn't it?"

"It helps," Mary agreed, trying to stop shaking as he wrapped her hand in gauze.

Having told him everything that had happened, Barbra knew he didn't believe a word of it.

"Doctor, she's locked herself in her room. If you could help me get the door open, you'll see for yourself. Her forehead is completely healed. I swear it."

Barbra stood behind him anxiously while he finished taping the bandage on Mary's hand.

He'll believe me in a few minutes, she thought. As soon as he sees Gretchen.

"You said your cut hurts more today, too, huh?" he asked kindly.

Mary nodded her head yes.

"Well, let's have a look." He zipped the tape open before Mary had time to brace for the pain.

Barbra instantly froze. "Oh, God, what is happening?"

Mary's wound was swollen and badly infected. Puss oozed out between the stitches. There was no reason it should have become infected, the doctor thought. Even if it had, it shouldn't have gotten this bad so soon.

"I'll have to drain it," he said, puttering around in

his bag until he had regained his composure. "I've got some antibiotics." He put the small plastic bottle on the counter. "Give her two of these a day for five days. That should do the trick."

Barbra held her trembling child as he pressed around the stitches, dabbing the thick drops of puss with a cotton ball.

"There." He swabbed the area with Betadine, then put on a fresh bandage.

Mary let go of her mother and let out a long sigh of relief.

Dr. Bernstein straightened up and looked at Barbra. How could a little girl put her hand on a red-hot stove and not burn herself? he wondered. The woman was probably so frantic she mistook one twin for the other. It was the only logical explanation he could think of.

"Will you help me get the door open?" Barbra asked. He agreed, but the doubt in his eyes convinced her he was just humoring the silly ravings of a distraught mother.

"Do you have a screwdriver and a hammer?" he asked.

"Why?"

"To knock the long bolts out of the door hinges." He smiled. "I don't usually carry those tools on house calls."

She didn't appreciate his bedside humor and left to find the hammer in the garage.

Fitting the point of the screwdriver up under the heads of the metal pins, he hammered each one up out of their casings. After jiggling the door, the hinges unhitched and it flopped open.

181

Barbra rushed around him. The room was freezing. She checked in the closet and under the beds, then closed the window.

Her daughter was gone.

Chapter IX

The Doll-Maker found the traffic in the big city streets of San Diego terrifying. Five times she had stopped to ask directions before she found the correct department store. Parking her rusty Winnebago in a loading zone in front of the main entrance, she marched inside and stopped at the perfume counter near the doors.

A blond, brittle-looking woman, whom the Doll-Maker thought needed more flesh on her skinny frame, cautiously approached the huge Mexican woman.

"Can I . . . help you?" she asked, as if it were obvious the old Mexican woman couldn't afford anything in the store.

"*Sí*. I wish to see your sales slips for my dolls."

The saleswoman wrinkled her brow and walked away, glancing over racks of women's lingerie for a security guard.

The Doll-Maker was in no mood to be snubbed by a woman whose face was painted to hide her natural features.

"Bill?" the saleswoman called, waving at the tall,

pock-marked man with the shiny brown suit. He scurried over.

"Bill, I think this woman is a little confused," the salesgirl began. The arrogance in her squeaky voice irritated the old woman. "Maybe you should show her . . . ah, well . . ."

The Doll-Maker had had enough.

With one sweep of her mighty forearm, she cleared the counter of all the perfumes displayed. Glass bottles crashed all over the floor. The sickeningly sweet blend of a dozen different scents immediately permeated the entire area.

"Hey, lady, you can't just . . ."

As soon as he tried to grab her, the Doll-Maker twisted his hand back at the wrist. He fell to his knees, his arm bent up and back, totally at the mercy of the crazy old woman.

Still clutching his wrist like a vise, the Doll-Maker helped him back up on his feet.

"Take me to the dolls," she commanded.

Two other security men quickly dashed to their comrade's rescue. But when he felt his hand being bent back again, he warned them to keep their distance. Staying about ten paces behind, they followed Bill and the old woman to the stairs and up to the third floor.

The saleswoman immediately called and warned the toy department. The assistant manager was waiting for them at the stair's door.

"Now what the hell is this all about?" he asked as the ever-growing entourage began to move through the aisles toward the Adoptable Doll display, complete with hospital cribs and a saleswoman in a pink nurse's uniform.

The Doll-Maker was tired of words and said nothing until she was standing before her dolls.

"I want to see your sales slips for the last month," the old woman demanded, staring at the fake nurse.

"Now see here," the assistant manager objected. "I don't know who you think you are, but . . ."

"I am the Doll-Maker. I made that doll there and the three next to it, the ones with the highest price. Senior Rodriguez, the president of Adoptable Dolls Incorporated, called you. He said I was coming."

"Oh, yes," the fake nurse replied. "Mr. Clark, our manager, told me to be looking for you tonight. I'll buzz him."

The Doll-Maker let go of the security guard. He quickly stepped back out of her reach.

"You mean you . . . you were expecting her?" he asked, stupefied.

"Of course we were," the phony nurse answered matter-of-factly. She faced the huge woman. "Please, come this way."

"But what about the perfume display?" the guard called out after them.

The Doll-Maker halted and spun around. All three guards instinctively jumped back behind the stuffed bear display.

"That is payment for your rudeness," the old woman hissed. "And the rudeness of the skinny woman with the painted face."

By the time the Doll-Maker left the store, she had Matt Foster's name, address, and telephone number, as well as an official apology from the manager, since Mr. Rodriguez said he would pay for the perfume display.

What she did not have, however, was the name or address of Matt's new girlfriend's apartment where he was staying for the weekend.

Tom Perkins was thinking about fishing as he drove through Canaan on his way home. In two years, he would retire, sell the house in Wilsippi, and move to his beloved cabin on the lake. He could fish in the early mornings right off the dock and have big-mouthed bass frying before the sun topped the mountains. Planning his retirement always kept him awake and alert on the long ride home. He was bone-tired. Tired of being a salesman for forty years. Tired of traveling. Tired of the rat race.

He knew this old mountain highway like his own driveway and sped up before he saw the sign that marked the end of the town's speed limit. Clicking off his brights, he squinted to see through the rain as two eastbound cars passed, blinding him momentarily. He was tired of this pot-holed highway and tired of the incessant rain. He flicked his brights on and started the long winding climb back up into the mountains.

A small blurry figure trotted precariously close to the edge of the road. He took pity on the hitchhiker, out in this cold rainy night, and decelerated.

"Holy Jesus," he muttered when his high beams reflected the little girl's long blond hair. The van bumped to a stop on the gravel.

Gretchen stared at the lights like a cat ready to dart into the woods. A door slammed and a heavyset, gray-haired man walked toward her.

"What are you doing out here?" The voice sounded friendly enough. "Are you lost?"

Gretchen cautiously held her ground.

"My God, you don't even have a coat on," Tom said. "You're shaking like a leaf. Come on. Get in the van and get warm. I'll take you home."

"No!" Gretchen stepped back.

"What's the matter?" He raised his hands in a gesture of surrender. "You run away from home or something?"

"No." She brushed back her dripping hair. "I'm going home to my father."

"O.K." He turned back to the van. "If you want a ride, hop in."

Gretchen weighed the alternatives. The warmth of the heated vehicle beckoned her closer. Waiting until the man was back inside, she approached the van and opened the passenger door.

Tom Perkins waved her in.

She stepped up toward the seat, keeping the door open. "I'm going to San Diego. Are you going that way?"

Having raised five children, he knew better than to laugh at such an absurdity. "That's a long ways away." He thought about telling her just how far, but decided she might not accept the ride if he did. "How'd you end up out here?"

Gretchen closed the door and sat down. "I didn't run away," she reminded him.

"Where's your mother?" He put the van in gear.

"She lives in the next town." Gretchen eyed him quickly to see if he believed her.

"In Wilsippi, eh?"

She didn't know the name, but nodded her head yes anyway.

"So how'd you get here?"

The van rumbled back onto the road. When she glanced out the back windows, Tom noticed the rain-drenched doll tucked inside her sweater. She turned and bent toward the heater, holding out her hands as if warming them in front of a fire. It took a few minutes before she stopped shivering. Pulling her doll out, she placed it near the heater.

"My mom hates me," she announced cryptically. "She kidnapped us from Daddy after the divorce and made us come up here. She kept me locked in my room so I couldn't even call him."

"That so." He kept his eyes on the road and let the little girl study him. "Did she lock up the other kids, too?"

"Both my brothers, yup."

"Listen, there's a blanket in back there. Why don't you wrap it around yourself?"

She wedged between the bucket seats, found the blanket, and returned, wearing it like a shawl. "To-day, I broke the window and made a rope out of my sheets and climbed down and escaped. I ran all the way here."

Tom saw no reason to tell her Wilsippi was twenty miles from Canaan or that she had been heading in the wrong direction to have just come from there. Why was she making this all up intrigued him. "You sure you don't live in Canaan? I mean, if you were locked up all the time, how would you know?"

"It wasn't Canaan."

Her defensiveness convinced him that was where

she really lived. "My name's Tom Perkins. What's yours?"

"Gretchen."

"Gretchen what?"

She overlapped the blanket and closed it with her knees. "Smith. Gretchen Smith."

"Nice to meet you, Gretchen Smith." He offered her his gnarled old hand.

Reluctantly she shook it. "How close to San Diego are you going?"

He couldn't help chuckling. "Not real close, I'm afraid."

"Can you drop me off at the highway that goes there?"

"No problem."

There was a small truck stop about a mile up the road. He decided to call the police from there. He had hoped she might tell him her correct surname so he could contact her mother directly. But . . . Smith?

The neon sign of Juan's Café blinked above them indignantly as they turned into the muddy parking lot.

"I have to call my wife to tell her I'll be late if I'm going to take you to the highway that goes to California." He switched on the overhead light. "Why don't you sit here and relax. If you're hungry, they've got good burgers here."

"I am, a little," she admitted.

"You like chocolate shakes?"

"Yeah," she said enthusiastically.

He opened the door. At that elevation, snow was beginning to mix with the rain. He grabbed his cap off the dash. "You keep by the heater. I'll be back real soon." He started to shut the door. "You like fries, too?"

"Uh-huh."

After ordering her food, he went back to the pay phone in the lobby. The police dispatcher told him they had received a call about a possible runaway named Gretchen Foster. The description checked out and he told them where she was. They said they would get a squad car there in ten minutes.

When he hung up, he saw Gretchen standing in the doorway.

"She said she'd put my dinner in the oven." He smiled, trying to decipher the strange, emotionless look on her face. "You want to eat in here?"

"I just wanted to see if I could get a strawberry shake instead of chocolate." She shoved open the glass doors. "I'd rather eat in the van. It's more comfortable."

He watched her trot back to his vehicle. Once safely inside, he decided she must not have heard his conversation and went to fetch her food. Even if she had, where could she go up here in the mountains? he thought. As he waited for her order, he kept watch on the van, just to be sure.

Gretchen saw him looking and waved, then pretended to lie down on the seat. Once hidden below the dash, she crawled into the back of the van and unlatched the rear door. She had heard him repeat her full name over the phone and knew she had been betrayed. Slipping outside, she snuck from one pickup truck to another until she was close enough to make a run for the four dented trash cans under the plywood awning behind the café.

From there, she could see the entire parking lot without being spotted and still keep out of the freezing rain and snow. A gust of wind bit her cheeks. She raised the blanket up over her head and pinned it under her chin like a hood.

The old man returned to his van. Within seconds, he was prowling the lot, calling her to come out.

A pair of headlights flashed across the face of the café and she hid further behind the end trash can.

It was the police.

She watched the old man run up to them. As he spoke, his arms flailed out wildly. The officers kept nodding at him while they reconnoitered the area.

Heading in opposite directions, the two policemen began to circle the wooded boundary of the parking lot with flashlights. Gretchen sunk down further into the darkness. It wouldn't be long before they had her trapped between them.

She tucked the bottom of her sweater into her pants to make sure the doll wouldn't fall out of its makeshift pouch. Keeping low to avoid the outside lights, she scampered into the woods. A long white beam swept across the trees to her right. She ducked behind some bushes and it passed over her. Another light cut above her from the opposite direction.

"Check this out, Jake." One of the officers was hovering by the trash cans. When his partner arrived, he shined his flashlight at the ground. "Those tracks look like a kid's tennis shoe to me." Both their lights followed the muddy trail until it disappeared in the overgrowth.

"Think she's out there?" Tom asked, looking for any sign of movement in the darkness.

"She ain't in the café. Or in any of the vehicles in the parking lot. Where else could she have gone?" the shorter officer surmised.

"Pretty scary place for a kid to hide. She must really be desperate."

Tom cupped his hands to his mouth and yelled out her name.

Gretchen crept further into the forest until the lights of the café were no longer visible.

The rain began to soak through her blanket. Huge droplets fell off the short hood, stinging her nose. She could still hear their voices, but was no longer able to determine their origin. Darkness completely enshrouded her. Between shouts, the wind whistled eerily around her and she started shivering again.

Suddenly a light tunneled into the bushes between the trees where she had been standing only moments before.

"There's some tracks over here, Joe," she heard one of the officers say.

"I'll never let them take us back," she whispered to her doll. "They'd find out. About you. Mommy saw how I hurt Mary. They'd make me tell. Then they'd take you away. I'll never let them take you. We'll hide and somehow we'll get to Daddy. He'll protect us."

As Gretchen felt her way forward, damp branches scratched her face and arms. In her imagination, she envisioned a myriad of sharp-fanged creatures lingering in the black shadows of the forest. But even that was nothing compared to the fear of losing her doll.

She trudged onwards, deeper into the mountains, away from the flashlights and the voices. She had no idea where she was. Or where she was going. Or what she would do when she got there.

All she knew was she had to escape.

For now, the darkness was her friend.

The chief of Canaan's five-man police force stopped at the Foster house before he drove up to Juan's Café to coordinate the search. He informed Barbra they might have received a positive identification. A girl fitting her daughter's description was last seen in the vicinity of a truck stop six miles east of town. The county police and the highway patrol were being called in and he assured her it wouldn't be long before she was found.

When she inquired why extra units were needed to find a ten-year-old girl in a small café, he told her his officers suspected she may have wandered into the woods behind the truck stop. There was the possibility she might be lost out there somewhere.

After he had left, Barbra checked on Mary. "I have to go out for awhile, honey. The police know where Gretchen is and I want to be there when they find her."

The calm facade Barbra was trying to sustain didn't fool her daughter.

"I'll only be gone a little while. Just go back to sleep. Everything is going to be all right."

Mary reached up toward her mother with her bandaged hand. "Don't leave me here alone, Mommy. Please."

"Nothing can happen to you. You'll be safe here."

"She wants to hurt me, Mommy. Please don't go away. Please!"

Barbra gathered Mary's clothes up off the floor. "I'll help you dress. We'll bring your blanket and you can sleep in the car. OK?"

As she drove out of town and started the climb into the mountains, Barbra Foster tried to make sense out of the day's alarming events. Before Dr. Bernstein left, he had explained his theory of mistaken identities. It may have been the only explanation possible, but he was wrong, Barbra concluded. Damn it, I know what I saw.

Suddenly the two-lane highway curved sharply around to the left. Her foot popped off the accelerator, but the car was already skidding. She jerked the steering wheel in the opposite direction. Instinctively one hand shot across the seat to brace her daughter. Sliding off the road at a forty-five degree angle, the back tires caught on the gravel bank and she was able to straighten out the Monte Carlo. When she gave it gas, the tires spun. The road was completely iced over. Slowing to a crawl, she continued her ascent, throttling the steering wheel like a vise.

Then how do you explain it? she asked herself when her heart had quit racing.

"I can't," she muttered out loud.

Mary sat up. "What, Mommy?"

Barbra gently eased her head back down onto her lap. "Nothing, honey."

"Mommy?"

"Yes?"

"Would you close your window?"

"It's not open." She pressed all four automatic window switches. "They're all closed."

"But I feel a cold breeze."

194

Without taking her eyes from the road, Barbra checked to make sure the quilt completely covered her daughter. "I'll turn up the heat, OK?"

Mary snuggled closer against her mother. "OK."

Barbra spotted the red flashing lights of the squad car parked on the opposite shoulder of the road below the neon sign and turned into the truck stop. Five police vehicles were lined in a row, to the right of the café, facing the woods. Their headlights pierced the darkness with a wall of light. She recognized the police chief talking to a couple of highway patrolmen and pulled up next to him.

"I'll leave the heat on. You stay here and keep warm. Be back soon." Barbra got out and approached the three men. Frozen mud crackled under her shoes. Beyond the vertical column of light, she saw other lights bobbing and flickering in the blackness and heard voices calling her daughter's name.

Chief Daniels excused himself and walked Barbra back toward her car.

"It's freezing up here," she said, turning up her coat collar.

"The man who picked up your daughter said she took an army blanket of his with her. It should help." He didn't want to tell her that a heavy snowstorm had been forecast in the mountains and it was going to get even colder.

"Where do you think she went?"

He led her to the footprints by the garbage cans, then pointed at the distant flashlights. "We're concentrating our search in that direction. There's a creek that runs up into the mountains right back there. The woods aren't as dense along its banks. I've got a man

195

on either side following it upstream. Eight other officers are circling the immediate vicinity where we think she went in. We're all keeping in touch with walkie-talkies. I'll be told the minute they find anything at all."

"What can I do?" she asked. "I want to help."

"Best thing to do is wait in your car. Or in the café. It's tough going out there at night. I don't want anyone else getting lost."

Barbra scanned the woods while Chief Daniels tried to think of a more positive final remark.

"In most cases, when someone is lost in dense woods like this, without specific landmarks, they tend to walk in circles. Has to do with which leg you favor. She couldn't have gone far. I'm sure of that."

Barbra shoved her hands into her pockets and shuffled back to her car. Her duty was clear. She didn't have time to worry about how Gretchen had burned her sister without burning herself or how her forehead had healed so miraculously. She forced all that aside now and concentrated on the more immediate problems at hand.

Gretchen had no coat and it had been over two hours since she had run away. She must be soaking wet, even with that blanket. It wouldn't take long before she started suffering from exposure in this weather. As soon as they brought her in, she decided she should take her inside the café and get her in some dry clothes.

No, she thought. With the heat on high, it would probably be warmer in the car. She should change her clothes there, wrap her in another blanket, get her home and give her a hot bath. And some brandy mixed with tea. And call Dr. Bernstein. He said he would be waiting at home. No, the police can call him. Then he'll be at the house when she arrives.

Barbra folded the second blanket and put it under Mary's head. All she could do now was wait.

An hour passed.

She watched the lights weaving through the woods. She went over her plan again. Then again. It was so hot in the car, she was sweating, but she kept the heater blasting because Mary was constantly complaining of chills.

Another hour passed.

Barbra felt like she was sitting in a sauna. Her back stuck to the seat when she leaned toward the windshield to catch Chief Daniels's attention. He shook his head and continued a conversation on his walkie-talkie.

"Mommy, I'm freezing," Mary said. She had both blankets over her, plus Barbra's coat, and the heater was still on high.

"How can you be?" Barbra felt her daughter's forehead. It was as cold as marble. She turned on the inside light. The girl's lips were blue and she was shivering.

Snow began to swirl through the parking lot, sparkling in front of the row of headlights. Barbra stared at it numbly, as if watching a black-and-white movie at a drive-in theater with a broken speaker hooked to the window. She could hear the buzzing of voices and the cackle of two-way radios, but it didn't seem real.

Nothing did anymore.

Out there, beyond the smudged glass, a perverse ceremony of darkness and flashing lights danced around her like some kind of cruel cosmic riddle. Trying to fathom the events leading her to this glass-caged insanity only further depleted the few threads of reality she had left.

A white-gauzed hand touched her knee. It made Barbra's entire leg vibrate.

Daniels trotted over as soon as he saw Barbra open her door. "We're doing everything we can, Mrs. Foster."

"I have to take my daughter home," she said, staring at his shiny badge. How could she tell him her daughter was freezing to death in a hundred-degree car. "She's sick."

"I understand."

She glanced at him through hair damp with perspiration. "I don't."

"You shouldn't be out here without your jacket." He took off his and draped it over her shoulders.

Barbra glanced into the woods behind him. "She is," she pointed out morosely.

"She'll be all right, Mrs. Foster. We've called in Search and Rescue. Their teams will be here any second now. You'll be notified at home as soon as we find her. By morning, this will all seem like a bad dream."

Barbra wanted to scrape that official, patronizing smile off his face with her nails. She handed him his coat and got back in the car.

If only it was just a bad dream, she thought, trying to gather enough of her wits together to simply shift the automatic transmission into reverse.

"I can't hear them anymore, can you?" Gretchen asked her doll.

The blistering wind ripped the blanket out of her grip but she caught it before it flopped away in the storm. Hunching down behind a tall, flat rock, she draped it over herself like a tent. There was almost no sensation left in her fingers and it was difficult to keep the blanket closed, but at least the terrible stinging was gone on her nose and cheeks. Even her toes didn't ache anymore.

"Maybe we should head back," she suggested to the doll. Her voice slurred. When she tried to stand, her mind reeled and she fell back against the rock. Pushing up weakly, she lurched forward and bumped into a huge wet tree trunk. The blanket fell from her numb hands.

"I wish everything would stop moving." She stumbled headlong into another tree. Pressing the doll against her, she shook her head. One foot at a time, she told herself, bouncing through the forest like a human pinball.

She had completely forgotten about the blanket.

"It must be getting warmer." She hugged the doll tighter inside her sweater. "I'm not shivering anymore."

A tree root looped up out of the ground like a miniature bridge, but Gretchen couldn't see it. She couldn't even see her doll's face when she tucked in her chin to kiss it.

The root caught her in the shin and her weight sent her sprawling into a thicket of blackberry vines. Thorns pierced every inch of her skin. When she tried to move, they dug in deeper. It felt like she had fallen into a giant spider web made of barbed wire.

"Mary, help me!" she screamed, battling the tangled branches as if fighting the squirming, suction-ribbed arms of a hungry squid. "Get it off me! Get it off!"

Abject terror renewed enough of her strength to roll out of the fierce grip of the vines. Her entire body stung as if she had been attacked by a swarm of angry bees.

She tried to rise onto her hands and knees, but splattered back onto her belly. The combination of pain and exhaustion was just too much.

Turning over onto her back, she closed her eyes and cried.

All she wanted to do was sleep.

That would stop the awful prickling on her skin.

Sleep, she thought, curling up around her doll and rolling sideways.

Sleep.

Snow began to dot her sweater, forming little white islands that grew together over her body like a fungus.

Groaning constantly, Mary drifted in and out of consciousness. No matter what Barbra did, she couldn't stop her from shivering. Even the electric blanket didn't help. Each time Mary awoke, she seemed delirious and kept complaining about the darkness and how cold the wind was.

Barbra watched the upturned corner of the quilt quiver by Mary's cheek. She began to shred the wad of Kleenexes in her lap as she prayed for the phone to ring. She had planned to wait until the police called before she contacted Dr. Bernstein, but was now debating whether to call him sooner.

When another tremor racked her daughter's body, she knew she couldn't wait any longer. Brushing the pieces of Kleenex off her slacks, she stood up. Her legs felt like broken springs.

Suddenly Mary catapulted up in bed and flung the covers away.

Barbra grabbed her. "What is it?"

The girl clung to her mother's arms. Her pale complexion and her frozen eyes made her look like a corpse. Barbra doubted she even recognized her then. Lifting her firmly, she tried to break her out of that morbid death mask. "Mary? You're here, Mary. At home. Safe with me, honey."

Barbra felt the awful spasms jolt her daughter's limbs. Mary's mouth twisted open. The cords in her neck stiffened and her lower jaw bulged.

Barbra's terrified gaze followed her child's as Mary looked down at herself.

Small patches of fresh blood began soaking through her pajamas.

"No!" Mary howled, squirming furiously in her mother's grasp. "Gretchen, no!"

After Dr. Bernstein finished examining Mary, he walked back into the living room. Barbra was sitting on the corner of the sofa, staring at a framed studio photograph of the twins when they were two years old. Her quiet sobs echoed in the still room. When she felt his presence, she put the photo back on the end table under the lamp.

To ask how she was holding up would be inane. Dr. Bernstein had absolutely no idea what to say to her. Or to himself. He had seen many unusual, sometimes even unexplainable, occurrences in his long career. But what he had seen tonight had shaken the very foundation of his faith in medical science. He was a doctor. Someone who had devoted his life to curing the sick. But there was a little girl in the next room, suffering terribly, and he could do nothing for her. It made him sick to admit it, but he was utterly helpless.

"I gave her a sedative, but I'm not sure I should have," he said, circling the sofa to face her.

"Why?" Her hands fluttered in front of her like moths around a fire. In the lamplight, her face looked whitish-pink. "Sleep would do her good. At least she wouldn't be suffering then."

Dr. Bernstein drew on all twenty-two years of his medical experience to retain a semblance of professional objectivity. "Mary has all the symptoms of hypothermia, Mrs. Foster. Shivering. Numbness and hardening of the extremities. A temperature far below normal. Speech is slurred. If she were in the woods and felt drowsy at this state . . ."

He shook his head. He knew she was thinking the same thing he was. Mary was suffering all the symptoms of her twin's exposure. Like a mirrored image, she was duplicating every aspect of Gretchen's plight. How could he tell her drowsiness was the last, final symptom of hypothermia? To give in to it was to sign your own death warrant. Once the body temperature goes below eighty-six degrees, respiration and heartbeat cease . . . for good.

All he told her was that if Mary were outside in the

cold, sleep would be very dangerous at this point.

"But she isn't," he added quickly.

"What about all those cuts?"

Running a shaky hand up through his thin hair, he slowly looked around the room as if to remind himself this was real. "They're not serious. They look like thorn pricks. I have no idea what caused them." He glanced out the sliding glass doors. It was beginning to snow there, too. "I have no explanation for any of this, I'm afraid," he admitted sullenly. "Hypothermia is caused by exposure. There is no medical reason for her symptoms. This goes beyond my original theory of sympathetic reactions. It can't just be psychological. How could she know what her sister is suffering? It's impossible." He rubbed his neck and looked at the color photo of the twins under the lamp. "Maybe they do have some kind of psychic link that binds them together. There's no other explanation I can think of."

Barbra lay her head back on the top of the sofa and stared at the ceiling.

"Then it's true," she said. She could no longer keep her worst fears buried in a surrealistic haze of disbelief. The truth was all too devastatingly clear now. She covered her eyes from the light. "What do we do?"

"I could take her to the hospital in Wilsippi."

Barbra sat up to look at him. "No. We have to wait for Gretchen. She'll want to come home. I should be here at home when she gets here."

He took off his glasses and massaged the bridge of his nose. "We can keep her just as warm here anyway, I guess. Do you mind if I stay and monitor her progress?"

"I'd be grateful if you would."

And what are we going to do if her temperature keeps going down? he asked himself, knowing he had already done everything he could.

Barbra pushed herself up onto her feet. "I'll make some more coffee."

"Do you want me to call the police?" he asked. "To check on . . . on how it's going?"

Suddenly it hit her.

She spun around in the doorway.

"You believe it, too, now, don't you? That she's suffering the same thing her sister is?"

"Yes."

"And if they don't find Gretchen? If she . . ." Barbra forced herself to go on. "If she dies out there? Will . . ."

Like some monstrous parasite, that final question devoured her heart.

"Will I lose them both?"

Chapter X

Although Dr. Bernstein had not told Barbra, his real reason for sedating Mary was based on intuition, a slim hunch actually, not on any medical premise. If the twins really were in contact, through some type of psychic, extrasensory phenomena, he had hoped that somehow that link might be broken if she wasn't conscious.

The sedative, at least, had worked. The girl was finally sleeping soundly. But his theory hadn't. For the last hour, Mary's temperature had still been falling. Her blood pressure and respiration were also steadily weakening.

Barbra didn't have to ask to know Mary's condition was deteriorating. It was written in the doctor's grim, stoic demeanor, no matter how hard he tried not to appear disheartened. She could see the growing sense of helplessness in his slow, ponderous gait and the way he continually paused in the twins' doorway, as if trying to encourage himself before entering.

While the doctor was examining Mary again, Barbra walked back into the kitchen and stared at the wall phone. She had been calling Matt since eight. It was almost eleven, but he still didn't answer.

Hanging up the receiver, Barbra pressed her cheek against the cold plaster wall.

Not both of them, she prayed. Please, God, not both of them.

"Mrs. Foster?" The doctor lightly touched her arm.

His voice, the soft touch, suddenly seemed so far away. Barbra slowly turned toward the intrusion. It was almost like looking through a thick pair of glasses.

"What's wrong?"

All he said was "Something's happening."

She followed him back to the girls' room. Mary's eyes were partially open and she was mumbling incoherently. Each time the doctor pulled the blankets up, she immediately kicked them off again.

"Is she awake?" Barbra asked, helping hold the covers up as Mary tossed and kicked.

"I don't think so."

Mary jerked her head up off the pillow.

"Keep away," she muttered, staring across the room at the closet.

Tucking in her chin, she started petting some invisible entity on her chest. Her pupils began to dance erratically as if searching for something deep in her mind.

"It's behind us," she wheezed. "It's coming."

It took all their strength to keep her from crawling off the bed.

"Go away!" she screamed, then fell back against the mattress and lay still.

Dr. Bernstein pressed two fingers against her jugular as Barbra watched her daughter's chest anxiously. She was still breathing. The doctor took his fingers away and nodded reassuringly.

"Whatever just happened helped," he said, cleaning his glasses on his shirt. "It raised her heart rate anyway. It's a good sign. I'll check her blood pressure."

Barbra stumbled to the dark window. Folding her hands on the sill, she bowed her head.

"Please, Gretchen," she whispered. "Let her go. Please let her go."

The wind bent the tips of the trees that rose above the top of the cliff a few yards west of Gretchen's body. The thin blanket of snow that had covered her fluttered away like sand on the ridge of a wind-swept dune.

"Mary?" Gretchen sat up and felt her doll. It's wet face nudged her chin. "Why did you wake me?"

Then she heard them.

The voices.

Hollow, dreamlike echoes in the wind.

Calling her.

Calling her name.

She forced herself to stand. For a moment, her legs felt like immovable iron anchors. She wasn't even sure if she was really on her feet or if she had only imagined trying to stand. The darkness seemed to pulsate around her. The ground heaved and dipped like a rope bridge strung above a deep gorge. Snowflakes twinkled in front of her eyes and disappeared before hitting the earth.

Stars, she thought, lost stars falling from the sky.

As she reached out to catch one, something crackled behind her. She spun around and fell into a snowdrift wind-piled against a thick clump of bushes.

She detected the brittle movement again, somewhere out in that blackness.

But where?

Whatever it was, it was after her. She just knew it. She could hear it snorting and pictured a huge, hairy creature raising his black nose to sniff out her scent.

"It's behind me," she cringed. "It's coming."

Frantic, the little girl started crawling across the snow toward the cliff. "It knows I'm here. It's calling me."

The wind snapped a dead branch off a tree to her right and it crashed to the earth. Gretchen pulled herself back up to her feet and screamed, "Go away!"

She tried to run, but her legs wouldn't respond. Limping forward, she tripped over a protruding stone and fell again. The doll popped out of her torn sweater.

"Mary?"

She searched the area in panic, like a blind girl for her cane.

Clawing the ground, Gretchen began to inch closer to the edge of the ravine.

Suddenly the ground dropped out from under her hands and she tumbled, head first, down the side of the cliff. A rock jabbed her ribs. Rolling over the stone ledge, she felt the softer bounce of earth and mud.

She tried to dig her hardened fingers into the sheer wall, but just kept sliding and rolling and sliding.

Wooden splinters pierced her limbs.

She had fallen into an old abandoned mine shaft.

A bitter cold shot through her body as she spilled into a dark pool of freezing water. Lunging up for breath, she started slapping the muddy walls in search of a handhold, but her strength was gone. She was barely able to stay afloat. In desperation, she kept inhaling mouthfuls of black, putrid water.

Like a deep well, the mine shaft was a vertical, forty-foot tunnel. Most of the steps on the ladder had rotted away years ago. What was left didn't reach the waterline.

Something slithered over her arm. She immediately stopped splashing, too petrified to move.

It skittered across her shoulder.

Gretchen spun around in the water, feeling for a ledge to save her from her watery hell.

There was no escape.

With her last futile grasp, she turned completely rigid. Her eyes bulged out grotesquely and her mouth dipped under the water.

It was biting her.

She felt little chunks of flesh being torn from her upper arm.

Then her shoulder.

Her body began to convulse in quick sharp jolts.

Reaching a state of terror no longer consciously endurable, she lost all control of her bodily functions.

The water line rippled against her eyes as the sharp yellow teeth tugged at the flesh on her cheek.

Barbra stood by the bed, helplessly watching her

daughter's unconscious agony. Her belly knotted each time Mary's face twisted in agony.

Suddenly the little girl's throat spasmed and she started spitting up green mouthfuls of bile. Barbra shrank back against the wall in horror.

Mary let out a ghastly shriek and began flailing at herself wildly. Barbra grabbed her wrists to keep her from hurting herself.

As Mary battled in her mother's grasp, she cried, "It's biting me! It's biting me!"

Barbra called the doctor while she attempted to pin her daughter down on the bed. Kicking and heaving and twisting, Mary finally broke away and screamed. Barbra crawled on top of her and forced her weight down on her squirming legs.

"Doctor, hurry!"

Suddenly Mary's cheeks ballooned. Arching up against her mother, she gagged in a futile attempt to draw in air. It sounded as if her entire wind pipe was plugged.

"Turn her over," Dr. Bernstein commanded, and they wrestled her onto her stomach. "It sounds like she may be drowning in her own vomit."

The doctor pounded the girl's back. Her face was quickly turning purple. Reaching around under her ribs, he clasped his fists together and jerked.

Like a drain pipe unclogging, Mary's throat gurgled and air hissed into her lungs.

Barbra sprang off the bed.

"Doctor, what is that?" She pointed at her daughter's upper body.

He had been so busy trying to keep her from choking to death, he hadn't noticed it before either.

Little chunks of flesh were missing from Mary's neck and shoulders. Blood oozed onto the pillows.

"They look like . . ." He drew his hands out from underneath the girl. "Bites."

Barbra fell to her knees by the bed.

"Gretchen, don't," she pleaded. "Don't take her with you. Please!"

A child's small voice broke the sudden, terrible silence.

Mary looked over at her mother and tears bubbled out the corners of Barbra's eyes.

"Mommy?"

"I'm here, baby." Barbra patted her cheek. "I'm here."

"Mommy?" Mary closed her eyes. "She's gone."

Barbra arose from her knees. "Who's gone, honey?"

The girl slowly peered over at the doctor. "I can't feel her anymore." She turned back to her mother. "She's gone, Mommy. Gretchen's gone."

"What did she mean, she's gone?" Barbra asked as they walked into the kitchen to get Mary more hot tea.

"I'm not sure," the doctor said.

"What do you think happened? How could those"—Barbra put the teapot back on the burner— "those bites just appear like that?"

"The same way the cuts on her body appeared." Dr. Bernstein folded his glasses and stuck them into their case. "From her sister." Leaning on the counter, he shifted his weight to his arms and stared out at the falling snow glittering around the lamppost by the

211

driveway. "Her temperature is almost back to normal. Blood pressure has risen. She's not shivering."

Barbra watched his bald spot slowly disappear under his hunched shoulders.

"Why?" she asked. "Why would it suddenly change like that?"

He shook his head limply, then turned. "Whatever was causing it doesn't exist anymore."

The mug she was holding slipped from her hands and crashed on the floor.

Barbra looked down at the glittering black puddle on the linoleum tiles.

"Gretchen's dead, isn't she?"

His silence answered for him.

"Hey, Ned. Over here," Hank called out. He spotted his partner's flashlight bobbing toward him and waved. "I think I found something."

Lifting his lantern above his head, he pointed at the snow-covered stone. Ned crouched down and picked up the frozen blanket.

"It's army surplus all right. That's what she had with her." He rolled it up and looped it through a strap in his backpack. "She must have lost it hours ago. There was at least two inches of snow on it."

Having worked as partners in Search and Rescue for ten years, neither had to comment on what that meant. They both knew the Foster girl didn't have a jacket.

"I'll call this in." Ned unhooked the walkie-talkie from his belt.

"Better tell them to concentrate the other teams in

212

this area." Hank circled the rock, extending his lantern to broaden the periphery of light. "We'll never find tracks in this blizzard."

"Maybe she left something else around here. If she was that far gone to leave her blanket, she could be pretty close."

Ned called out her name and they listened to its echo fade into the mountains.

"Should we start circling out?" Hank asked. "The other teams should be moving from the southeast, so let's head west."

His partner nodded and they split up in opposite directions.

Almost immediately, Ned spied something odd in the contour of a snowdrift between two tall firs. Stopping, he nervously flicked off the snow, dreading what he might find.

A small foot suddenly appeared. He lowered the flashlight. There were no toes. Only a tiny pink swollen-looking stub.

"Hank!" he yelled, shoveling aside the rest of the drift.

His partner jogged toward the light between the trees. Holding up his lantern, he knelt beside his friend.

"Jesus Christ." Ned scooped it out. "It's a doll."

They looked at each other pensively. Any joy they might have shared, knowing they were close to finding her now, was tempered by the grim knowledge that they probably would be rescuing a corpse, not a scared, shivering, grateful little girl.

Ned called Control and told Chief Daniels about the doll. It fit the description Ted Perkins had given him.

"Let's check up there." Hank pointed westward. Ned shoved the doll into his pack and followed his partner.

Suddenly Hank turned. He was standing at the edge of a ravine.

"Watch it, Ned. There's a cliff here. I thought there were bushes, but they're the tops of trees."

He walked the precipice, looking for broken branches, rocks cleaned of snow, any kind of sign of a fall.

About ten feet down, something reflected the light. He bent over and lowered his lantern below the edge of the cliff. Ned crouched beside him and shone his flashlight in the same vicinity.

"Something sure crashed through those bushes." Ned squinted to see through the falling snow. "What's that dangling over there?"

"Looks like it might be part of a sweater," Hank suggested.

"Break out your rope and tie it around that tree."

Once the rope was secured, Ned helped Hank with his repelling gear. It would have been a simple procedure if their fingers weren't so numb.

"I'll take the lantern. Follow me with the flashlight. Those rocks look pretty loose below that line of shrubs."

Hooking the rope around his back, Ned braced his feet against a rock as his partner began his descent.

"It's part of a sweater all right," Hank announced. "Wait a minute. I see something over here. I'm going down further."

Ned's flashlight no longer illuminated his friend.

The tension on the rope was the only way he knew he was swinging over to the right.

Repelling out and down, Hank landed on a small stone ledge. It was slippery and he clung to the rope until he was sure of his footing. Giving himself extra line, he climbed down between the crack in the cliff to the next ledge.

"Hey, Ned," he called.

"Yo!"

"I think there's a cave here. Either that or an old mine shaft."

"Don't go down there, Hank. Wait until the others get here."

Hank hitched up the last thirty feet of rope, tied on a lantern, and lowered it into the tunnel. Its yellow glow was sharply reduced by the width of the shaft, but he could make out the remnants of a wooden ladder. After letting out the rest of the rope, he bent down into the tunnel.

In the inky depths, he could see the reflective glare of water. He swung the rope to move the lantern off the wall.

"Oh, Jesus," he groaned.

The body of a small girl was floating facedown in the black liquid.

Then something moved.

Two orange eyes flashed up between her tangled blond hair.

Jerking the rope again, he leaned over further to get a better view.

A brown rat scurried down the girl's back.

* * *

The Doll-Maker lay in bed staring at the ceiling of her trailer. She had parked her Winnebago in an abandoned gas station next to a pay phone two blocks from Matt Foster's apartment building. For the last three hours, she had been trying to make contact with the man who had bought her doll, but no one had answered the phone or the buzzer at the apartment building under the name Foster.

The night was frustrating, the long wait aggravating, but that was not why the old woman lay sweating in the dark trailer.

Something far more terrifying had dried her throat until she could barely swallow . . .

La muerte . . . Death.

It had swept over her with a sudden, chilling fury.

The child-mother, the evil one . . . the life-giver to her doll, was dead.

So why do I feel her damp, clammy hands, those gray fingers of hate, still clutching my baby's throat? she kept asking herself, horrified.

My Mary should be free now. Free of the evil one.

Yet her voice, that dark, shrill voice of vengeance, touches her still.

Even from the land of the dead, she cries out.

Cries out not just to the doll, but to the other child as well.

Somehow, the pain, the fear, the dying itself has touched the innocent one.

But how?

How can the evil one still reach out like this?

Now, more than ever, she knew she had to find her doll.

And purify it.

Before it was too late.

Before the evil one would gain enough strength to rise up from the grave and fulfill her final wish.

But how? she kept asking.

How can my doll have such power?

How can the evil one touch it still?

What special link does she have with the living child?

Then it struck her.

The child the evil one despises somehow gives her strength, through the doll, because her heart remains open to the dead girl.

Is there a connection, a bond between the two children that holds as much power as the doll itself?

The old woman bolted up from her pillow, her eyes flaming with the final, terrifying knowledge why.

Gemelos . . .

Twins, she wept.

Two parts of one whole.

It was the only explanation.

That is why the doll has the power to hurt the other, the one not her life-giver.

There must be a powerful bonding between the children. Now strong enough, with the aid of my doll, to breach the walls of death itself.

And the doll must help her life-giver.

For she had not yet fulfilled the child-mother's malevolent wish . . .

The total destruction of her flesh and blood.

"Ayee!" the woman moaned. "Is there nothing more terrible for a mother than to know her child will be the vessel of another's destruction?"

I must find the doll, she told herself frantically.

And stop the transition.

I must!

Dr. Bernstein parked his Seville in back of Bob Tyler's funeral home and opened the door for Barbra. The embalming room in the basement also served as the town morgue. Supporting her by the arm, he led her to the stairs where Chief Daniels was waiting.

The chief had driven to the Foster residence just before midnight to tell Barbra they had discovered a girl's body that fit her daughter's description. The child had drowned and they needed a positive identification by a member of the immediate family. He said it could wait until morning, but Barbra had insisted the doctor drive her to the morgue at once. She had to know whether it was Gretchen or not.

Dr. Bernstein reevaluated Mary's bizarre recovery as they slowly trooped down the cement stairway. All the girl's symptoms of hypothermia had disappeared within a half hour after her choking fit. He would have called it miraculous except for the fact that she never should have had the symptoms to begin with. After the girl was out of danger, he had decided to stay with Barbra because he had been expecting the chief or one of his officers to show up and didn't want Barbra to have to face them alone. She had been through hell already.

But the worst was yet to come.

Daniels led them through the brightly lit hall to a side room adjoining the morgue. They had lain the body there on a table so the girl's mother wouldn't have to see her on one of the shallow, bowl-like metal embalming tables that funneled down in the centers to let the blood and excess fluids drain out.

Bob Tyler and another officer were waiting by the body. It was covered with a clean white sheet. Barbra squinted in the glaring overhead lights as Daniels walked up next to the table. Dr. Bernstein watched her muscles flex and loosen as she tried to gather enough courage to approach the body. In the last few hours, he had gained a great respect for this woman. She had incredible fortitude, reserves of strength he doubted even he had.

"Can you make it?" he asked, lightly rubbing her lower back.

She nodded and took his arm. Together they approached the head of the table. Barbra couldn't take her eyes off the horrifying imprint of the small figure under the thin sheet.

Daniels looked at the doctor and waited. He hated this place. It reeked of death and anguish and tears. For the next few moments, no one breathed.

With the slightest flick of a finger, Bernstein gave him his cue. Daniels lifted the end of the sheet, exposing the body from the neck up.

"Is this your daughter?"

Barbra had been warned about the bites, but she hadn't been prepared for this. Half of Gretchen's left cheek was eaten away. An empty socket was all that was left of one eye.

Pushing the two men aside, she stumbled to the far wall and collapsed. The doctor quickly crouched next to her and held her while she retched.

Between the violent dry heaves, she kept spitting up the words, "It's her. It's her."

* * *

Dr. Bernstein drove Barbra home and put her to bed. She was in a mild state of shock, but still coherent enough to refuse any type of sedation. She had Mary to think of. She had to be alert and ready to comfort her daughter whenever she needed her.

"I want her with me," Barbra told him.

"I'll examine her again. Then I'll carry her in. OK?"

Barbra clutched his wrist. "It didn't happen. She didn't die. She didn't."

Denial was not that uncommon under circumstances like this, but he hadn't expected it from Barbra. It was a frightening complication.

"Mrs. Foster," he said quietly, "you did confirm it was Gretchen. You gave them a positive identification."

"But Mary didn't die with her." Barbra pulled herself up on his arm like a rope. "She's still alive." Falling back onto the mattress, she began to cry.

"Thank you, God," she whispered, closing her eyes. "For not taking them both."

Then he understood. It had nothing to do with denial. The poor woman was just grateful she hadn't lost both her children. It was probably the most positive thing she could hold onto right now, he thought. As sad as that was under the circumstances, at least it was something. Something good and real and true amid such terrible tragedy.

Dr. Bernstein slowly backed out of the room. *It'll be hard*, he thought, *but she'll get over it*. Realizing there had been a point tonight when he had thought

220

Mary would die too, he wondered if he would get over it as well. All his years of experience, his skills, his knowledge, had been absolutely useless tonight. Whatever happened in this house had nothing to do with science or medicine as he knew it. It went beyond that into dimensions he would never understand.

Guided by the night-light, he wound his way between the twins' beds. With a sense of awe, an almost frightening reverence for the strange, unworldly power that had touched the girl sleeping before him, he reached under the blanket to feel her pulse.

Mary opened her tired eyes. "Where's Mommy?"

He smiled, as grateful as her mother that she was still alive. "I'm going to take you to her as soon as I examine you. Would you like to sleep with your mommy tonight?"

Mary nodded.

"Okay. Just relax. I'm going to pull down the covers and put this around your arm to take your blood pressure." He switched on the lamp and she turned away from the glare.

After tonight, he had thought nothing would ever shock him again. But what he saw now froze the very marrow of his bones.

He blinked and looked again in order to believe it.

The multitude of small abrasions that had covered her body were gone. So were the bite marks around her neck and shoulders.

He unwrapped the gauze bandages from her hand. The burns were completely healed.

Shaking, he checked the stitches above her eyes. The cut was still there, but it was no longer swollen and hadn't the slightest trace of infection.

As he carried her into Barbra's room, he began to wonder if any of this had really happened. He would have liked to dismiss the entire episode as some type of crazy mass hallucination shared by himself, this girl, and her mother.

The vision of Gretchen's half-eaten face convinced him it was no illusion.

At least it's over, he thought morbidly, lying the girl next to her mother. Your twin can't hurt you anymore. Not from the grave.

Chapter XI

The funeral had been set for Wednesday at two o'clock. Matt Foster and his parents flew into Seattle Wednesday morning and rented a car to drive to Canaan. Barbra had offered to let them stay at her house that night, but her hospitality had been curtly refused. Matt told her they planned to drive back to Seattle immediately after the funeral. They had a return flight booked Thursday afternoon and had made reservations already at a hotel near the airport.

For Mary's sake, Barbra had pleaded with Matt not to go back to Seattle that soon. Since Barbra's mother had died, his were the only grandparents Mary had. Although he had been staying with them in their house in the north end of San Diego since Sunday, they had refused to speak to her over the phone. They would only talk if Mary was on the line.

Matt made it very clear all three of them blamed Gretchen's death on her. His parents were even more stubborn than he was. He was their only son and, in

223

their eyes, could do no wrong. They never had tried to hide the fact that they didn't like Barbra. She had stolen their little boy. Even worse, she had belittled him by earning more money than he did. For twenty years, Barbra had tolerated their snide innuendos because of the twins, but there was no love lost between them. She considered Matt's father a weak, insensitive man who had let his wife dominate both he and his son for over forty years. But it was Grandma Foster's influence on Matt that had finally turned her against them. She had spoiled him until it was ingrained in his personality that everything in the world should be handed to him on a silver platter. She was the real reason Matt had gone through so many jobs. He had expected every company to promote him instantly. Not because of hard work, just because he deserved it. After all, he wasn't like other people. He was special. He was Harriot Foster's son.

Barbra hadn't spoken to them since the divorce, although they did call the children once a month. Since Matt could do no wrong, she had been the obvious villain in the divorce. Barbra had expected that. But she thought their differences would have been temporarily reconciled because of their mutual tragedy. For Mary's sake, if nothing else. Since they had been a family for almost twenty years, she had thought they would support each other in such a time of need.

At first, their abject refusal to speak to her had created the response they hoped it would. Barbra was devastated. She had reached out, in desperation, and they had kicked the ground right out from under her. In their minds, the courts should never have allowed her custody, never allowed her to take their son's children away from them. And now they had the grizzly proof they had been right.

For two days, Barbra had wondered the same thing. Was it her fault? Was she a bad mother? But after two long evenings with Michael pointing out to her that her ex-husband and his parents seemed more interested in proving themselves correct than in trying to do what was best for Mary, her initial fears had turned to disgust. It was an oversimplification, but, in essence, he was right. Even as a single, working mother, raising her child alone, she was still a better family unit for Mary than the three other Fosters put together.

That knowledge gave her the added courage to face the funeral, knowing they would be there loaded with all the hate and guilt they could muster for the occasion.

Barbra looked out the back window of her Monte Carlo as they followed the gray hearse through Canaan's graveyard to the big black square canopy on metal stilts that marked the empty plot. The Fosters' rented car trailed behind them at an unusually long distance. The only other vehicle in the small procession was Dr. Bernstein's Seville. Each time the wiper cleaned the rain off the windshield of the rented car, she could see Harriot Foster's grim, tight-lipped old face staring back at her.

The hell with you, she thought. Facing forward again, she took Mary's hand and kissed it. If it wasn't for Mary and Michael, Barbra didn't think she would have been able to get through the last three days. Even though the loss of her twin was extremely difficult for

Mary to cope with, she was doing better than Barbra had expected. The hardest part was trying to answer the simple question: Why? Why had her sister died? There was no simple answer.

And Michael, dear Michael, had been a god-send. He had taken over for her at the mill and came to check on them every evening after work. He didn't come bearing pat answers or trite condolences, only a shoulder to lean on. His mere presence comforted them more than any words ever could. When they needed him, he was there. Barbra would never forget that. And she would never forget that the Fosters weren't.

Michael parked far enough behind the shiny gray limousine to give them enough room to roll the small black coffin out the back. When he started to open his door, Barbra pulled him back by his sleeve.

"Not yet," she said.

Matt and his parents paused to look into the Monte Carlo, then marched solemnly up to the gravesite. She nodded to Michael and he slipped around the car to open the door. Taking his hand and Mary's, Barbra waited to follow Gretchen's coffin.

Rain pattered on the canvas while the pastor spoke his brief sermon. Dr. Bernstein stood at the end of the grave, sadly watching the way the two groups of people deliberately averted their eyes from each other. The death of a child is terrible enough, he thought. Why do they have to do this to each other, too? It should be a time for forgiveness. Not for blaming. Or for hate.

After the funeral, Dr. Bernstein met Barbra by her car to offer his condolences. While she was thanking him for everything he had done, her ex-husband left his parents by their car and walked over.

"You did much more than you had to, Dr. Bernstein," she said. "I'll never be able to repay you for all your support."

Bernstein waved the comment aside, a little embarrassed by the fuss she was making about, what to him, was his duty.

She took his arm. "You are a kind man. And a good doctor. I won't ever forget how much you helped my daughter . . . and me."

Michael Striker inched closer beside Barbra as Matt approached. He saw no reason to hide his animosity and stared openly at the man he had already grown to despise. Matt stopped and faced him, but quickly looked away. Michael could look extremely intimidating if he wanted to. And he did.

Since the beginning of the funeral, Mary had been wondering why her grandparents and her father hadn't spoken to her. She decided it must have something to do with how people were supposed to behave at funerals, but it still hurt her feelings.

Matt squatted between the doctor and Barbra and said hello to his daughter. Mary ran into his arms, relieved he had finally come over.

"Oh, Daddy," she cried, hugging him around the neck. "It's so terrible. I miss her so much."

He lifted her and stood up. Without looking at any of them, he said, "Grandma wants to say hello to her only grandchild. If you'll excuse us."

The bastard, Michael thought, wishing he could have five minutes alone with him in a dark alley to make him swallow that word "only."

Dr. Bernstein considered the obvious taunt cruel and unwarranted. He could see how deeply it had struck Barbra. Although she had pretended to ignore it, he noticed the way her fingernails had dug into the palms of her hands when he said it.

"I take it you're not on speaking terms," he stated to break the tension.

"I guess not," she admitted.

He forced a smile. "So . . . Mary looks well, considering." It was a stupid lead-in and he decided to get straight to the point. "Does she remember any of it yet?"

Barbra's pupils locked into the corners of her eyes to keep track of her daughter. "She still doesn't remember a thing after coming home from the truck stop. Not even your being there. She remembers feeling cold and waking up in bed with me. That's all."

"Most psychiatrists would scream bloody murder if they heard me say this, but maybe it's for the best," he theorized. "Remembering won't change anything now. Maybe it isn't even supposed to be part of her memory. She was living her sister's experiences then, not her own. Actually, I hope she never remembers. What good would it do?"

Barbra finally looked at him. "None at all."

Grandma Foster bent down and hugged Mary. Her wrinkled hands were cold and rubbery. Mary had to breathe through her mouth to keep from being overpowered by her stale perfume.

"My poor baby. My poor, poor baby."

It was the only thing Mary had heard since her father had brought her over. She allowed herself to be kissed and fondled, but it didn't feel right somehow. Her grandmother pressed her cold, powdered face against hers.

"Mary, how would you like to come live with us for a while?" the old woman asked, sneaking a look at Barbra.

Mary glanced up at her father as she backed out of her grandmother's chilly embrace.

"Right now?" she asked, confused by the offer.

Matt grinned and crouched down. "Sure, honey. Today. You could stay in a fancy hotel tonight and fly to San Diego with us tomorrow in a big jet."

"Is Mommy coming?"

The way her father stared at Grandma Foster made Mary uneasy.

"I don't think so, baby," her grandmother stated. "I'm sure she couldn't leave her job. That's always been most important to her."

"But she hasn't even gone to work since"—Mary glanced at the bright yellow machine shoving mounds of dirt over her sister's grave and started to cry—"since Gretchen died."

Suddenly they were all around her, talking at the same time. She couldn't move and it frightened her.

Grandma Foster's voice overrode the others. "Mary, honey, you have to come with us. We can take care of you. Your mother can't. She never could. If she hadn't taken you both away, none of this would have happened. Your sister would still be with us. Your mother isn't capable of caring for you. She's proved that beyond a doubt. Not the way you should be. Now get in the car, honey. We'll take you home. With us. Where you belong."

"I don't wanna go. I wanna be with Mommy." Mary felt six hands shoving her toward the back seat of their car. "Let me go," she whimpered, trapped.

"Now, baby, just relax. This is for your own good," she heard her father say.

Mary bit the closest hand pushing her and elbowed her way free.

"Mommy!" she screamed, fleeing across the grass. "Mommy!"

Barbra swept her into her arms before Matt could catch her.

"Mommy, I want to stay with you," Mary pleaded. "Don't make me go with them, please!"

Barbra cradled Mary's head against her shoulder. "No one is going to take you anywhere, honey. Don't worry."

Before Matt could get within ten feet of them, Michael had squared off, blocking his path, his big fists swinging menacingly at his sides like sledgehammers.

"She should come home with us, Barbra," Matt snarled, not daring to take another step. "You're not a fit mother. You've proved that. For the child's sake, Barbra, let her come with us."

Her fiery eyes focused on Matt.

"Go to hell," she hissed. "And take that damn witch of a mother with you."

"I feel awful," Barbra said. She was still in her black dress.

The neck of the bottle of Chivas Regal kept clinking against the rim of the highball glass as Michael attempted to pour himself a drink.

"I should have hit him," he growled.

"No." Barbra looked at her drink as if it were some strange, alien concoction. "It would only have made things worse. I shouldn't even have said what I did." She put down the glass. Just the thought of alcohol reminded her of her ex-husband. She poured it down the sink.

"You sure as hell should have said it. And more!" Michael tapped his knuckles on the edge of the counter. "They tried to kidnap your daughter, for Christ's sake."

"They only thought they were doing what was best for Mary." She rubbed her burning eyes. If she had had any tears left, she would have shed them, but she felt strangely barren of emotions, like a bitter old woman who had buried her heart long before they had buried her body.

"Why are you standing up for them now?" Michael asked, annoyed. "The whole way home you were too livid to speak. Now you're taking their side?"

He could see Barbra sinking inside herself and grabbed her firmly to make her face him. "What they did was unforgivable. Trying to steal Mary at your daughter's funeral." When she lowered her gaze, he shook her. "Barbra, anyone that could do something as cruel as that doesn't deserve pity or understanding." He slammed his palm against a cabinet and it popped open. "They deserve a fucking kick in the teeth. And that's it."

"Michael, they're not your family. They're mine. So don't tell me what they do or don't deserve."

He let go of her and backed away. Her sudden

coldness frightened him.

"They're not your family either. They're not in-laws anymore. You're divorced, remember?"

Barbra jabbed a finger toward his chest. "Who are you to tell me what . . ." She turned and leaned down over the sink, trembling. "Oh, God, Michael, I'm sorry. I shouldn't take it out on you."

"Or yourself," he added, encircling her waist and drawing her back against him.

"It's not me I'm worried about." What anger she had left melted as he held her. "It's Mary. You're right. They're not my family anymore. But they are hers. Good or bad, they're all she has, besides me. It doesn't matter if they despise me. Or if I despise them. In their own way, they do love Mary. And she loves them. And now they've scared her and I've scared her and the poor thing is lying on her bed crying and I don't know what to say. She's just lost her only sister and the people that love her most are tearing her in two."

The last of her bitterness drained and she wept on his shoulder like a lost child. When she was done, Michael helped her to the sofa in the living room.

Even in the last three days, Mary had never heard her mother crying like that. She walked up to the sofa and hugged Barbra from behind.

"Don't cry, Mommy."

Barbra squeezed her eyes closed and patted Mary's arm. "I can't help it, honey. I hurt inside."

"I hurt too, Mommy." Mary slid over the top of the sofa and sat in her mother's lap.

Barbra tucked her daughter's head against her breast. "I know, honey. I know."

Mary's big blue eyes reflected the pain she had seen on her mother's face. "I'm glad they didn't want to come over here, Mommy. They said mean things about you."

Barbra wiped her cheeks with the back of her hand. "They didn't mean it, honey. They're just hurt. The same as us. And when people are hurt, sometimes they do things they don't mean."

Michael edged around the coffee table and headed into the kitchen. This was between mother and daughter.

"They tried to make me go with them. I didn't want to, but they pushed me." Mary lowered her gaze. "I didn't mean to, but I . . . I bit Grandma."

"You bit her?"

Mary nodded. "On the hand."

Barbra choked back her sudden amusement.

Mary was puzzled. "You're not mad?" she asked cautiously.

Barbra shook her head.

Mary smiled. "I bet Grandma is."

The picture of Mary's teeth clamped into that old woman's hand struck a chord of poetic justice that tickled Barbra. It was the last thing she could have imagined doing, but she was laughing through her tears.

She stopped as abruptly as she had started. It wasn't really funny. It was merely the perverse symbol of the entire pitiful confrontation.

"I'm just sorry it had to happen at all," Barbra said, gently brushing back Mary's hair.

"Will Daddy hate me now?"

The innocence of her question tore Barbra apart.

"No, honey. He still loves you. He'll always love you. Don't ever think that, please."

"But he said those mean things. He made it sound like it . . . was all your fault."

"I know. But that's between him and me. It has nothing to do with you."

Mary could tell her mother was about to cry again and threw her arms around her.

"It wasn't your fault. Daddy was just mad, that's all," Mary argued, hoping it would comfort her. "Gretchen was being hurtful, Mommy. She was always . . . hating so much. She did it to herself." Mary drew back. "Mommy, she kept trying to hurt everyone. It was her own fault. She did it to herself. It wasn't you or me that made her run away. It was her, Mommy. Just her."

Michael stared at the little girl from the doorway, impressed. When Mary cuddled up against her mother to kiss her again, he felt an aching deep in his throat.

"I love you, Mommy," Mary said. "I love you more than anything in the whole world and I never want to leave you. Not ever ever."

"I love you, too," Barbra assured her. "More than you know."

A silent tear trickled out of Michael's eyes.

"I know this is a bad time for you, ma'am. I'm real sorry about your daughter." The tall, ruffled-looking man kept switching the crumbled brown grocery bag from one hand to the other. "My name's Hank Landell. I was one of . . ."

"You were the one that found her." Barbra remembered. She opened the door further. "Would you like to come in?"

"No, ma'am." He spotted the little blond girl peeking at him from the living room. It was like seeing a ghost. "I just thought . . ." He stared down at the bag. "You might want this. It kinda got lost in the shuffle. My partner found it in his truck and didn't know what to do, so . . ." He handed her the paper bag. "Amy, my wife, she washed it for you and, well . . ."

Barbra opened it. It was the doll.

"That was very thoughtful of you and your wife, Mr. Landell. Thank you."

He shoved his hands deep into the pockets of his baggy jeans. "I'm sorry we didn't find her sooner. Real sorry."

"I know you did your best, Mr. Landell. Please thank your partner and the others for me, too."

As he got into his pickup, Hank Landell thought about all the rude, drunken slurs he had heard about the "city girl" who had taken over at the mill. She wasn't at all like some of the mill workers had described. He hadn't expected to be thanked like that, not when they had failed. But she had meant it and it made him feel better.

If any of those assholes say anything obnoxious about her while I'm around, he decided, turning onto the street, they'll be spitting teeth for a week.

"Who was that?" Mary asked.

"It was one of the men who found Gretchen." Barbra handed her the bag and Mary sat up curiously. "He brought this over for you."

Barbra had considered hiding the doll in a closet for a few weeks before giving it to her daughter. Upon opening the bag, she had instantly pictured Gretchen drowning in the mine with the rats. But Mary didn't know the details of her sister's death, only that she had drowned, so that vision would not torture her young mind like it did hers. She just hoped it never would. That was why she had requested a closed coffin funeral. Not even Matt knew about the rats.

Mary lifted out the doll and Barbra tried to read her reaction. For a long time, Mary just held it in her lap and stared.

"Gretchen really loved this doll," she said quietly. "I was jealous when she got it. I shouldn't have been jealous. It made her happy and she was almost never happy."

Barbra stroked her daughter's thigh. "It's yours now, honey. To remember her when she was happy."

"It's Gretchen's." Mary lay the doll aside and gazed up at her mother. "Daddy gave it to her. I couldn't take it. She'd get mad."

"No, she wouldn't. She'd want you to have it. Really she would."

Mary started to reach for the doll, but pulled back. "It was so special to her. I . . . I should leave it for her."

Barbra was worried that she may have made a mistake. "She's not coming back, honey. She's gone. It's yours now."

"I know." Mary gently lifted up the doll. "But it's still hers. It will always be hers."

Resting back against the arm of the sofa, Barbra pulled Mary up between her legs and held her.

"When someone you love dies, it's good to keep a few things you knew were special to them. When you look at them and touch them, they make you feel close to that person. Like I do with my daddy's gold pocket watch you like so much. They make you feel sad, but in a good kind of way. Remembering the ones you love keeps them alive, inside, in your heart, and that's what's important. Keeping their memory alive. Then they live inside you and they never really die, not completely, not as long as there is the love and the memories. Can you understand that?"

"I think so." Mary leaned over her mother's leg and put the doll on the rug. "It's Gretchen's, but I'll keep it for her. Is that OK?"

"That's just fine."

"And when I play with it, I'll always think of Gretchen." Mary tilted her head to one side and looked up. " 'Cause it was her favorite toy in the whole world. And she loved it very very much. As long as I have it, she'll never really be dead. She'll always be here with me. 'Cause I'm keeping her doll safe for her."

Barbra lay in the darkness of her room, unable to sleep. The way Mary had tucked the doll into Gretchen's bed and reminded it that, together, they would keep her sister alive, reassured her that she had done the right thing.

But the scene also had triggered a flood of memories that she had hoped to escape from, at least in sleep. Memories of the twins each suckling from one of her ripe, swollen breasts. Memories of the day

Gretchen had taken her first step and the day she said her first word, "Daddy."

Oh, Matt, she thought, tugging all three pillows up against her as if they were the child's body. Why? Why did she have to die? And why did we have to end up enemies, so full of malice we can't even talk at a time like this? Why, Matt? Why?

She pulled the pillows tighter. I loved you once. With all my heart. I loved your boyish charm and all your dumb college jokes. I even loved your insecurity when you failed at a job and needed to hold me to keep the fear away. Then the twins were born, and I wasn't working and it wasn't all just one big childish game anymore. You had two hungry children and a wife and a new house and all your charm and all your good looks couldn't pay the bills. Then the jokes weren't so funny and the drinking took over.

You hated yourself for not being able to provide what we needed and you started hating me because I could. But money wasn't what I needed, Matt. I needed a father and a husband. Why was that so hard for you, Matt? It's such a simple thing.

And, in the end, you tried to take the one good thing left between us away. I needed you today, Matt, more than I ever needed you before and you . . . you . . .

Barbra couldn't go on.

She didn't want to start the hating again.

When Michael came to her mind, she fought to keep him there. He has that same boyish charm, she thought. It's what I first liked about him. I guess he reminded me of you, Matt, in the beginning, before it went sour. But he accepts things the way they are. And he accepts

238

me the way I am. And you never could do either, Matt. What hurts the most is I know you tried. In your own way, you tried. And I waited. God, how I waited. For ten years, Matt. Ten long years.

Suddenly Barbra drew away from the pillows. Her maternal instincts were tingling. That keen sixth sense focused on the soft whispering that floated in the darkness.

"Mary?"

She threw off the covers, grabbed her robe, and hurried into the twins' room. Switching on the ceiling light, she saw the beads of sweat glistening on her daughter's face. The girl grimaced.

Halfway to the bed, Barbra stopped to stare at the black rocking chair with the gold trim Gretchen had loved so much when she was first starting school.

It was swaying up and back by itself. Each time it creaked, Mary whimpered and her body twitched.

The doll was sitting on the seat.

"Mary, wake up." Barbra gently shook her. Her entire body was damp.

Mary's eyes flashed open.

"Keep her away, Mommy," she cried. "She came to hurt me again."

"Who wants to hurt you?"

When Mary heard the creaking, her face shot toward the rocking chair and Barbra felt her daughter shudder.

"Why'd you put it there?" she asked, clutching her mother's arm.

"I didn't. I just came in. You were having a bad dream. You said someone wanted to hurt you."

"I did?"

Mary tried to remember. She vaguely recalled her sister entering their room and sitting down in that chair. Her face was torn and bloody and she was carrying the doll. She couldn't remember anything else, except the feeling of utter terror when she had awakened and seen the doll where Gretchen had been. For a split second, it had looked just like her sister.

Or herself.

Barbra wiped the sweat off her daughter's forehead with the sleeve of her robe. "You must have put the doll there, honey. When you were half asleep."

Mary stared at the chair. "It was Gretchen, Mommy. She put it there."

"You were dreaming, that's all."

Barbra lifted the covers back up and Mary turned onto her side.

"I know I should keep the doll for Gretchen. But I don't want it here right now."

"I'll put it in your closet."

"No." Mary rolled onto her back and looked up. "Not in here. I don't want it in here when I'm sleeping."

Mary's frightened expression convinced Barbra she should have waited before giving her the doll. It was too soon. But she had seemed so happy about it earlier.

"I'll put it out in the garage. How's that?"

"OK." As Barbra picked up the doll, Mary added, "When I saw Gretchen come into the room, her face looked awful. It was all bloody and . . . and she only had one eye."

Barbra felt as if a small bomb had just exploded in her intestines. No one had told Mary about the rat.

She had purposely made sure of that.

"It was only a dream," she said soothingly. "Just a dream."

"I know dreams aren't real." Mary sighed. "But I didn't put the doll there. I didn't."

Chapter XII

The Doll-Maker had been keeping a watchful vigil on Matt Foster's apartment for over a week. But after the funeral, Matt had decided to stay at his parents'. The one time he had stopped at his apartment to pick up his clothes, the Doll-Maker had been in the grocery store buying another week's worth of canned food.

Time was running out.

She could sense the dead girl's soul, her life-essence, fighting to reach out from the grave to the doll. And through her to her living twin.

Three times, she had conducted cleansing ceremonies to try to stop the dead girl from contacting the doll, but the girl's power was too strong. Without the doll, the old woman's fiercest incantations to Mictlan-cihuatl, the goddess of the nine levels of the underworld, the land of the dead, were useless and she knew it.

There was only one choice left. She would have to break into the apartment to find out the doll's location. She was certain that neither the living twin nor the doll resided in the apartment or she would have felt stronger vibrations, the close emanations of the doll's life energies. But it was her only lead.

She knew it would be dangerous for her, as an illegal immigrant, to risk a possible confrontation with the gringo authorities, but it had to be done . . . now.

At 3 A.M., eight days after she had left the factory, the old woman parked her Winnebago in a dark alley three blocks from Matt Foster's apartment building. She had already planned her escape route. The trailer was a half block from a back street that connected with the big highway that wound southeast, back over the mountains, toward the Adoptable Dolls factory in the desert. If anything went wrong, she would be on that highway leaving the city in less than five minutes.

The steel-framed glass door of the building was locked as usual when she tried to open it. After making sure no one was on the street or in the well-lit lobby, she braced her three-hundred-pound frame, locked both hands on the handle, and yanked.

The steel deadbolt cracked with her first mighty tug. On her second heave, it snapped. Ducking inside, she scurried to the stairs and ran up to the third floor.

From the names listed on the outside buzzer, she knew Matt Foster lived in apartment 312. Moving with unusual stealth for a woman her size, she quietly slinked down the hall to his door. Even with its double lock, the wooden door was easy to break open. It only took one well-placed kick.

For a moment, she waited just inside the doorway, listening. When she was sure no one had heard, she closed the door and turned on the lamp by the sofa.

Hurrying to the big, roll-top desk by the living room window, she began to shuffle through his letters.

An address . . .

She needed to find an address.

She could barely read English and had to rely on searching for a name, the woman's name, the mother of the twins. She just prayed that his ex-wife had not changed her last name back to her own or had remarried.

Suddenly she heard the creak of a door and the soft rustle of footsteps in the hall. She quickly turned off the lamp and hid in the dark corner next to the door.

A hand slowly edged the door open and she saw the blue cuffs of a police uniform. If she waited any longer, she knew she would lose the slight edge she now held, the element of surprise.

Before the officers knew what hit them, three hundred pounds of desperate, frightened flesh slammed into them like an avalanche. The first officer smashed back into his partner, knocking him into the opposite wall in the hall.

In a flash, the Doll-Maker leaped past them and was opening the stairway door.

The first policeman, rolling over on his side, unflapped his standard .38, aimed, and commanded her to halt.

A shot rang out and the officer heard a muffled cry.

"Tim, whatever that was, I hit it," he yelled, trying to untangle himself from his partner. Tim was out cold, having cracked the back of his head against the wall.

The policeman pulled himself to his feet, still groggy from the fall. He tried to run after the suspect, but his legs were wobbly and he was having trouble focusing. By the time he had reached the stairs, he heard the door slam closed two flights down.

Shaking his head to clear his vision, he began to follow the trail of blood.

"We couldn't have picked a better day," Barbra said, spreading the blanket out on the grass.

Mary put the wicker picnic basket next to the ice chest. "It's pretty warm in the sun. Maybe we could go swimming."

The wide Snohomish river was shallow and calm where they were picnicking. In a month, its mighty currents would be heaving and churning, beating back the eroded clay banks to enlarge its muddy spring carapace.

"Take off one of your tennis shoes and dip a toe into the water," Barbra dared. "Then tell me about swimming in the Northwest in February."

Mary skidded down the arched embankment, shaped like the curl of a long, breaking wave, and limped up to the water's edge with one shoeless foot. After barely wetting her toes, she cried, "Never mind."

The water was as cold as snow. Sitting on a flat dry rock, she retied her sneaker. There wasn't a cloud in the sky. Snow-peaked mountains rose above the false, tree-lined horizons to the north and east like massive skyscrapers. The sheer power they exuded gave Mary goosebumps. Across the river, a brown mare and her colt frolicked in a big high-sloping field.

Mary hurdled the bank and plopped down on the

245

blanket beside her mother.

"Everything is so green and bright and pretty," she said.

Barbra began laying the food out between them; cold chicken, sausage, cheese, potato salad, Jell-O with fruit slices, and a loaf of freshly baked French bread. Mary popped a can of root beer and searched under the mustard and napkins for her favorite snack. It wasn't in the basket. She rechecked the array of food on the blanket, then glanced at her mother, disappointed.

"What are you looking for?" Barbra asked.

"The Fritos. I thought I put . . ."

Barbra reached behind her back and held out the bag she had hidden while Mary was testing the water.

"With this veritable feast here before you, all you want are"—she glanced at the Fritos with playful disdain—"these?"

As quick as a frog's tongue, Mary snapped the bag from her mother's hand.

"I like 'em," she said, tearing it open. "They're my favorite snack."

Barbra grinned teasingly. "And they're so good for you, too."

Mary barely acknowledged the sarcasm as she devoured the corn chips by the handful. Barbra divided the Jell-O into squares and gave them each a section on a paper plate.

Mary grabbed a spoon. "Jell-O goes good with Fritos," she said with a gourmet's appreciation.

Barbra chuckled. "What doesn't?"

Just seeing her daughter happy made Barbra feel wonderful. The weeks following the funeral had been rough. There were times when one of them would suddenly turn sullen during a conversation and immediately the other would sense it, too, and both would become quietly immersed in their own tragic memories. It was to be expected. After ten off-and-on days like that, they had agreed it would be best to get back to their daily schedules.

It seemed to help.

All the children in Mary's class had signed a sympathy card and Janet had brought it over the Saturday before Mary returned to school. The following Monday was Valentine's Day and Mary had come home with a shopping bag full of Valentine cards, two from secret admirers not even in her class. She was elated. Mrs. Bixby called Barbra that Wednesday to reassure her that Mary was adjusting well and that all the kids were trying very hard to be extra nice. It had warmed her old schoolteacher's heart to see just how kind and understanding children could be and she had wanted to share that feeling with Barbra. The call created the desired effect Mrs. Bixby had hoped it would.

Barbra knew she would never totally get over the loss of her child. But she didn't expect miracles and was content to take life one day at a time. She was relieved to discover the mourning periods seemed to lessen as the weeks progressed.

Getting back to a routine helped Barbra even more than it did Mary. Redesigning the mill to accommodate the new computerized robotics was complicated and that challenge was just what Barbra needed. Becoming emerged in her work again was her best therapy. The Japanese technologists were extremely polite and innovative and together they were an impressive team. Even Old Man Hopkins liked the "little Nips," as he called them, because they knew how to enjoy themselves, as well as how to show proper respect. Barbra suspected his appreciation had blossomed the night he had taken them out to dinner and they had proceeded to drink him under the table—that and the fact they always bowed ceremoniously when they greeted him. It seemed to bolster his aristocratic illusions.

Her greatest comfort, however, was Michael Striker. Before she returned to work, he had already solved a rather sticky emotional problem with some of Old Man Hopkins's elderly cohorts. A few of them had fought in the Pacific during "The Big One," W.W. II, and weren't exactly comfortable taking advice from Orientals. But when Michael had spread the rumor that the leader of the Japanese team had lost his entire family in the bombing of Hiroshima, even the most ardent of the opposition became sympathetic, even a little remorseful. It wasn't true, of course, but it was a brilliant diplomatic coup and even Old Man Hopkins started to return their frequent bows after that.

Remembering the first time Michael had pointed that out to her suddenly made Barbra laugh. Mary grinned curiously, waiting for an explanation.

"Just thinking of something at work," she explained between guffaws.

"I bet," Mary said, her big eyes challenging the validity of her mother's statement.

Barbra stopped. "What do you mean?"

"You weren't thinking of work," Mary commented

matter-of-factly.

"Oh, yeah?" Barbra shook a chicken leg at her daughter. "Since you're now reading minds, what was I laughing about?"

Mary sucked a mouthful of Jell-O in and out of her teeth until it liquified, then swallowed. "You were thinking about"—she wrinkled her nose—"your dreamboat."

Barbra feigned confusion. "My what?"

"Your Dreamboat, Michael Kissy-Face."

"Well, I never." Assuming the haughty pose of the perfect Southern belle, she fanned herself with the chicken leg.

Spitting out a section of grapefruit, Mary giggled. A small formation of ducks tilted down across the skyline like a moving connect-a-dot drawing of a jet and skidded to a landing in the river. Behind them, above the trees that fenced the western perimeter of the park, two black crows dipped and circled, then disappeared in the woods.

When her daughter was quiet again, Barbra asked, "What do you think about him?"

"Who?" Mary questioned innocently.

Rolling her eyes, Barbra answered, "Michael, honey."

"Who?"

"Michael," Barbra stated loudly.

Mary threw back her head. "Ohhh." Then frowned. "I thought his last name was Striker."

"It is." It took Barbra a moment to get the joke. Eyeing her daughter, she sighed laboriously. "So much for dumb puns. What do you think about him?"

"I think . . ." Mary pondered dramatically. "I think he's been hanging around a lot."

Barbra tapped her fingers on the lid of the potato salad. "Let's be serious for a minute, OK?"

"OK."

"Do you like him?"

Mary nibbled on a piece of sausage. "He's kind of funny."

"What do you mean—funny?"

"I mean, he's funny. He makes me laugh." She could see her mother wasn't in the mood to be teased, at least not about Michael. She put down the sausage. "I like him a lot. I really do. He treats me like a grown-up. And he's interested in stuff I do. You know, not like the way some grown-ups ask you about school and your friends, but you know they think it's just dumb kid stuff and aren't really listening. He listens." She grabbed a slice of sharp cheddar cheese and sandwiched it between two Fritos. "What do you think of him?"

Barbra laid the chicken leg on her plate and looked at Mary seriously. "I like him a lot, too."

Mary smiled impishly. "I kinda figured that."

Realizing she'd been taken in again, Barbra tossed her crumpled napkin at Mary. The girl ducked, scooped up a chunk of Jell-O and aimed the spoon at her mother like a tiny catapult.

"Don't you dare," she warned half-heartedly.

"You started it."

"But I was . . ."

Before she could finish, Jell-O had splattered against her neck. Barbra leaped across the blanket, but Mary rolled away and was on her feet before she

250

could reach her.

The chase was on.

Mary was agile as a rabbit, but was no match for Barbra's long-legged stride. Before she could hop down the embankment to the river, Barbra had tackled her. They tumbled over the edge and landed on their rumps in the cold hard mud. Laughing uproariously, they helped each other up the bank. Their rear ends were soaked to the skin.

For the next hour, they lay, belly down, on the blanket, eating and talking, while the hot sun dried their pants. Boys were the main topic of conversation. Mary had never really thought about them much, but between Michael and the two secret Valentine cards, they were beginning to intrigue her. There was one boy, a sixth-grader with brown curly hair and green eyes, who had started talking to her lately. He always acted weird when he was near her, like he was trying to show off all the time, but she liked him and hoped one of the anonymous cards was from him.

By the time their rear ends had dried, they were too gorged with food even to look at the homemade cookies still in the basket. A few cumulus clouds drifted over the mountains. Each time one blocked the sun, it instantly became chilly. Mary's underwear was still damp and her buttocks itched incessantly. Sitting up, she jerked her hips back and forth against the blanket. It only made it worse.

Checking to make sure no one else was in the small park, she finally stood up, unsnapped her pants, and reached back under her panties to scratch herself properly. Her look of relief reminded Barbra of a puppy being rubbed on its stomach.

"Mom? There's something important I want to ask." Mary zipped up her pants.

"About Michael?" Barbra finished stacking the paper plates and started wrapping the leftover food.

"No." Mary sat facing her, cross-legged. "About Gretchen."

Barbra quickly packed the rest of the food and gave her her full attention. A light breeze swished through the trees. On the wide brown river, a small wooden rowboat lazily drifted into view. Two elderly men kept casting their lines and reeling them in, as content with the process and the river itself, as with catching fish.

Mary knew what she wanted to say, but it was difficult to begin. She picked a red apple out of the basket and began to polish it with her sleeve.

"I loved my sister." She said it as though there might have been some doubt. Barbra remained silent to let Mary think it out. "We shared so much, but"—she studied the waxlike sheen of the apple—"I wonder if we were ever really that close. If I ever really knew what she felt or what she was thinking. I always thought I did, but now I don't."

Barbra wanted to draw her daughter to her and hold her, but there was something in the girl's posture that said she needed to do this on her own, without comfort or prodding. When Mary looked her straight in the eyes, Barbra suddenly felt as if she were sitting next to a wise old woman who, like Merlin, had been living her life backward and who, behind the childlike mask, had knowledge of a long and complicated life.

"I used to feel sorry for her because nobody ever liked her in school. In her whole life, she never had a friend. But now I'm not sure she really cared. I think she did, but she never tried to make friends. She was always mad at everything." Mary rolled the apple up and down her thigh. "Even us. She took us for granted. She almost never tried to be nice. The only person she really liked was Daddy. And I think that was only because he was always giving her things and getting her out of trouble. Not because she really loved him. Only because she could use him. Like she used me to get out of trouble sometimes." She tossed the apple back into the basket and sighed. "I know I shouldn't say these things. I mean, she's gone and it's not nice to talk bad about her, but . . ."

"It's good to talk about it," Barbra interrupted. "Sometimes it's hard to get it out, but once you have, it makes you feel better."

Mary hoped she was right. She watched the rowboat until it passed out of view behind the hill, then continued.

"She wanted to hurt me. I loved her, but I don't think she loved me. I don't really think she loved anyone. She was so full of hate, there wasn't any room left for love. When I saw her in the kitchen by the stove, I could feel that. The hate. It was awful. If you hadn't stopped her, she would have kept burning me. I know it."

"Your sister was sick." Barbra didn't want to mar Mary's memory of her twin, but it was necessary Mary knew she was not alone in her sad conclusions. "Emotionally sick. We can't blame ourselves. It was in her since she was born. It was like part of her was missing. The sweet, loving part."

"There were times when she was nice to me. But only when she wanted something." Mary kept staring out at the slow, wallowing river. "I was scared when she ran away."

"I know, honey." Barbra caressed her daughter's knee. "We all were."

"But I wasn't scared for her, Mommy." Mary turned toward Barbra. "I was scared for me. Scared she was going to hurt me even more. Out there where no one could stop her. Sometimes I dream about it. I dream she's making me so cold I can't stand it. Then she starts biting me on the neck like a vampire or something. The dream is always the same."

Barbra wondered if she should tell her daughter what happened the night Gretchen died, but concluded it was still better left as a bad dream.

"I understand why you were scared. You had a right to be. It's only natural."

"It's more than that," Mary confessed. "I was glad when she died. I was so scared, I was glad. I loved her, even though she hated me, but I don't really feel bad that she's dead. It's like I feel she deserved it. Like God was punishing her for hurting everyone all the time." Mary lowered her eyes. "That's not right, is it? I should feel terrible that she died. She's my sister. My twin. But I don't."

Barbra was stunned by Mary's honesty. Not because of what she said, but because of what it unlocked in her own heart. Mary's words were like keys slipping into the bolted latches of a massive door she couldn't open herself. What shocked her most was that it had taken the innocent self-judgment of her daughter to finally force it open.

"I'll tell you a secret," Barbra said, humbled by her daughter's insight. "Gretchen scared me, too. I was her mother. And I loved her. But when she died, the first thing I thought of was how glad I was you didn't die too. Even when she was lost out there in the mountains, I was more frightened for you than I was for her."

"Why were you scared about me?" A big white cloud hid the afternoon sun and Mary crawled up next to her mother for warmth. "Was it because we always felt each other's pain?"

"Yes," Barbra conceded, not wanting to elaborate.

"But it wasn't, Mommy. Not then. It had changed. Gretchen had changed it somehow." Mary tugged out a handful of grass and sadly tossed it in the wind. "All those times when she was worried about me hurting myself, like on the jungle gym, I thought she really cared about me, at least a little. But it wasn't that at all. She was only worried about herself. As soon as she could hurt me without hurting herself, she burned me. I don't know how she did it, but she did."

Barbra wasn't sure she completely followed that but didn't want to dwell on it. "She can't hurt you now, honey. It's over."

"I know." Mary leaned closer against her mother's side.

"It's just you and me now," Barbra comforted. "And we'll never hurt each other. Not ever."

Mary rolled off the blanket just as the sun reappeared.

"Just me and you," she agreed, tearing out another tuft of grass. "And Michael."

Mary threw the grass at her mother and giggled. The chase was on again.

* * *

Victoria Martinez saw the headlights of the Winnebago enter the trailer camp, zigzagging from one side of the road to the other.

Swerving toward the dry riverbed, it crashed into a large old mesquite tree. Screaming at the other trailers in camp for help, she dashed to the Doll-Maker's aid.

"*Madre santa*," she gasped, tugging the old woman's head off the steering wheel. Her dress was soaked in blood, as was the seat and the towel stuffed against her breast. "I will call a doctor."

"No," the Doll-Maker groaned weakly. "No doctor. No one is to know. Especially the authorities." With the last of her ebbing strength, the huge woman reached out and grabbed the sleeve of Victoria's blouse. "Go to El Ramos. You know of this town?"

Victoria nodded.

"Ask for Socorro. Tell her I need her. She will come. She has powerful medicine, that *bruja*."

Victoria tried to help the old woman up from her seat, but couldn't budge her. "Holy Woman, can not your dolls help you? They saved *mi bebé*. Can they not save you?"

"My dolls are for the children. No others. Not even me." The old woman pushed Victoria toward the door. "Take the car from George Perez. Now go. The others will help me until you return with Socorro."

With that, the Doll-Maker slumped against the window and passed out.

Mary stared into the gaping black hole. It seemed to be as deep as the earth itself. The sound of dripping water echoed in its depths and a crown of thorns rimmed its mouth like sharks' teeth.

From the bowels of the pit, she could hear her sister calling her.

. . . Mary . . .

Suddenly the earth began shaking. Mary teetered on the brink of that horrifying abyss, unable to uproot her feet and flee.

. . . Mary, help me . . .

Gretchen's ghost-like voice began sucking at her like a vacuum, pulling her toward the hole.

. . . Give me your hand . . .

The ground rumbled. Footsteps, like volcanic tremors, pounded the land.

Something gigantic was behind her.

Its hot breath washed over her like a desert wind. It stank of decay.

Mary spun around and saw Gretchen's doll. It was as big as a ten-story building, as big as the mountains themselves.

When it smiled, Mary could see waves of blood gushing between the gape in its rotting teeth. Rivers of red arteries and blue veins pumped through its huge, translucent fingers as it slowly reached down to crush her.

"Don't touch me!" Mary screamed.

Suddenly she was falling.

The walls of the damp black tunnel raced by as she tumbled further and further into its unfathomable depths.

. . . Save me, Mary . . .

Her sister's voice exploded around her like an air-raid siren.

Awakening in a cold sweat, Mary searched the shadows of her room to make sure she wasn't still in the abandoned mine shaft. Spotting the big panda bear by the closet, she breathed more easily.

It was just a dream.

Or was it?

. . . Mary . . .

The girl twisted around in bed.

"Who's there?" she asked timidly.

. . . Mary . . .

The voice seemed to be coming from the hall.

. . . I need you . . .

She pulled the blankets up in front of her like a shield.

. . . Come to me, Mary . . .

"No," she whimpered. "Go away."

. . . Mary, we're waiting . . .

The blankets dropped from her hands.

. . . It's time, Mary . . .

Her little body jerked. Then jerked again.

"Gretchen, don't," she pleaded, helplessly watching herself walk out into the hall. "Let me go, please?"

She couldn't stop herself. Her limbs seemed only to respond to the voice beckoning her from the darkness. Like a human marionette, she was shackled by invisible strings that controlled her body's every movement.

She tried to scream to her mother, but even the chords in her throat no longer responded to her will.

Her mind reeled with terror as she watched herself open the door to the garage.

Gretchen, don't. Please Gretchen, don't!

Her silent screams pounded her brain uselessly.

. . . Touch us, Mary . . .

The twin suddenly found herself standing in front of the tools hooked on the garage wall.

Looking up at the metal shelf, she saw the doll's orange eyes glowing in the dark like a hideously carved Halloween pumpkin. Her consciousness shrank from the ghoulish sight.

. . . Touch us with your blood . . . fresh blood . . .

Moving of their own accord, her hands reached down toward the trimming shears hanging on a nail. Holding them in her fist like a knife, she jammed their pointed end deep into her thumb.

She could hear the blood dripping into the wheelbarrow under the shelf.

Like a mindless creature risen from the dead, she reached up and dabbed each of the doll's eyes with her torn thumb.

Chapter XIII

The Doll-Maker had been in a coma for nine days. She was a strong old woman but had lost a great deal of blood. The bullet had entered through her left breast and passed cleanly through her rib cage, never touching bone but piercing her left lung.

The people at the factory prayed for her twice a day at the small chapel, actually an old trailer, gutted and fitted with makeshift benches and a crucifix of pine cut from a mountain tree to the east. Between prayers at the church, some of the workers, the Indians from the hills of central Mexico, also went up into the mountains each evening to pray in the ancient way, the way of the Doll-Maker, to plead with the old Aztec gods for their Holy One.

On the tenth day, as they trudged back from the mountains, their prayers were answered. The old woman had opened her eyes and spoken.

Everyone from the factory gathered outside the Winnebago waiting. The back window beside the bed squeaked open and the face of the Doll-Maker peered out at the crowed.

A silence swept over the desert camp as the people's

souls cried out in joy.

"Victoria," the woman's feeble voice commanded, "*vien aquí.*"

With bowed head, Victoria obediently entered the trailer. "You asked for me?"

The Doll-Maker beckoned her closer. Socorro, the medicine woman, led her to the side of the bed. Victoria bent her ear closer to the Doll-Maker's mouth.

"There is a phone number," the old woman began. Victoria glanced at the medicine woman. Socorro handed her a slip of paper. Victoria took it and again leaned down to hear the Holy Woman's words.

"Call this number. Keep calling every day, every hour, until the man, Foster, answers. Tell him you are from the factory that makes the Adoptable Dolls. Tell him, in your best English, that you have lost some of your files in a fire and that you need the addresses of all the dolls' owners. Tell him it is part of our service to send birthday cards to the adopted dolls. If he objects, tell him it was you who accidentally started the fire and you will lose your job if you don't get every single address. Beg if you have to. As soon as you get it, come to me."

The Doll-Maker pulled Victoria even closer to her face. "Promise, on your child's life, that you will do this faithfully until you have the address."

Victoria nodded. "On the life of *mi bebé*, who breathes now only because of you, I pledge I will do this thing."

"*Es bueno.*" The old woman breathed out heavily. "Now go. We must let Socorro, that old *bruja*, make her medicine so I will be strong again. Strong enough to battle Mictlancihuatl. Much time has been wasted." Slowly her eyes closed. "Too much time."

"I think I got a nibble," Mary whispered excitedly. "Something's tugging at the line."

Michael Striker secured his fishing pole between two rocks and hurried to her side.

"Keep the line taut," he instructed.

Mary pulled her pole up a few inches. The tip bobbed again and the line jerked out, rippling the still water.

"He's tasting it all right," Michael agreed. "Don't get overeager. Feel him out. That a girl."

Mary squeezed the cork-wrapped handle, too nervous to breathe. The line slackened and she glanced at Michael in disappointment.

"He'll be back. He's a smart one. Wants to make sure he doesn't taste any hook before he goes for it."

"I think I lost 'im." Mary looked back at the spot where her line met the surface of the water.

"Be patient. Keep the line taut. That's it." Michael stood close behind her, holding her waist as if she were an extension of the pole. "When you feel him strike again, give it a quick snap to drive the hook in good. He's a little wary of the bait, so you have to make him take it."

Mary could feel the vibrations in the pole as it began nibbling again. She jerked the line up hard and suddenly felt the full weight of the fish.

"I got 'im," she cried. The line started to reel out as the fish circled toward the middle of the lake. She couldn't take her eyes off it. The metal reel was singing. "Now what do I do?"

Michael laughed. "Take it slow and steady. Get one hand on the reel, there, so you can wind him in." His big fists engulfed hers so he could pace the first easy upward tug, then the quick reeling in. "Just keep pulling on the pole and reeling on the downward stroke. Beautiful. You got it."

Mary was surprised at the power of the fish. It took most of her strength just to yank back the pole. Each time she did, the fiberglass rod warped almost into a V.

"Isn't it gonna break?" she queried.

"It was made to bend like that. If it didn't it would snap in two. Just keep pulling and reeling. That's the way. You look like a pro now."

Suddenly she saw the silver and blue trout twisting and wiggling in the clear water near a white rock.

It jumped.

For a moment, it just hung in the air, glistening. Mary almost dropped the pole, she was so awed by its beauty and power.

"Don't let it tie up your line on that rock," Michael instructed. "Pull it in. Pull it in."

Mary was still stunned. "It was so pretty. Did you see it?"

"He's a big one. But if you don't keep pressing 'im, you're gonna lose 'im. Keep it tight." She quickly reeled in the slack. "Now you got it."

Michael let go of her to get the net, then crouched on the bank.

"Reel 'im in a little more. That's it." He scooped under the fish and snapped up the net. "Got 'im!"

Mary was ecstatic. "Mommy, I caught one!"

Barbra looked down the hill and waved.

"I think we've got the makings of a real country girl there," she announced.

Mary grinned proudly as she followed Michael to the blue plastic bucket.

"You want to unhook him?" he asked, holding out the squirming trout.

She wrinkled her nose, but nodded. "How do you do it?"

He showed her how to hold the fish so the fins wouldn't cut her and she wrestled the hook out with his snub-nose pliers.

"It's got little teeth," Mary gasped, examining the inside of its cream-colored mouth.

"Better to bite you with, my dear." Michael flipped it into the bucket. They now had two fish.

"Mine's bigger," Mary pointed out, watching them fight for the limited space available. "Boy, that's really neat. I like fishing."

She baited her own hook and went back to the shoreline.

"As soon as I catch one for Mom, we can have them for lunch," she said with the assurance of a professional angler.

Michael reeled in his line and laid down his pole. "I'm going to see how your mother's doing. Think you can handle it alone?"

"No problem."

After hiking halfway up the hill, he stopped to survey the area. He had bought this land three years ago. Five acres with two hundred feet of lakefront property. He had already begun drawing up plans for his vacation home with the architect who owned the adjoining property to the north. In his mind, he was standing in the living room, the loft behind him, the kitchen below it, and to the right, the two-story framed glass wall jutting out in front of him like the prow of a proud old clipper ship. Stepping through the sliding glass doors of his imagination, he envisioned himself on the L-shaped deck with the hot tub around to the left by the master bedroom, and gloried in the spectacular view of his six-mile-long, hourglass lake. Gazing past the wooded shore to the east at the mountains rising in the distance, he felt as if their only function was to protect his sacred land.

It had been foggy and overcast when they had made the two-hour drive north to Lake Ketchican, but by midmorning it had burned off. There were scattered clouds to the northwest, but they seemed content to play among the mountain peaks. Only a few small mavericks broke away to drift over the lake.

"Sunshine two weekends in a row," Barbra commented as Michael approached her little oasis. "Must be a record for February." A small rock cliff rose behind her and protected the clearing from the wind. It was hot enough to sunbathe, so she had tied her shirt up under her breasts and put on her cut-offs.

"Catchin' some rays, huh?" Michael sat on the blanket, unbuttoned his heavy cotton shirt, and faced the sun.

Barbra felt like a teenage mountain girl secretly rendezvousing with her logger boyfriend because their families had been having a blood feud for generations.

"We can't go on meeting like this, Billy-Joe," she warned. "Daddy said he'd use both barrels on ya if he caught you within a mile of his little girl. Remember

265

what he and Uncle Jim did to your cousin, Bobby-Jake. Wouldn't want that to happen to you, Billy-Joe. You're too damn pretty."

He gave her his best country grin. "Don't worry, Sally-Sue, I got a lookout down by the lake. They'll never find us."

"Want some of Daddy's homemade brew? Fresh off the still?" She handed him a bottle of cold Beck's beer.

After trading sips, they lay on the blanket, shoulder to shoulder, and enjoyed the heat of the sun on their pale winter skins.

"She's having a ball, isn't she?" Barbra said.

"I think she's gonna be bugging me to take her fishing every weekend. She loves it." He rolled onto his side and propped himself up on one arm. "Has she had any more nightmares?"

Barbra shaded her eyes to look at him. "Not in the last week. Not since we had that talk during the picnic. I told you about that."

"She's a real little trooper."

Barbra sat up and saluted. "OK, Sarge."

Michael yanked her arms out from under her and pinned her to the blanket.

"Don't get snotty with me." He scowled teasingly, pressing his body down against hers while she pretended to struggle.

Then her movements changed and their bodies seemed to mold together in slow, rippling undulations. Pushing back her hair, he kissed her neck and the soft lobe of her ear.

"I love you, Barbra," he whispered. "I love you so much it hurts."

For the last two weeks, he had been waiting for the right moment to say it. She felt his hand move up across her belly and untie the knot in her shirt.

"What about Mary?" she asked, arching up against him as he slipped one sleeve back over her shoulder.

"She won't leave until she gets another fish. We'll hear it when she does, I'm sure."

She rolled away and stood up, letting her shirt flutter down off her arms.

"Let's take us and the blanket up on the cliff. Just to be safe," she suggested.

He was not about to argue logistics.

Mary Foster's mother was in love.

She had suspected that since they had talked about Michael Striker during the picnic last Saturday. But now Mary was sure. Something had definitely changed while she had been down at the lake fishing. She couldn't exactly pinpoint what it was, but it was there in the way her mother had kept looking at Michael while he was building the fire, and in the way they kept brushing against each other like cats afterward, and in the way they exchanged long, hungry glances while they ate. It was as if they shared a special secret that was only for them and no one else.

Something had changed all right, Mary thought, but she wasn't sure she liked it. For the first time in her life, she felt left out by her mother.

She had liked Michael ever since the day she had met him. Her mother always seemed to radiate when he was around and that pleased her. She understood about men and women and how they needed each other. She wanted her mother to be happy, but she suddenly felt threatened.

As they drove home from the lake, Mary pretended to sleep in the back seat while she tried to sort out her confused emotions. When she peeked out one eye and saw her mother's head resting against Michael's shoulder, part of her was glad, but part of her was livid.

A small voice in the back of her mind kept telling her that her mother didn't love her anymore. That only Daddy loved her.

For a moment, she found herself wishing she had gone with her father that day at the funeral. It was as if that small voice was feeding on her jealousy and growing stronger with each brief flash of anger.

The strangest thoughts kept bursting into mind. Thoughts she had never had before. Jarring fits of hatred racked her heart as the thoughts became clearer.

Mommy doesn't love me.

She never loved me.

She only loves . . .

Mary.

Suddenly the girl jerked up from the seat and cried, "I'm Mary."

Barbra twisted around, startled by the odd statement. Michael glanced in the rear-view mirror and smiled.

"Nice to meet you," he said. "I'm Michael. And this is Barbra."

The headlights of a passing vehicle caught Mary's frightened expression.

Barbra reached over the seat. "What is it, honey? Did you have a bad dream again?"

Mary sank back down on the folded blanket and said nothing.

She knew she hadn't been dreaming.

But why would she think such horrible things? She had never doubted her mother's love before. Never.

But Gretchen had.

As soon as they arrived home, Mary made a beeline for the television, turned it on and sat down on the floor. Barbra picked up the jacket Mary had discarded en route and hung it in the closet with hers and Michael's.

"Is there something special on?" Barbra asked.

"No." Mary started switching channels randomly.

Her behavior surprised Barbra. It wasn't like Mary to toss her clothes around or to be that intrigued with television. Gretchen had been the family's TV junkie, not Mary.

"Why don't you get changed and wash up?" Barbra suggested. "I don't want everything you touch to smell like dead fish, OK?"

"Do I have to?" Mary whined.

"It would be nice."

Mary stomped down the hall and banged open her bedroom door.

Barbra couldn't understand this at all. She was acting just like her sister. She looked at Michael. "She was having such a good time today. I wonder what upset her?"

"She's just tired and a little cranky."

Barbra hoped that was all it was.

Mary flipped on the light in her room and started toward her chest of drawers, wondering why she was making such a big deal out of nothing. She didn't even like TV that much and there was nothing good on anyway.

As she opened her underwear drawer, she suddenly had the oddest feeling she was being watched. She slowly turned around toward her bed.

Gretchen's doll was sitting on one of her pillows.

When she tried to scream, her throat locked. Riveted to the floor, she began to hyperventilate as the doll's face transformed itself into a mirror image of herself.

Blood began to drip out of one of its eyes like tears.

Throwing her arms up to cover her face, Mary was finally able to shriek, "Mommy!"

Barbra ran into the bedroom. Mary let out a flurry of muted grunts and pointed at the bed. Barbra didn't see anything particularly unusual, just a stuffed toy, a coloring book, and Gretchen's doll.

Michael watched from the doorway as Barbra calmed Mary down.

"Breathe in slower," Barbra coaxed, stroking the child's back. "Relax. That's my girl. Now tell me what happened."

Mary gulped in air and swallowed.

"Shhhh." Barbra gently patted her hair. "There's nothing to be scared of. Just relax."

Mary waited until she was sure she could speak. "Mommy, throw it away. I don't want it in the house."

"Throw what away?"

"Gretchen's doll. It was staring at me and then it started bleeding and its face changed and . . . and . . ."

The little girl shook her head once, then started crying.

Michael picked up the doll. It seemed normal enough to him. Barbra looked over her daughter's shoulder and he shrugged. There wasn't any blood on it anywhere.

"Want me to throw it out?" he asked.

Mary raised her head. "Take it away. Put it in the garbage can. I don't want it. I never want to see it again."

Michael wasn't sure what to do. His eyes questioned Barbra and she nodded.

"OK. I'll toss it in the can and latch the lid. Will that make you feel better?"

"Uh-huh." After Michael left, she rubbed her eyes. "I'm sorry," she murmured softly.

"About what, honey?"

"That I want to throw her doll away. You said it would be nice to remember her by. But I don't want to remember. And I don't like that doll. It gives me the creeps."

"That's all right. Don't worry." Barbra smiled to let her know she understood. "I never really liked that doll either."

"Mommy, the garbage man comes tomorrow, doesn't he?"

"Yup. Real early in the morning."

"Would you ask Michael to put the can out at the end of the driveway before he leaves?"

Barbra stood up. "I'll tell him to right now, OK?"

271

As Mary wiped her nose, she shook her head gratefully.

"How's she doing?" Michael asked, putting the last glass in the dishwasher.

Barbra wrapped the bologna sandwich in a plastic bag and put it in the refrigerator.

"She wasn't hungry. I sat with her until she went to sleep. She seemed better after she watched you take the garbage out. Strange, isn't it?"

"Poor kid really looked scared there for a minute." Michael dried his hands. Pulling Barbra to him, he asked, "And how are you doing?"

She leaned back in his arms, her hands flat against his broad chest.

"I'm worried. She'd been doing so well this week. Not one nightmare. I had thought the talk we had last Saturday had been a turning point. She seemed content after that, as if she had finally sorted out all her conflicting emotions. But that damn doll triggered something. I don't know what, but obviously she hasn't completely dealt with her sister's death. There's a lot of pain still stored inside her. We saw that tonight. She's been scared of that doll since the day that man brought it back to the house. The doll reminds her of too much, I guess. I don't know how, but I think she knows, at least unconsciously, how her sister died. It's like she keeps reliving her sister's death, and what she went through, too, in her dreams. Consciously she doesn't remember any of it. The hypothermia. The choking. The bites. Not any of it. But it's beginning to surface. She told me the doll frightened her because it started looking like her and because one of its eyes was bleeding. Maybe what she was seeing was an unconscious vision of her sister's face. I saw Gretchen at the morgue and it wasn't pretty. The worst part was her eye. I was hoping, like Dr. Bernstein, that it wouldn't happen, but now I'm sure she knows everything, even about the rats. Don't ask me how."

The image of her daughter's mangled face turned Barbra's stomach. She eased out of Michael's embrace and poured herself a glass of cold tap water.

"It's a horrible thing for anyone to live with, especially a child," Michael said. "But maybe it's good. It had to surface sometime if it was part of her memory. Maybe seeing the doll again caused a kind of catharsis. It's rough, but it could be a healthy sign she's finally coping with the last terrifying aspects of her sister's death. In doing so, she's also forced into facing her own mortality. Children don't usually have to look death straight in the eyes like that. In a way, death has no meaning to them. Most people never do face it. Not really. But when an identical twin, a carbon copy of yourself, dies, part of you has to die, too. She's actually holding up pretty well, if that's what is happening."

Barbra considered his theory. "Could be. Must be awful for her, though."

"When I was a kid and I'd watch a scary movie, sometimes I'd wake up and swear I saw animals in the corner of my room. I mean I could really see them. Then I'd blink a few times and it would turn out to be a coat or a shirt I'd thrown over a chair. Mary's been through a lot more than a scary movie. And she's

273

working it out. It's hard, but it's better than keeping it stored inside and letting it slowly eat away until it's released in other, more unhealthy, ways."

Barbra sighed heavily. "I hope you're right. But I'm not going to take any chances. Not with Mary. Maybes just aren't good enough. I've learned that lesson too well."

"What are you going to do?"

"I'm going to call Dr. Bernstein in the morning and tell him what happened. I think he'll agree I should make another appointment with the psychiatrist. Just to be safe." She looked at Michael with grim determination. "I couldn't live with myself if I didn't do everything possible to insure Mary's health and well-being."

Michael watched her weaken as she gazed down at the floor.

"I love her and I need her. If anything ever happened to her, I . . ." Her moist eyes lifted, fluttering to hold back the fear. "I just couldn't cope anymore. She's all I have left."

Michael hugged her tightly. "You have me, too," he reminded her softly.

Chapter XIV

An internal alarm clock awoke Mary an hour earlier than usual. It was five to six. She could remember having another nightmare sometime during the night, but didn't recall the details. Pushing off the covers, she slipped out of bed. With sleep-heavy eyes, she searched the floor for her fluffy pink slippers. It was her habit to always take them off by the foot of her bed, but this morning they weren't where they should be.

Scratching her little round tummy, she walked barefoot to the front window in the living room and turned on the outside light by the driveway. It looked cold outside in the dark and it was raining. Icicles, like short stalactites, dangled from the black lamp-post.

In the distance, she could hear the deep mechanical rumblings of a truck starting up. It stopped, then started again. It was coming up the hill toward her house.

When she saw the dirt-smeared, heavy-looking yellow truck pull up to her driveway, she pressed her face against the glass. A short burly man in a yellow rubber rain coat and matching pants hopped off a small platform on the back and proceeded to dump both metal garbage cans into the truck. Like a train conductor, he waved an all-clear sign and the vehicle ground into first gear.

Mary leaned away from the window, satisfied.

"You're up early," Barbra said, tying her robe.

Mary jumped back. "I didn't hear you get up." She laughed uneasily.

Barbra smiled and glanced out the window. Seeing the back end of the garage truck disappear up the hill, her smile faded, but she forced it back before she turned.

"Making sure they do a good job, huh?"

Mary nodded, a little embarrassed that her mother had caught her.

"Well, since we're both up so early, what do you say we make ourselves a big breakfast? How about some pancakes and sausage and eggs to start off the new week? Just like the lumberjacks."

Mary was glad her mother had changed the subject. "I can make the eggs. Over easy like we like 'em, without breaking a one."

"You're hired." When Barbra flipped on the kitchen light, she noticed the back door wasn't completely closed. "That's strange. I could swear I locked that right after Michael left." She shut it. "Doesn't help the heating bill." Rubbing her arms, she started for the refrigerator. "It's a little nippy in . . ."

Suddenly she stopped and bent down. Mary glanced around the counter to see what had interrupted her.

Barbra lifted up one of her daughter's slippers.

"How'd these get so wet?" She peered at Mary curiously. "They're soaked right through."

Mary threw up her hands. "I don't know. Maybe they got rained on because the door was open."

"Huh." Barbra furrowed her brow, then shrugged it off. "I guess so. Pretty dumb of me not to have made sure I locked it." She tossed the slipper back on the floor. "Well, Chef Show and Tell, shall we get on with it?"

After breakfast, they adjourned to their respective bathrooms to get ready for work and school. Because of the downpour, Barbra decided to drive Mary instead of her taking the bus. With briefcase in hand, she waited by the door to the garage.

"Come on, honey. It's almost eight o'clock," she called impatiently.

Mary ran into the kitchen. "I can't find my backpack."

"Think, honey. Where do you usually put it when you come home for the weekend?"

"In my room. On the chair."

"It's not there, huh?"

"Nope." Mary began scouring the living room. Barbra checked the pantry, then hurried down the hall. "Did you check the closet in here?"

"No. I've looked in my bathroom and in my room."

Barbra pushed aside an assortment of spring jackets and summer dresses.

"Here it is," she announced. "On top of the box of swim gear."

Mary cocked her head. "Why would I put it there?"

"Don't ask me." Barbra handed her the pack.

"Let's get a move on. Don't want to be late for school."

Janet, Linda, and Mary finished lunch early and trotted back to their classroom to get their coats for recess. There had been an assembly that morning about child abuse and afterward Mrs. Bixby had led a discussion with the fifth graders about what to do if an adult tried to touch them in their private areas. The whole school had been talking about it during lunch and while the three girls were leaving the small cafeteria, they had heard a sixth grade boy make a crack about Becky Hopkins's private parts becoming public last weekend in his dad's barn. Jack and Billy were the only ones who laughed.

"I think he was lying," Janet said as they put on their coats.

It had stopped raining and there were already some boys out on the asphalt court trying to shoot baskets without letting the ball bounce off the metal backboard into the puddle that stretched to the foul line.

"I bet it is true." Linda disagreed as they ambled down the hall. "My brother said he saw her with an eighth grader at the movies. They were in the balcony kissing and everything."

"Gross." Janet made a face and they laughed.

"She's started to wear a bra now, too," Mary said.

"No?" Janet stared at Mary. Neither one of them moved when Linda opened the door to the playground.

"I saw it," Mary stated. "Last Friday, before gym. Ask Anne, she saw it, too."

Linda examined her own flat, flagpole figure. "What's she need it for? She doesn't have anything yet."

"She's got Kleenexes," Mary said.

A flurry of one-liners kept them giggling all the way to the jungle gym.

"Wanna climb it again?" Janet asked. "In memory of your first day, Mary."

"It's too wet." Linda zipped her jacket up. "Hard to believe it was warm and sunny yesterday. It's colder than a witch's tit." Her two friends' mouths dropped open simultaneously. "That's how my uncle puts it," she defended.

"So what should we do?" Janet inquired, since her last idea had obviously been voted down.

"I'm gonna go get my gloves." Mary stared back across the field. "See ya in a minute."

Because of the assembly and the subsequent discussion in class, there had been no schoolwork that morning. Mary's backpack was still under her desk, unopened. Her gloves and stocking cap were inside.

Grabbing the shoulder straps, she heaved it up on her desk. It surprised her to realize she hadn't noticed how bulky it was before. And what was it doing in the hall closet? She had never put it there before. And her slippers? She never took them off in the kitchen. She always left them right by her bed.

Mary stared at the backpack, disturbed by the day's strange occurrences. Maybe her mother had put a surprise in it, she thought. She certainly had found it easily enough. She must have stashed it in the hall closet to hide the surprise until today. Her curiosity aroused, Mary eagerly unstrapped the top flap.

Suddenly she stepped back, tipping over her chair. Its metal posts clanged on the hard floor. The pack rolled over onto its side and Mary covered her eyes.

Looking between her fingers, she saw the doll's head flop out onto the desk.

. . . MARY . . .

Her sister's voice assailed her from every corner of the room.

"Leave me alone," she pleaded. "Please. Just go away."

. . . Mommy's little helper . . .

"Stop it!" Mary screamed, covering her ears.

. . . Mary, Mary, quite the fairy . . .

Mary swept up the backpack and strapped it closed.

. . . How does our garden grow . . .

She shook the pack violently.

"I'll make you stop," she hissed through clamped teeth. "You're dead. You belong with the dead. Not with me!"

The little girl ran out of the room and down the long hall, holding the pack like a football.

"I'll give you back," she cried, slamming the school's front door open with her shoulder. "Where you belong."

Frightened yet determined, the little girl darted across the street toward home.

"Phone call on line two," the intercom crackled.

"Who is it?" Barbra asked.

"It's your children's . . ." The receptionist could have kicked herself. "It's Mary's teacher, Mrs.

Foster."

Mrs. Bixby told Barbra that her daughter had not returned to class after recess and that two of her friends had seen her running down Bank Street going north, away from town.

Barbra buzzed Michael in his office and asked him to meet her at her car immediately. She would explain why when he got there.

As fast as her little feet would go, Mary sprinted up the well-worn trail between Cove Road and her street. Tall fir trees loomed above her, blocking the sky with a thick ceiling of intertwined branches. The winding trail was dark and shadow-strewn.

Mary knew the path well because it was the neighborhood shortcut to and from school. There was a clearing just past the fork where one trail split off and curved down to a dry streambed. Mary pushed aside the underbrush and made sure the clearing was empty. Carefully avoiding the blackberry thorns, she edged between the brush toward the split alder perched on two entangled fir trees. The ground was soggy and her tennis shoes made suction noises as she crossed the small clearing. After breaking a rotten, flat-bottomed branch off the dead alder, she slipped around a deep puddle and began stabbing the soft earth with the stick.

Gnarled, moss-heavy trees scratched against each other in the wind. The digging was easy in the pliant, rain-drenched ground. As she shoveled heavy clumps of dirt, she used her foot to kick them out of the ever deepening hole. The tops of the fir trees swayed above her like monstrous, swishing seaweed.

She stopped when her fingers began to tighten into knots from the feverish exertion.

It was done.

The grave was ready.

She dropped the pack into the hole.

"Now you can rest in peace, Gretchen. I'm giving you back your doll."

A sudden gust of wind brushed through the trees. Branches clawed and scraped at each other.

. . . Help me . . .

She ignored the faint cry.

Like a miniature bulldozer, she used the inside of her sneaker to plow the upturned earth back into the grave.

Then she heard a strange scratching noise and stopped.

It wasn't the branches in the wind.

It was coming from . . .

Her eyes bulged downwards.

. . . from the grave.

Falling to her knees, she frantically shoveled the rest of the dirt into the hole with both hands.

. . . You'll never be rid of me . . .

Mary glanced around the clearing in horror.

. . . Never . . .

Leaping to her feet, she stomped the earth to pack it down.

The voice was gone. She wiped the sweat from her brow, exhausted.

There, she thought. It's over.

Then she felt something push up under the sole of her shoe.

"I returned it," she sniveled, backing away. "It's all yours now."

Thorns pierced her legs and she swallowed a scream. She couldn't take her eyes off the shallow grave.

Like some unholy weed, a pudgy pink finger broke through the tight black earth.

The ground around it started to tremble.

In a frenzy, Mary fought her way through the bushes toward the trail, but when she heard the ghoulish laughter, her head snapped back.

A hand burst out of the dirt and reached toward her, quivering.

Barbra and Michael searched the house thoroughly.

"She's not here," he said. "Want to drive around and look for her?"

"In a second." Barbra ripped a piece of paper off the pad by the phone. "I'll leave her a note in case she comes home while we're gone."

She was shaking so badly she could barely write.

Michael walked up behind her. "Calm down. She's just playing hookey. It's nothing serious. Take it easy."

"Mary loves school," she argued. "She wouldn't take off like this unless something was wrong."

"We'll find her. Don't worry."

His last statement struck a frightening chord inside her. It was the same thing Chief Daniels had told her the night Gretchen had died.

Mary threw her forearm against the back door and

it banged open. Stumbling into the kitchen, she bent over and clutched her ribs. Her sides ached as she struggled to catch her breath. The muscles in her calves were as hard as wood. When she tried to straighten up and walk, a sharp pain shot up her legs.

The house was as quiet as death.

She spotted the note on the refrigerator and shuffled nearer to read it. Her mother had been home, but had gone out to look for her.

Mary prayed she was back already.

"Mommy?" Using the counter as a crutch, she hobbled toward the living room. "Mommy, are you home?"

A familiar voice answered her from somewhere in the house.

"Mommy?" She looked in the dining room, then checked the living room.

No one was there.

. . . Mary . . .

"Mommy, is that you?" she asked in a hushed tone.

. . . I'm here, Mary . . .

The girl pulled at her hair nervously. "Where?"

. . . Here, Mary. Here in your room . . .

As she limped down the hall, the door to her bedroom slowly creaked open. The foot she was favoring slid on something slippery and she looked down.

A path of mud in the hall led straight to her room.

. . . Come in, Mary . . .

The little girl froze.

"Is that you, Mommy?" Holding her fists up against her chin, she bit into one of her thumbs.

"Mommy, I'm scared. Come get me. Please?"

. . . Mary, I'm waiting . . .

Warily, she crossed the threshold into her room.

The doll, blackened with dirt, stared at her from her bed.

. . . Come closer, Mary . . .

A sickening gurgle bubbled up the girl's throat.

. . . You've been such a bad little girl . . .

Then she fainted.

Chapter XV

Having searched the streets of Canaan for over an hour, Barbra decided to check at home again. She still couldn't rid herself of the haunting feeling she had been through all this before.

Michael had tried to convince her everything would be all right, but he knew she didn't believe it. There was only one way to convince her and that was to find Mary.

Barbra slammed the car into park and Michael lurched against the dash. Before he could look up, she was already out the door, running toward the house.

"Mary?" Barbra checked in the kitchen. Halfway across the living room she noticed the trail of mud.

"Mary, are you here?" she asked excitedly.

The little girl sauntered out of her room.

"I got your note," she said, smiling happily. "I've been waiting for you."

Barbra sprinted down the hall and swept her

daughter up in her arms.

"Where have you been? Why did you leave school?" Letting Mary down, she cupped her pretty, smiling face. "Oh, baby, you're safe. You're OK. Nothing's wrong, is there?"

The girl shrugged nonchalantly. "No, Mom. I'm fine."

Michael remained in the living room, relieved to see mother and daughter together again.

"So why did you leave school?" Barbra asked, finally feeling at peace again. Her eerie sense of déjá vu had left as soon as she had seen her child.

"I had a stomachache. I'd called you at work, but you were gone for lunch. So I walked home."

"That's funny. I should have gotten your message."

Barbra crouched down. She couldn't stop touching her daughter. It was as if she needed to reassure herself the girl was real.

"I didn't leave a message," the twin countered. "When they said you weren't in, I just hung up."

"Why didn't you go to the nurse?"

The girl had been rehearsing her answers for the last fifteen minutes.

"I don't like her. She thinks I'm strange. Ever since that time Mary and"—she waved that aside—"Gretchen and I cut ourselves, she's been looking at me kind of funny. So I didn't want to see her."

"I understand." Barbra hugged Mary again. The little girl pulled her head back, waiting for her mother to let go. "I'm just glad you're all right. You had me worried to death." Barbra stood up. "Next time you don't feel good, if you don't want to go to the nurse, you tell Mrs. Bixby. You got that?"

"Yes." The girl ran her fingertips along the door frame and pouted. "I'm sorry. I didn't mean to worry you. I don't see what the big deal is, though. I came right home."

Barbra glanced back at the muddy trail. "Through every puddle on Highline, no doubt."

The girl was prepared for that, too.

"I didn't notice my shoes were muddy until I was in my room. I'll vacuum it up. I promise."

Again Barbra squatted down to hold her daughter. "How's your tummy now? Does it still hurt? Did you get sick? Throw up, I mean?"

"No." She stepped away from her mother. "I feel fine now."

Barbra checked her forehead. "You sure?"

"It must have been something I ate for lunch. But it went away." Her mother's loving concern made her want to laugh. All her lies had worked perfectly. "Really, Mom. I'm fine. Just fine. Can I go back and play in my room now?"

"First I want you to promise you'll never leave school again unless I know where you are going and with whom. All right?"

The girl stared down the hall at Michael. When he smiled, she turned away.

"I promise," she said, skipping into her room.

Barbra joined Michael by the sofa. "I guess I overreacted a little, didn't I?"

"Not at all." Michael put his arm around her. "You had ever reason to be worried."

"I know I'm overprotective with Mary, but . . ." She leaned her head on his shoulder. "But I can't help it."

"That's perfectly understandable." He kissed her forehead. "But now she's home and everything is all right. So relax and quit shaking."

The little girl took a washcloth from the shower, poured warm water on it, and soaped it up. She could hear her mother in the kitchen preparing lasagna for dinner and knew she wouldn't be disturbed. Strutting across the hall, she quietly closed her bedroom door.

Taking the doll out from under her bed, she put it on the chest of drawers below the mirror and washed off the worst of the dirt.

"You're mine now," she said, gloating.

But she wasn't addressing the doll. She was looking at herself in the mirror.

"Forever and ever."

Let me out, Mary cried.

Her silent words merely echoed inside her head.

The twin finished cleaning the doll and hid it in the back of the closet under a pile of dirty clothes. The upper third of its damp face stuck out above a crumpled pair of corduroy pants. The child slid the door partially closed and a thin horizontal line of light pierced the doll's one uncovered eye.

Gretchen, please! Mary pleaded. Don't leave me here!

The little girl glanced over her shoulder at the closet.

"I won't go back," she stated emphatically. "I won't. Not ever."

When she heard her mother coming down the hall, humming, she snatched the washcloth off the chest and tossed it in the corner behind Mary's bed.

"How's my big girl doing?" Barbra asked, peeking around the door as she opened it.

"Fine," the twin answered. "When's dinner gonna be ready? I'm famished."

"Pretty soon."

Just looking at Mary, safe and happy and at home, made her feel more contented. Barbra smiled.

The girl frowned suspiciously. "What's so funny?"

"Nothing, honey. I'm just glad you're here, that's all."

"Oh."

Mary watched out of the crack in the closet door. Through the bloody specks in the doll's one black unblinking eye, she spotted her mother.

Her consciousness screamed out in torment.

Mommy!

"I just wanted to tell you how much I love you," Barbra said, kissing the girl's cheek.

Help me, Mommy! Please!

"I love you too, Mommy," the twin lied.

Mommy, I'm here! Mary howled from her soft-sculptured prison. Here in the doll!

Barbra looked in the mirror at her daughter as the girl brushed her long curly blond hair.

"I'd better check the lasagna," she said on her way out.

Don't leave me here, Mommy!

The door clicked shut.

MOMMY!

The twin reached into the closet, picked up the doll, and cradled it in her arms. Rocking it like a baby, she started to sing.

"Hush little Mary,
don't you cry.
Mama can't hear you . . ."
She tossed the doll back into the pile of dirty clothes
"And neither can I."

Chapter XVI

"I thought you liked to play kickball?" Janet asked, a little perturbed by Mary's constant refusal to participate in any games. Standing behind Mary, Linda shrugged her slender shoulders, as perplexed as her friend.

"It's just a kid's game. It's stupid," Gretchen objected. For the last week, she had been trying her best to keep up the facade, pretending to enjoy all the things Mary had, but she was becoming increasingly frustrated. Possessing Mary's limbs and senses did not give her the innate abilities to perform those tasks like her sister. Mary had always been good at athletics and Gretchen had expected that same level of coordination now that she was in control of Mary's body. To her dismay, she had discovered that her sister's quickness and agility were not inherent in her body, but a part of her spirit, her mind . . . the one aspect of her twin she could never truly possess.

Reluctantly she followed the two girls as they ambled away from the field of play.

"So what do *you* want to do?" Linda asked.

"I dunno." Gretchen no longer attempted to hide

her obvious boredom.

Glancing behind Mary, Janet questioned her tall friend with a look of disappointment. It was getting harder and harder to have any fun with Mary around. The first day they had met her, Janet and Linda had thought they had found a kindred spirit. They had become instant companions. But something had changed in the last week. It was difficult to pinpoint exactly what, but that sense of shared interests no longer seemed to exist between them.

Linda stopped by the big square pyramidlike jungle gym. Suddenly her face lit up.

"Let's climb it," she suggested eagerly. "For old times' sake. Just like the first day you came to school, Mary."

Janet jumped up on the lowest rung.

"First one to the top wins," she called out.

Linda scrambled up after her, laughing. When they both leaped up on the final square, they discovered Linda's plan hadn't worked. Their friend was still on the ground. Linda sighed loudly, sharing the frustration she sensed in her buddy's slumped posture.

"I would have won," Gretchen yelled up. "But I didn't want to. I don't like this jungle gym."

The two girls watched her walk off by herself.

Linda swung down to the lower rungs. "I'm getting sick of this."

Janet lowered herself next to her friend and shook her head in agreement. It saddened her to realize she was beginning to share the same opinion.

"We've tried and tried," Linda complained bitterly. "But it's like she doesn't even want to be our friend anymore. Like she could care less. Everything we want to do is either stupid or boring." Linda hopped down on the wet grass. The clouds were darkening and it looked like it was going to pour again, as it had all morning. "I say the heck with her. I know it's hard, losing her sister and all, but she didn't act this way last week. Or the week before. If we're not good enough for her, she can go play with someone else for all I care."

Janet reluctantly agreed. She was tired of being called stupid, too. As she watched their companion edge along the fence, purposely avoiding the other children, she finally gave up.

"She's been acting as weird as her sister used to," Janet commented morosely. "She never even laughs anymore."

That seemed to sum up both their feelings. There was really nothing more to say. For a moment, they stood shoulder to shoulder in silence, each quietly grieving the loss of their friend.

Gretchen wrapped her fingers through the wire fence and stared at the dark woods beyond the block of the houses east of school. Things were not going as she had planned and it angered her. Once she had taken over Mary's body, she had thought everyone would like her. Just like they had her sister. And at first, they had. But as the week progressed, her circle of friends, Mary's friends, began to diminish. One by one they deserted her. And now her two staunchest allies had turned against her as well. She had seen the way they kept glancing at each other behind her back. They had the same look on their faces that all the others had.

If they still believe I'm Mary, she pondered, why

don't they like me? The dilemma was impossible for her to understand. She had expected the jealousy she once fostered toward her sister, and the intense hatred that produced, would no longer affect her now. But it did. If anything, her anger had only grown in recent days. To her dismay, she realized she was still competing with her sister . . . and losing.

Utterly confused, her fury grew. She would get them, she decided, all of them, for being so cruel to her.

Slinking around the kickball game, Gretchen edged toward the back door of the school. When she was sure no one was watching, she dashed inside. The hall was deserted. Keeping close to the wall, she ran to her classroom and peeked in the door.

Crouching below the windows, she scurried to the back of the empty room and stood up by the model of Canaan they had finished two weeks ago. It was her class's pride and joy.

Like a giant, vengeful god, displeased with her people, she destroyed the miniature replica, delighting in each crushing whack.

Having righted the terrible wrong she felt had been done to her, she happily scampered out the front door, undetected.

Or so she thought.

As soon as she circled around the buses and entered the gate to the playground, she felt it . . .

A presence.

Someone had seen her.

Scowling, she surveyed the grounds. Not even the teacher on duty had noticed her yet.

But she knew she was being watched.

Somewhere.

By someone.

Suddenly she twisted around. It was as if she had heard someone calling to her. Yet she knew no one had. It hadn't been an audible greeting, she had just sensed it.

Peering between two buses, she spied a small, broken-down mobile home across the street. In the shadow of the driver's seat, she could see a dark face staring back at her.

When their eyes met, she felt it again . . . a strange probing sensation, like a weak electrical current tingling under her skin.

The door to the Winnebago opened and Gretchen instinctively backed away, her adrenaline pumping furiously.

The Doll-Maker never took her eyes off the blond girl as she poured her great bulk out of the driver's seat.

It was her. There was no doubt in the old woman's mind. The moment the child's eyes had met hers, she had known.

I must make absolutely sure, she thought. I must talk to the child.

Although she had instantly felt the connection, that ethereal bonding between the child and the doll, she couldn't be sure which twin it was. Since they both were an integral part of the doll, how could she?

But her instincts told her to be wary. That was a bad omen.

In her heart, she prayed she was wrong, but each time the child glanced back, the old woman's soul spoke to her of fear . . .

And evil.

"I told the teacher on duty about it," Gretchen continued between bites from the carrot her mother had given her while preparing a dinner salad. "But that fat lady was gone by the time I found Mr. Price and got him to look."

Barbra had been listening with only half an ear as her daughter recounted the day's events. Michael was coming over for dinner again. Vivid mental pictures of last weekend's lovemaking kept interfering with her daughter's story.

Gretchen could see she didn't have her mother's undivided attention. Guessing why, she still held her temper. Her sister had liked Michael Striker. Even if Gretchen didn't, she had to at least pretend she did.

Until Easter vacation, she reminded herself. Then she would be reunited with her father and her plan would be complete. She would finally be rid of them both. Her sister and her mother. And she would never come back . . . never.

"When's Michael getting here?" the girl asked, grabbing a few slices of cucumber.

"Any time now."

Gretchen despised the way her mother's face illuminated when she mentioned Michael Striker. She wanted to lash out, strike at her mother, break something, anything, to show her displeasure. She innocuously crushed the cucumber slices in her hand and tossed them in the garbage instead.

Barbra covered the salad bowl and put it in the refrigerator. "If that woman comes to school again and you see her watching the kids, tell the teacher like you did today. But I wouldn't worry about it, honey. From what you told me, nothing much really happened."

She doesn't care, Gretchen chided. She didn't even listen.

The little girl stomped out of the kitchen before her anger completely took over and she did something she would later regret. As much as it irked her, she had to remain docile, even be nice at times, like Mary always had been. And being nice could be so very hard sometimes.

As soon as Gretchen had entered her room, she heard the doorbell ring.

"That jerk is here again," she announced to no one in particular.

When her mother opened the door, Gretchen didn't hear Michael's usual deep, resonant hello, but the odd cacophony of a woman with a thick Spanish accent.

"I have to come to see if you might need a housekeeper," the Doll-Maker explained, edging past Barbra to peer into the living room. "My cousin lives in Canaan. I moved here to be with her. She is old and sick and has no one to take care of her."

"I'm sorry to hear that," Barbra admitted. "Won't you come in?"

The old woman nodded, already inside the door. Closing her eyes momentarily, she opened her inner sense to the vibrating auras within the house . . . searching, touching, beckoning.

The doll is here, she concluded. I can feel her.

"I have been stopping at all the nice houses in this

neighborhood," the Doll-Maker continued uncomfortably. To tell lies was bad. It caused waves to disrupt the eternal flow of the spirit-world, the land of shadows and intuition. But lie she must. She had no choice. "I am strong. A hard worker. And I am honest. I do not steal."

Barbra had been considering getting a housekeeper, but hadn't been ready for a stranger to suddenly knock on the door and offer her services.

"Do you have references?" she asked, slightly intimidated by the mere size of the woman.

"*Sí.*" The Doll-Maker took out a piece of paper. "This is the address and phone number of my last employer, Mr. Rodriquez. He will vouch for my . . ." She quickly snapped her fingers. "What is the word . . . integrity?"

"That's the one." Barbra checked the address. "You moved up here from California." She smiled to break the odd tension she kept feeling. "So did we. From San Diego."

The Doll-Maker returned the smile. "A place of warmth and sunshine." Then, circling around the sofa in the living room, "Do you have children?"

"Yes, I have two . . ." Barbra felt a sudden, painful twinge. "I have a ten-year-old girl, Mary."

The Doll-Maker quickly turned her face away. She did not want the woman to see how shocked she was by that. The living twin's name was the same as her doll's! To her, all names had special powers. This was strong medicine linking the other twin to her doll.

But it was not a good sign. Not for the innocent one, she thought sadly.

The short silence that followed was broken by a

squeal of tires. Barbra walked to the door. She did not feel comfortable having this woman in her house and was glad Michael had arrived.

As soon as she opened the door, Michael swept her up in his arms and kissed her. Then he spied the huge old lady watching.

"Oh . . . sorry," he whispered to Barbra under his breath. "I didn't know you had company."

"Michael this is . . . Ah, Mrs. . . .?" Barbra realized she didn't even know the woman's name.

The Doll-Maker bowed slightly. "I am Mrs. Perez."

"Michael Striker," he returned, nodding back to her.

Barbra closed the door and took his arm. "Mrs. Perez is here about a job. She cleans houses and has been checking the neighborhood for possible employment."

"Sounds good to me." Michael laughed. "It'll give you more time to spend"—he winked mischievously—"Doing other things."

Barbra pinched the inside of his bicep playfully and they both chuckled.

The Doll-Maker hid her amusement, enjoying the strong vibrations of the love that emanated from the couple. One does not have to have special powers to see that, she thought. It is written in their smiling eyes.

If the evil one has taken possession of her child, she certainly does not know it, she concluded.

Suddenly the back of her neck tensed.

The child was close by . . .

Watching.

The Doll-Maker slowly turned, focusing all her senses on the little girl.

Gretchen froze by the end of the hallway, her mouth agape.

Barbra let go of Michael and walked proudly over to her daughter. "This is Mary. Mary, this is Mrs. Perez. She's come about cleaning the house."

Barbra tried to lead her daughter into the living room, but the girl wouldn't budge.

"Mommy, that's the woman," Gretchen stated in an agitated tone. "The one at school that was watching me."

Barbra's skin prickled, her mother's protective instincts suddenly aroused.

"Is that true, Mrs. Perez?" she asked suspiciously.

The Doll-Maker grinned. "*Sí.* I stopped at the school for the little ones. It is good for an old woman to watch children playing. It warms the tired heart."

Barbra detected a slight loneliness in her voice and felt sorry for the old lady.

"There now," she said to her daughter. "She wasn't staring at you. She was just watching the kids in the playground." Then, more quietly, so only the girl would hear, "That's not so weird, is it?"

Gretchen was by no means convinced. She knew the old woman hadn't been watching the other kids.

Only her.

She tugged her mother down closer. "I don't like her here, Mommy. You're not gonna hire her, are you? She gives me the creeps. Make her go away, OK?"

The urgency in her daughter's plea startled Barbra. She had been through too many ordeals already. If she

301

didn't like Mrs. Perez, that was enough for Barbra. Her daughter's happiness was her first and primary concern.

Barbra patted the girl's head and walked back to the front door.

"It was kind of you to come, Mrs. Perez. I'm sure there are a number of people around here who could use your services, but I'm afraid I really don't need a housekeeper. There's only my daughter and I. I can take care of the house by myself. With Mary's help, of course."

Ignoring her statement, the Doll-Maker strode toward the little girl.

"Do I scare you so?" she asked, squatting down to face the child. When Gretchen tried to pull away, the old woman grabbed her wrist. "How can I hurt you, little one?"

Gretchen tried to yank her hand away. "You don't scare me," she lied, tightening her shoulder muscles to keep from shaking.

The Doll-Maker arose and her huge shadow engulfed the girl.

In that brief instant, Gretchen felt the horrifying chill of the netherworld from which she had escaped touch her soul.

. . . Gretchen . . .

Her sister's voice flickered in her mind.

. . . Let me go . . .

The skin on her scalp tingled as she forced that frightening whisper back into the dark void beyond.

"Now if you'll excuse us, Mrs. Perez?" Barbra moved between the woman and her daughter. "I have a dinner that's going to burn if I don't get back to it."

The Doll-Maker looked deep into Barbra's strong blue eyes. Barbra suddenly felt exposed. And oddly vulnerable. Pushing her daughter further behind herself, she threw her shoulders back and raised her eyebrows in a deliberate gesture of defiance.

Without another word, the Doll-Maker turned and walked out the door.

Her ploy hadn't worked, but she had found out what she needed. Having been in physical contact with the girl, there was no longer any doubt.

The worst had come to pass.

The evil one had escaped Mictlancihuatl, Goddess of the Underworld.

She lives again, the holy woman thought.

Within her twin's body.

As she headed back to her trailer, the Doll-Maker wept for the innocent one, the one called Mary, knowing now that her soul was trapped in a state of limbo within the doll. A most terrible place of darkness, a shadow-world between the living and the land of the dead.

As she wiped away her tears, she opened herself to that nebulous shadow world and heard the lost child's wails of torment.

Willing her spirit to go further toward the gates of that black, dimensionless world in limbo, she called to the one named Mary.

"I will save you, little one," she whispered, hoping her words would break the barrier between them.

Returning to her place with the living, she sadly added to herself . . .

If I can, child.

If I have the power.

Gretchen couldn't stop trembling after the old woman had gone.

"She's left, honey. Don't be scared," Barbra coaxed, kneeling to hug her.

"Who is she? Why did she come here?" Gretchen queried.

"I told you already," Barbra soothed. "She's just a poor lonely old woman, that's all."

Michael bent down next to the girl. "She was kinda huge, wasn't she?" He smiled to break the tension. "And more than a little scary looking."

When he tried to stroke the girl's hair, Gretchen slapped his hand away.

"She didn't scare me," the girl growled. "I just don't like her. That's all. It's none of your business anyway. You're just . . . just . . ."

Pushing them both away, Gretchen dashed to her room.

Barbra straightened up and looked at Michael. Her daughter's outburst had embarrassed her. It wasn't like Mary to lash out at anyone like that, especially Michael.

"I'm sorry," she apologized. "I don't know what got into her. She's been doing so well lately, but . . ." Barbra glanced back down the hall. "Maybe it's just me, but . . . well, recently, Mary's been acting oddly at times, a lot like her sister used to. I guess she's compensating for her loss by taking on bits of Gretchen's personality. Maybe it helps make her feel less lonely."

"That's understandable." Michael shrugged.

"Don't worry about it. It doesn't bother me."

"I think I should go check on her. Be back in a minute."

Gretchen heard her mother coming down the hall and braced herself against her welling anger. She knew she shouldn't have gotten mad, but she just couldn't help it. She hated that awful man touching her.

Only Daddy can touch me, she thought. Who the hell does he think he is?

When her mother peeked in, Gretchen took a deep breath to help squelch her temper.

"Are you OK?" Barbra asked.

Gretched forced herself to grin. "I didn't mean to get mad, Mommy," she explained. "But that fat lady did scare me and Michael teased me about it."

"He wasn't teasing you, honey. He was trying to help, that's all. To make you feel better."

Gretchen reluctantly nodded, as if she understood. "Do you want me to go apologize?"

"That's not necessary. Michael understands. He's not mad."

"OK, I won't then." Gretchen was relieved not to have to do something so abhorrent to her nature.

"Are you sure you're all right now?" Barbra asked.

"I'm fine . . . really."

When Barbra turned to leave, Gretchen ran up to her.

"Mommy, can I call Daddy? I haven't talked to him since . . ." She lowered her head in a pretense of mourning. "Since the funeral."

Barbra had been waiting a long time for that question. Even after what Matt had tried to do at the funeral, she still couldn't let her child be denied her father and only grandparents.

"Sure you can. I think he's still at Grandma's. Their number's in my book by the phone."

Gretchen waited until her mother and Michael were in the kitchen before entering Barbra's bedroom. She wanted to make sure no one but Daddy could hear her.

If only I could tell him it's me, she thought sadly. Not Mary. It would make him so happy.

After talking to her grandparents for a few minutes, Matt came on the line.

"Daddy?" she asked, wishing he could tell by her voice who it really was.

"Hi, Mary. How are you?"

Gretchen's heart shuddered. "Daddy, when will I see you? Can I still come for Easter?"

"I have to talk to your mother about that, honey. But I hope so."

"Oh, Daddy, I have to come. I don't want to be here, Daddy. I don't like it here. I want to be with you. I want to come for Easter and stay. I don't want to come back, ever. I want to live with you, Daddy. Not with Mommy. Please Daddy, I won't tell. Let me stay with you? Please? Please?"

Although totally surprised by Mary's strange plea, Matt was too overjoyed to question it.

"It'll be our little secret, honey. Don't you worry, I'll work it out. Just don't mention it again. OK?"

"Then you'll let me live with you and Grandma?"

"If that's what you really want."

"Oh, I do, Daddy. I do."

Gretchen was ecstatic. Everything was going as

planned. In her imagination, she pictured her mother crying at the airport when she learned her daughter was not coming back from San Diego. She relished the cruel fantasy until her father's voice interrupted the vision.

"I'd better talk to Mommy, Mary. To make sure you can come down first."

Gretchen immediately yelled to her mother to come to the phone. Barbra excused herself and began the slow march toward her bedroom. She knew she would have to talk to Matt again someday. And she dreaded it.

Might as well be now, she decided, steeling herself to the distasteful task. Gretchen eagerly handed her the phone.

"Hello, Matt." She greeted in an absolute monotone. "How are you?"

Gretchen flipped over on the bed and listened. The conversation only lasted a few minutes, but her mother hadn't raised her voice once. As soon as she hung up, Gretchen was dying to ask her about Easter. It took all of her willpower not to. She didn't want to sound eager. She would bide her time, wait a week, maybe two, then ask. She couldn't let her mother become suspicious. As difficult as it was, she would have to wait. It was almost more than she could stand, but she watched her mother leave the room and said nothing.

"Michael, you didn't happen to see a piece of paper lying around here anywhere?" Barbra asked, searching the living room.

"No. Why?" Michael joined the quest and checked the dining room.

"Here it is." Barbra quickly read the address on Mrs. Perez's reference. Her face paled.

"What's wrong?" Michael asked, seeing the color recede from her cheeks.

Barbra handed him the paper. "Check the address."

It was simply a street number in a town in California. "So what about it?"

Barbra slumped down on the arm of the sofa, staring at the paper. "Matt told me he gave my address to that Adoptable Dolls factory because they had lost some of their files. He said it had something to do with sending birthday cards to the dolls' owners."

"And?" Michael pushed.

Barbra opened the drawer of the end table next to the sofa, took out the doll's fake birth certificate, and showed it to Michael.

One eyebrow rose as he met her gaze.

"They're the same," he said, perplexed.

"Mrs. Perez's reference obviously came from the doll factory." Barbra put both papers down. "That woman, whoever she is, must have been the one who called Matt for my address. But why? Why would she come all the way up here? This doesn't make any sense, Michael."

Barbra quickly phoned her neighbors and asked if Mrs. Perez had offered her services to any of them. No one had even heard of her. And no one knew of any Mexican family living in Canaan either. Her story about having a cousin here must have been a lie.

Barbra stared at Michael in disbelief. "Who is she? What does she want from me?" She rubbed her temples to ease her sudden headache. "Michael, I'm frightened."

Looking over his shoulder, Striker stared uneasily out the front window.

"I think we should call the police."

Chapter XVII

The police assured Barbra that they'd keep their eyes out for the woman. But as of yet, she hadn't broken any laws, so there wasn't much they could do. They certainly couldn't arrest Mrs. Perez because she offered to clean Barbra's house.

The puzzle haunted Barbra all through dinner. After Michael left, she spent half the night in her office, working, because she couldn't sleep.

The next morning, Barbra drove her daughter to school and had a talk with Mrs. Bixby. The twin's teacher promised not to let Mary out of her sight until Barbra came back to pick her up after school.

Having done everything she could to protect her daughter, Barbra finally left for the mill.

Most of the day was spent staring out her office windows, wondering what the connection could be between that Mrs. Perez and her family. What worried her most was that she couldn't find an answer.

She even called Mr. Rodriguez, president of Adoptable Dolls, but all he would tell her was that, yes, Mrs. Perez had worked for him, and, yes, he had given her a reference. But he had no knowledge of her whereabouts now and had never heard of any family named Foster before.

When Barbra picked up her daughter after school, Mrs. Bixby escorted her to her car and told her no woman fitting Mrs. Perez's description had been seen anywhere near the grade school today. It didn't alleviate Barbra's anxiety, but it helped.

After stopping at the grocery store, they drove home.

"Are you still hungry?" Barbra asked, turning in their driveway.

Gretchen quickly finished her ice-cream sandwich. "Yup."

Barbra pointed her thumb at the groceries in the back seat. "There's a super king-size bag of Fritos on top of one of those bags back there."

Leaning over the front seat to have a look, Gretchen wrinkled her nose. "Nah, I don't like them. What else we got?"

Barbra parked the car outside the garage and looked at her daughter, shocked. "You . . . don't like Fritos?"

Gretchen realized she had made another blunder. "I grew out of them, I guess," she quickly amended.

"In one week?" Barbra was absolutely amazed. For the last four years, Fritos had been Mary's favorite snack food. Again she wondered if somehow Mary was compensating for her sister's death by taking on certain character traits of her dead twin. Gretchen really had never liked Fritos. She only ate them so Mary couldn't have the whole bag to herself, Barbra remembered sadly.

"I'll eat some if you want." Gretchen offered to console her.

"Don't force yourself on my account." Barbra opened the back door and gathered a bag in either arm. "Can you carry the little one?"

Gretchen grabbed the last bag and the six-pack of Pepsi and followed her mother to the front door.

Leaning one knee up against the door frame, Barbra searched her purse for the right key. The bag shifted and Barbra swung sideways against the door to rebalance it.

Suddenly the door flew open and the bag spilled onto the floor. Having lived in San Diego for almost twenty years, Barbra had acquired the habit of always locking the house when she left in the morning. Because of Mrs. Perez, she had double-checked the door that morning and was positive she had locked it.

Not wanting to worry her daughter, she said nothing and nonchalantly examined the lock. The dead bolt was cracked and the square wooden hole in the door frame was badly chipped. It didn't take a detective to see that the door had been kicked in.

"Mary, go back to the car and see if there's any more groceries on the floor."

"I already checked," the girl informed her. "There isn't any gro . . ."

"Mary, do as you're told," Barbra barked. Her tone of voice convinced Gretchen not to argue, even if she knew there weren't any groceries left in the car.

Having gotten her daughter out of the house, Barbra grabbed the baseball bat out of the hall closet and began to check each room.

Whoever had broken in was gone.

When the girl returned, Barbra asked her to pick up the groceries on the floor and put them away. Before Gretchen could object, Barbra told her not to argue . . . just do as she was told.

"Aren't you gonna help?" the girl asked, gathering up an armful of frozen vegetables.

"In a minute. I have to make a phone call first."

Barbra hurried to her bedroom and closed the door. First, she called Michael at the mill. He said he'd be right over. Then she called the police. The dispatcher told her a squad car would be at her house in five minutes.

While she waited, Barbra made a quick inventory of her most precious possessions. Nothing of value seemed to be missing. She wished there had been. At least that would make sense. The alternative, that someone had broken into her house for reasons besides theft, was much more frightening.

Michael parked his 280Z behind the squad car and followed the two officers into Barbra's house. Just having Michael beside her made Barbra feel more secure. After checking the lock, one of the officers left to question the neighbors. The chief remained to go over the details one more time with Barbra.

"And nothing is missing?" he asked after she had recounted the events of the last twenty-four hours.

"Nothing that I can find." Barbra wouldn't let go

of Michael's arm. He understood and stayed by her side, a sentinel of strength. As terrible as the circumstances were, he liked being needed so desperately by the woman he loved. The woman he would protect with his life if necessary. The way his powerful muscles flexed, tensing into granite as she spoke to the chief, conveyed that commitment to her far more than words ever could. It was extremely comforting to know she was not alone anymore. She would finally let herself admit how scared she was. Not having to keep up a facade of courage was a great relief.

"There is something missing, Mommy," a small voice informed them from the hallway. All three adults turned in unison toward the little girl.

"My doll," Gretchen explained. "Someone went through my closet and stole my doll."

The officer looked at Barbra incredulously. "A doll?"

"It was an expensive doll," Gretchen defended, seeing the doubt in the policeman's face. "Daddy sent it to me."

"Michael threw it out, honey. Don't you remember?" Barbra reminded her.

Gretchen wanted to argue, but knew better. Losing the doll terrified her. In the last two days, she had felt Mary's presence creeping into her consciousness more and more often. It was as if her sister's life essence was somehow growing stronger. When she had discovered her doll was missing, an eerie premonition had immediately permeated her being. Her will was strong. She was still in control, but she couldn't shake that sudden sense of impending disaster, as if her sister, in that dark, horrifying place of limbo, was now lurking just beyond her material senses . . . waiting, just waiting to take her back.

Chief Daniels felt a twinge of pity for both the child and her mother. He had been at the morgue when Mrs. Foster had identified her dead child's body.

"That's odd," he mentioned under his breath as he wrote on his pad.

His partner suddenly burst through the door, out of breath.

"What'd you do, run to all the neighbors?" The chief joked.

No one laughed.

"Mrs. Justin, the lady across the street? She said she saw a large Mexican-looking woman enter this house." He scratched his head. "She didn't think much of it at the time because Mrs. Foster had called her yesterday asking about the new cleaning lady in town. She said the Mexican woman went to the door with a bucket full of cleaning utensils and a mop or something. She thought Mrs. Foster had hired her to clean the house. She said it looked like she had a key. She opened the door easily enough. Just pushed it once, she said."

"That's a little hard to believe." The chief fingered the cracked wood on the door frame. "It'd take a defensive lineman to break this door open with one shove."

"That's what she said, Chief," the officer concluded. "Her description fits that Mrs. Perez to a tee."

Michael felt Barbra shudder and pulled her closer

315

to his side.

"But why? Why would she break in just to steal a doll?" Barbra asked.

"Maybe she was looking for something . . . else." The chief glanced at the little girl, then back at her mother. Barbra understood immediately.

"Mary, why don't you go play in your room?" Barbra pointed down the hall. It was not a request.

"But I wanna stay and . . ."

"Didn't you hear me?" Barbra interrupted, staring at her daughter for emphasis.

Reluctantly the girl did as she was told. Barbra led the group into the kitchen and swung the door closed.

"Now what exactly do you mean, Chief?" She locked herself around Michael's arm and waited. The chief tapped his holster, trying to think of a way to ease into his theory. He decided to be blunt.

"Maybe she was looking for your daughter, Mrs. Foster." He took a deep breath and waited until the shock wore off. "You said the woman had a reference from a factory in southern California, in the area east of San Diego. You told us yesterday that your husband lives in San Diego. We contacted the police department there. It seems someone fitting Mrs. Perez's description broke into your husband's apartment. But they haven't been able to contact him."

"He's been staying with his parents since the funeral," Barbra explained. "I have their address. But what does that have to do with it? They must have a hundred break-ins in that city."

"Maybe nothing at all," the chief admitted. "But there might be an explanation. Let me ask you one

316

thing first. What, exactly, is your relationship with your ex-husband, Mrs. Foster? I mean . . . are you on good speaking terms? Or is there some animosity between you?" He was not putting it well and he knew it. "What I'm trying to ask, is . . . Is there a problem between you two concerning the custody of your child?"

"Yes, there is, Chief. He tried to take Mary by force at the funeral." Having begun to follow his line of questioning, Barbra's jaw went slack. "You don't think he would try to . . . to . . ."

"Kidnap your daughter?" the chief filled in. "It's the only connection I can come up with. There's a lot of private detectives that hire out to do just that."

"But why would someone he hired break into his apartment?" Michael asked.

"I admit that's puzzling." The chief rubbed his wide chin. "And I don't have an answer. But like I said, it's the only explanation that makes any kind of sense. Maybe the break-in was just a ploy, to throw us off the track. This Mrs. Perez, if that's her real name, obviously came to Canaan to find you, Mrs. Foster. And your daughter. You told us she seemed very interested in Mary when she was here yesterday. And before that, the only time she's been seen, was at the grade school. You said your daughter felt the woman was watching her, not the other kids. And your husband did admit to giving your address to a woman on the phone. It's all rather circumstantial. It wouldn't stand up in court, but . . ."

Barbra unlatched herself from Michael and gripped the edge of the sink.

"That bastard," she hissed. "I wouldn't put it past him."

"Do you think she'll try again?" Michael asked nervously.

Barbra spun around, waiting for the answer.

"To tell you the truth, I doubt it. She knows we're looking for her now. She's probably halfway back to California. We'll radio it in. She shouldn't be hard to spot in an old Winnebago."

"What should I do?" Barbra asked. "In case she didn't leave?"

"We'll keep a watch on your house, Mrs. Foster. At least until we're sure she's gone. We can arrest her on suspicion of breaking and entering. And we'll contact the San Diego police again. They have a warrant out for her as well. But we can't do anything to your husband really. Except warn him. And, hopefully, scare him out of any further attempts. Once he sees the police know about his plan, if that's what's really going on here, I'm sure he'll realize the futility of any further attempts."

Barbra was beginning to feel better. At least there was an explanation now. And it did seem logical that the woman would have given up at this point. Any vestige of pity she once had for Matt was finally gone for good. After his incessant, almost feverish apologies over the phone, Barbra had been considering letting Mary spend Easter with her father. In a way, she was glad this had happened now. Matt had shown his true colors. She would never again trust a word her ex-husband uttered. If she had let Mary go to San Diego, she realized she might never have seen her

318

daughter again.

"I'm staying here tonight," Michael informed Barbra after the police had left. "I'll sleep on the sofa. Nothing will get by me. Don't you worry about that."

Barbra hugged Michael gratefully, then stepped away.

"I'm going to call Matt. And tell him his stupid plan didn't work, and that as far as I'm concerned, he can rot in hell before he'll ever see his daughter again."

As he watched her leave, Michael decided he, too, would have to talk with Matt Foster . . . man to man. In no uncertain terms, he would explain to Mr. Foster just how easily he could break both his legs if he ever bothered Barbra or her daughter again.

Michael Striker was not one to make idle threats.

After hearing her mother pass by, Gretchen took her ear from the door. Barbra's final statement still echoed in her mind. If her mother had her way, she would never see her father again.

She can't do that, Gretchen wept. She can't keep me from Daddy!

The utter helplessness of her predicament horrified her. The one person who could have saved her was gone. All she really wanted was to take me back to Daddy, Gretchen thought. No wonder she kept watching me at school.

Why didn't I talk to her at the playground? Gretchen angrily accosted herself. Why? If I hadn't been so stupid, I would be on my way to Daddy right now. And that woman has my doll. She stole it so I'd have it when she took me to daddy. Somehow, Daddy knows about the doll. He must. And that means he knows it's really me. Not Mary . . . ME! Why else would he ask Mrs. Perez to take the doll? It's not Mary's. He must have recognized me over the phone!

I knew it.

I just knew he would.

Gretchen crashed her little fist against the wall, chastising herself again and again for being so dumb.

"Oh, please," she cried, staring out the window. "Please come back for me, Mrs. Perez. Please!"

"I won't," Gretchen groaned, her spine arching up off the mattress. "I won't go back there."

For the third night in a row, Gretchen was battling those black howling demons in her dreams, ghouls from the shadow world, who came to her in her weakest hours, when her unconscious was freed by sleep to roam the farthest boundaries of the living, boundaries that held her twin at bay in that dark, terrifying place in limbo . . . her place. The cold lonely grave from which she had fled.

. . . Gretchen, come back . . .

She could hear their jackellike barks of torment beckoning, entreating, tugging at her will.

. . . Gretchen . . .

"No!" Her entire body erupted in puddles of sweat

320

as she desperately barricaded herself from the dark forces now scratching at the gates of her consciousness.

Beyond those horrifying cries, a dim, frightened voice began reverberating against her skull.

. . . Gretchen, let me go . . .

The howling dimmed as Mary's pleas grew louder, until her sister's cries were like clanging cymbals.

. . . Gretchen . . .

. . . for both our sakes . . .

. . . Come back . . .

The child's head snapped off the pillow. Her eyes flared open and scanned the room until they locked onto her big, one-eyed bear in the corner by the closet.

They can't make me, she reassured herself, waiting for her mind to return from that land of nightmares. And neither can Mary. I'm in control. Not her. Me!

. . . Gretchen, please . . .

The girl ripped the covers up and her shoulders trembled.

"Leave me alone," she hissed through her teeth, her jaws locked. "Damn you."

Sucking in her breath, she waited, her senses keyed on the slightest rustle.

The only sound was the swishing of branches against the side of the house and the heavy thumping of a heart . . .

Mary's heart.

"My heart," she growled, incensed by that thought. "Mine! Mine! Mine!"

The next morning, Michael followed Barbra to the grade school. The police had already contacted the principal, but Barbra wouldn't leave until the unmarked car had parked across the street from the buses.

For Mary's sake, she had tried not to make a big deal out of the break-in yesterday. Although Matt had denied everything over the phone, she hadn't believed a word of it. But she saw no reason Mary should know what her father had done.

The man is sick, she thought, sitting at her desk, unable to concentrate on her work. Sick! Sick! Sick!

She hadn't been in the office for more than twenty minutes when her secretary buzzed.

The police were on line two.

Like a caged pigeon, Barbra's heart fluttered against her breastbone as she picked up the receiver. "This is Mrs. Foster."

"The chief would like you to come down to the station immediately," a faceless voice informed her.

"Why? What's wrong? Is Mary all right?"

"Yes, Mrs. Foster. Your daughter is fine. But would you please come right away. Chief Daniels said it was better not to discuss this over the phone."

The chief met Barbra in the station parking lot.

"Now what's going on?" Barbra demanded, getting out of her car.

The chief opened the passenger door of his vehicle. "Would you come with me, please?"

Huffing to show her frustration, Barbra did as he

322

asked. As soon as he closed the door, she asked him to explain all this secrecy.

He started the engine and drove off. "I can't explain it, Mrs. Foster. Just wait. You'll see soon enough."

He tried to think of a way to prepare her for what she was going to see, but he just couldn't. It was too grotesque to put into words.

When he turned into the graveyard, Barbra glanced over at him suspiciously. He noticed it, but kept his jaw locked and said nothing.

Halfway up the hill, across from the big stone mausoleum, he stopped the car. Barbra immediately recognized the area. She had often parked in the same spot to put flowers on her daughter's grave.

Rain careened down over the windows, fogging them on the inside. The chief silently pointed to her right and Barbra rolled down her window.

"Oh, God," she muttered. Her intestines coiled together like a ball of rattlesnakes. "Who would do such a thing?"

Gretchen's gravesite was in a shambles. Piles of dirt were scattered everywhere, as if some huge animal had dug it up with its paws.

"It's gone," the chief stated quietly, feeling as sickened as he had when he first saw it. He could barely continue without become nauseous. "Your daughter's grave has been robbed."

Barbra was in a state of shock. She couldn't speak, couldn't move, couldn't think.

"We'll get her," the chief, said, hoping, somehow, it might help. "Don't worry. We'll find that Perez woman. And get the coffin back."

As soon as he got to the station, Chief Daniels asked the dispatcher to call Dr. Bernstein.

"Tell him it's an emergency," he commanded before running back to his car.

Barbra Foster looked catatonic. Too many things had happened, he thought, sliding in beside her. What mother could stand up to such continuous horror?

Seeing her daughter's pillaged grave site had finally pushed Barbra over the edge. Her strength was gone. She couldn't even raise her arms without assistance.

The doctor arrived at the station minutes after the dispatcher had called. Together, he and the chief helped Barbra to her car. Dr. Bernstein gave her a sedative and sat with her until it began to take its effect.

"Is she going to be all right, doc?" the chief asked as he escorted Bernstein out of hearing distance.

"She's a strong woman," the doctor stated. "But she's been through a lot. Too much, I guess. I think she'll be able to handle it, though. She just needs to shut out the world for a little while. To regroup inside. I gave her enough Tuinals to put a horse to sleep. She'll be out for a few hours, at least. It should help. I'm going to drive her home."

Shoving his hands into his pants pockets, the chief checked the area to be sure they were still alone. "Doc, I don't want this getting out. The town would be in a panic. Two of my officers are erecting a tent over the grave site so no one will see it. I'd appreciate it if you keep this to yourself, at least until we find the woman who did it."

"What woman?" the doctor said angrily. He liked Barbra Foster and had learned to respect her over the last two months. He would have enjoyed getting his hands on the ghoul who robbed her daughter's grave . . . and the hell with his Hippocratic oath.

The chief explained the entire episode. Dr. Bernstein could hardly believe his ears.

"At first, I thought this Mrs. Perez was hired to kidnap Mary Foster. But it just doesn't fit anymore. Nothing fits." Again the chief quickly scanned the parking lot. "Doc, we've got a sicko on our hands. A crazy woman. And I have the awful feeling she's still around here somewhere. I don't know why she's doing what she's doing, but she's obviously psychotic. And dangerous. If this gets around, I'm afraid we could have a lynch mob on our hands. To tell you the truth, I couldn't blame them. No one's safe in this town until we find her. We've called in back-up units from the county and the state patrol. There can't be that many places to hide a Winnebago, for Christ's sake. We'll find her, all right. But until then, we've got to keep this quiet."

"I understand, Chief." The doctor glanced back at Barbra's car. "I'd better get her home and put her to bed. What about her daughter?"

"I was going to have one of my men watching the school take her home. But that might cause too much speculation."

"Call Michael Striker at the mill," the doctor

suggested. "He's close to them both. No one would think it odd if he picked her up. I'd like to have the girl home as soon as possible, though. I want her there when her mother wakes up. I have a feeling she'll need her. She's a tough woman, Chief. With her daughter there, she should come around. It'll give her a reason, an incentive to face this . . . I hope. It did before, at least. When her other twin died. She'll need all the love around her she can get right now."

The chief nodded. "I'll get on it right away, Doc."

The Doll-Maker began chanting as she pried open the dirt-encrusted coffin. The dank odor of decaying flesh attacked her nostrils.

"Mictlancihuatl," she wailed, closing her eyes. "I sing the song of the dead. Hear me. One of your children has escaped thy lair. Hear me, Goddess of the nine spheres. Call this child that lays before me. Call her back. For she has tampered with the soul of her living twin. And it is blasphemy to break the natural order of the worlds, here or hereafter."

The Doll-Maker lifted two small clay dolls above her head.

"Tezcatlipoca," her voice rang out. "Giver of life. Thy child-doll is in my left hand, the hand of giving. For a hundred generations she has guarded your secrets. Feed her with thy power." She put the doll by the left ear of the withered corpse. "Speak to this rotting skull, oh, giver of life. Help me protect the innocent one."

Lowering the other doll, she pressed its head

against the lips of the corpse.

"Xipe," she chanted, "Flayed-one, god of sacrifice, Blood god, hear me! Thy child-doll, ancient of ancients, made in the dawn of our people, is in my right hand, the hand of power. She has kissed the dead." Twisting the girl's skull slightly, she placed the clay doll by her right ear. "Prepare the alter, Xipe, for a sacrifice." Raising her big fists high, she again pleaded with her gods. "Tezcatlipoca, Xipe, whisper thy sacred promise in the ears of the dead. Know, too, my words are from Ometéotl, god of gods. He entreats you, through my child-dolls, to do my bidding. Prepare, my gods, for the Ceremony of the Dead."

From her pocket, she took a short sacrificial knife of pure gold, its handle shaped like the skull of a jaguar, and cut a clump of dry, stringy hair from the dead body. Holding the hair aloft in one hand and the soft-sculptured doll in the other, she screamed.

"It is I who have sinned. My doll, whom I loved too much, to whom I gave too much power, holds the soul of an innocent one in limbo. Do not let her be punished for my indiscretions. I beseech you, let the child go. Send the evil one back to Mictlancihuatl. If payment is due, let the burden fall on me."

Closing her eyes, she let her inner self slip away. Reeling through that trembling vortex between life and death, she forced herself to stand before the gates of limbo once again.

The terrifying cackle of demons in that darkness beyond attacked her soul, some bidding her to enter.

Back! her mind cried. Get back to thy pits in hell. Let the child come forth and speak.

Concentrating all her powers, she tried to make contact.

Help me, child. Help me find her weakness. I must know how to make the evil one flee thy body. Child, do you hear me? I must know.

Suddenly she felt something gentle but frightened touch her spirit.

A faint voice called out from that black void.

. . . Pain . . .

Speak, child, her soul kept screaming at the gates. I know of your agony. Speak!

But the voice was gone.

Bringing herself back to the place of the living, the Doll-Maker shivered involuntarily, one word still echoing in her skull like a death chant . . .

. . . Pain . . .

Throwing her head back in anguish, tears streaming from her dark eyes, she began to wail like a sick animal.

"Ayee! Tonight, when the full moon touches the pinnacle of heaven, I will bring the living corpse, the possessor of your body, my child, to make the sacrifice. Ayee! Ayee!"

Michael Striker paced the living room, unable to sit still. Each time he passed the bay window, he checked the driveway to make sure the unmarked police car was still there.

It was one-thirty in the morning.

As soon as the chief had called him this morning, he had left the mill without a word to anyone. By the time he picked Mary up at school and drove her home, Dr. Bernstein had already put Barbra to bed. After a short conference in the kitchen, they had both decided it was best not to let the girl know what had happened, only that her mother was sick and needed rest.

The first time Barbra awoke, she was hysterical and Dr. Bernstein had immediately sedated her again. Michael had sat by the bed all day and half the night, holding her cold, limp hand. Each time she moaned in her sleep, her fingers dug into his. It was tearing him apart, but he couldn't bear to leave her side.

After fourteen straight hours of that, he finally had to get up and stretch. Keeping all the lights out, he went into the dining room and knelt by the oak table to pray. Then he began to pace. All he really wanted was to crawl under the blankets, hold Barbra against him, and weep. But he wouldn't. If he allowed himself to shed a single tear, he knew he would never be able to stop.

So he paced.

And paced.

When he felt his courage weakening again, he dropped to his knees and prayed a second time. His chest felt like an empty cavern lined with sharply barbed hooks. Nothing mattered to him anymore, except Barbra. If it would have helped, he would have gladly sawed off one of his arms to ensure her recovery.

As he prayed, a slight sense of calm ensued. In that brief moment, he knew the only thing that would really help Barbra was his love. With all his being, he opened himself to that love, hoping, praying, pleading that such a love as his would somehow work miracles.

A sharp snap, like the sound of metal cracking, and a sudden rush of cold air interrupted his concentration. Spinning around, he saw the open glass door to the porch and leaped to his feet. His eyes frantically searched the shadows.

By the time he saw her, it was too late.

With one mighty sweep of her arms, the Doll-Maker knocked him clear over the sofa. Half-conscious, dizzy, his limbs as weak and pliable as willow branches, he forced himself up and crouched, fists raised, ready for battle. Momentarily blinded by the blow, he turned, ducking and swinging at the darkness around him.

Suddenly a massive forearm locked around his neck. He slammed his elbows back into the intruder.

The blows had no effect.

Bright silver stars started flickering around him. He felt as if he were falling through a vortex in the night sky.

He tried to scream out, but his windpipe was blocked.

In a few moments, he had lost consciousness.

Making certain he was still breathing, the Doll-Maker gently laid him on the floor.

"I have no fight with you, brave one," she whispered.

Staying away from the front window, she silently stalked down the hall. Cracking open the twins' door, she gazed upon the sleeping child.

Gretchen's eyes shot open. "Who's there?"

"Shhhh, child. Do not be frightened," the Doll-Maker cajoled.

Gretchen sat up and pulled the covers to her chest. To the Doll-Maker's surprise, the girl was grinning.

"It's you," she exclaimed excitedly. "I knew you'd come back. I knew it."

The Doll-Maker had not expected such a welcome. "We must go, child. Quickly."

Gretchen jumped out of bed and put on her slippers. "Daddy sent you, didn't he? Are you gonna take me to him? He hired you to come get me, right?"

The Doll-Maker saw no reason to deny it. Not if it would make the girl come willingly.

"Yes, child. It is so. But we must hurry. Be silent now. The police are everywhere. We must travel through the forest, but it is safe there. The spirits of the great trees speak to me. Come."

Michael Striker fought the darkness with all his ebbing strength.

Open your eyes, his consciousness cried out. Open them!

One lid fluttered and his right hand twitched. Each breath he took burned his throat like a hot poker.

"Move, damn it!" he muttered.

Forcing himself to roll over on his belly, he tried to get up on his hands and knees. The floor seemed to roll and pitch underneath him, but he finally succeeded.

When he tried to stand, however, he immediately fell back down. Crawling across the rug, he reached

331

up and opened the front door.

The police were out of their car and running up the driveway by the time the door hit the outside of the house.

Chapter XVIII

Chief Daniels was furious. His people had let an old woman, a grave-robber, slip through their web of sentries. Unable to look Barbra in the eyes, he stared at the floor as he spoke.

"We've called in every available unit in the whole damn state. We've even called in the fire department and Search and Rescue. There's got to be near a hundred vehicles combing the county. We've got road-blocks on every back alley and horse trail leading out of town. She can't escape."

Michael squeezed Barbra's shoulder, wishing there was something he could say, anything that might give her hope. Still groggy from the sedatives, she kept gulping coffee as she leaned against the counter. She hadn't spoken since Michael had awakened her with the news of Mary's kidnapping. To her, words had become useless.

Only one thing mattered now.

Finding her daughter . . . safe.

Before the crazy woman . . .

Barbra couldn't finish the thought.

"I . . . I'd better get going," the chief stammered. "I'm not doing any good standing here."

Before he could take two steps, Michael grabbed his arm. "I'm going with you."

Suddenly Barbra broke her silent vigil.

"So am I," she said, swaying forward dizzily.

Sitting between the chief and Michael, Barbra remained mute. Her entire consciousness focused on the static reports constantly blared over the two-way police radio. Every street, dirt road, and abandoned driveway was checked and rechecked as the perimeter of the search grew in ever-widening circles away from Canaan.

An hour passed.

Then another.

And still no sign, not one clue as to the whereabouts of the mad woman or her trailer. A trigger mechanism somewhere in the farthest reaches of Barbra's psyche had been activated. Like a safety valve, turned to keep her mental circuits from overloading, it kept shutting off her imagination each time she thought about her daughter's peril.

Gretchen's death had been difficult enough. Losing Mary would literally destroy her. That terrifying truth had immediately registered in her subconscious when she had been told of Mary's kidnapping. Her entire being had, in essence, been put on hold.

To wait the final verdict.

If the worst happened, if Mary was found dead like

334

her sister, that mental safety valve would click off entirely, letting her consciousness slip away from the world of reality, a world too devastatingly harsh to be worth living in any longer.

"Home base . . . home base," the radio monitor cackled. "This is Officer Philips, Highway Patrol, car twenty-seven. There's fresh tire tracks on an old dirt road two miles east of Canaan. Off Route six. Do you know the road? Over."

Chief Daniels suddenly slammed on the brakes. Michael threw his arm in front of Barbra to keep her from crashing into the windshield.

"Damn," the chief muttered. Then, picking up the microphone, "That leads to an old abandoned lumber camp. Shut down in forty-six. Check it out, Philips. Over."

"There's a tree blocking the road, home base. It'd take at least six men to move it. From the looks of it, it hasn't been here long. Someone chopped it down with an axe. The cuts are fresh. I'm going to have to walk in. How far to the camp? Over."

"Stay right where you are, Philips. I'll have six cars there in five minutes. Over."

"OK, home base. I'll wait. Over."

Switching on his siren, the chief shoved the gas pedal to the floor. Route six was only a mile down the highway.

The old lumber camp would be the perfect place to hold a Winnebago, he thought, angry with himself for not having considered it sooner. It's got to be the place. We've checked every damn inch of road in a ten-mile radius. She's got to be there.

Officer John Philips had three children. When his eldest son had been old enough to join the Boy Scouts, he had volunteered what little time he had left to be an assistant scoutmaster. He loved kids. Staring up at the dirt road, he knew he couldn't wait, not even five minutes, not with a kidnapped child in the hands of a grave-robber.

Hopping up over the tree trunk blocking the road, he began to jog along the edge of the path. Obscene mental images of the blond girl's plight kept him running at a gallop even after the sharp pains had begun to stab at his ribs.

"I'm tired," Gretchen complained. "I don't think I can walk any further."

The Doll-Maker halted at the foot of the hill leading to the lumber camp. Sweeping the girl up into her arms, she carried her the rest of the way.

The full moon suddenly emerged from between two black clouds, illuminating the forest in a pale green hue. A hundred yards ahead of them, the dilapidated camp seemed to glow in its light.

Stopping in front of the mess hall where her trailer was hidden, the Doll-Maker peered up at the night sky. Like a beacon calling to her from worlds beyond, the full moon spotlighted her upturned face. Dark clouds, like ghostly tentacles, encircled it, making it seem even bigger and brighter.

Ometéotl watches, the holy woman thought, trans-

336

fixed by the eerie glow from the heavens.

"What are we doing here?" Gretchen asked, after the woman had put her down. "When am I going to see Daddy?"

There was no reason to lie anymore. The moon was at its peak and they had made it to the camp, undetected. It was time to begin the sacrifice.

"I was not sent by your father, little one," she told the girl.

Gretchen shivered, hoping it was a joke. "But Daddy hired you. I heard the police tell Mommy."

"I was sent by another," the woman stated.

"What do you mean? Who sent you?" Gretchen was becoming frightened by the strange glazed look in the woman's eyes. "Quit teasing me and take me to my daddy."

"I will take you to your parent." The old woman picked up a handful of muddy earth and chanted something in a foreign tongue. "Your new mother. The one you denied. From whom you escaped . . . Mictlancihuatl."

Before Gretchen could flee, the old woman locked onto her arm.

"Let me go!" the girl pleaded, kicking wildly. "Let me go!"

The Doll-Maker dragged the screaming girl into the half-fallen building. Moonlight tunneled through a myriad of cracks in the roof.

Suddenly Gretchen stopped kicking. Her eyes blazed with horror at what she saw.

Her open coffin was lying on a long wooden table. Nine bright candles flickered around it, illuminating the decaying corpse within.

Her corpse.

"NO!" Gretchen howled, her body convulsing in sheer terror.

Binding the girl's arms behind her back, the Doll-Maker lifted her up on the table next to the coffin.

"Daddy!" Gretchen cried, squirming against the bonds.

Having prepared the sacrificial table already, the Doll-Maker quickly tied the girl's legs, neck and forehead against it securely. Unable to move, Gretchen followed the woman with her wide, frightened eyes.

The Doll-Maker edged the table closer to the coffin until it was directly under a large hole in the roof. Moonlight washed over the girl's body, causing it to shimmer in its unearthly radiance. Her big blue eyes began to redden in the glow. In seconds, they were the color of freshly spilled blood.

Pleased that the forces of the moon were with her, the old woman climbed into her trailer and returned with the doll. Seeing it again gave Gretchen a brief glimpse of hope.

"She's mine," the girl stammered. "Give her back."

"All in good time, little one," the woman said. "All in good time."

Rounding the final bend in the road, Philips halted. He could see lights flickering in the large building slightly to the left of the center of camp. Unsnapping his holster, he rechecked his .38, clicked off the safety, and cocked it back. As he headed up toward the side of the old mess hall, he suddenly felt a strange sense of calm for the first time in his career when faced with a possible shooting in the line of duty. In that brief instant, before his fears for the child's safety started to eat at his guts again, he knew that he would have no moral qualms whatsoever killing a psychopathic grave-robber. Even more startling was the realization that he hoped it would actually come down to that.

"What do you want from me?" Gretchen began to weep. "Please give me my doll and let me go."

"Do you wish to be freed?" The Doll-Maker set the doll between the coffin and the bound child.

Sniffling back her tears, Gretchen nodded. "Yes."

"Then free your twin. The one whose life you have stolen."

Gretchen's spine turned to ice. "I . . . I don't know what you're talking about."

The Doll-Maker leaned down, her face inches from the girl's.

"I ask you again. Free your twin."

Gretchen closed her eyes tightly and bit her lip. Then, in a voice trembling with horror, "Let me go. You're . . . you're crazy. Please, don't scare me anymore. Just let me go."

The Doll-Maker arched back, tugging her own hair out by the roots.

"Ayee!"

The chilling cry echoed through the camp. Gretchen could feel its vibrations attack her skin like hailstones.

Suddenly the girl's eyes riveted on the old woman's outstretched hands.

The Doll-Maker now held a short knife. Its golden blade shimmered in the candlelight as she cut open Gretchen's pajamas.

"Thy soul is tainted, little one. Thy heart is black with evil. Let thy sister go!" She raised the knife above her head.

"NO!" the girl screamed.

"Ther ⋯ ⋯ agony of the living dead," the woman ⋯

Lowering ⋯ , she slowly ran the tip of the blade across Gretchen's chest, slicing the skin like paper.

Gretchen howled in agony.

The child's torturous scream tore into Philips's ribs like a red-hot poker. Knowing he didn't have time to be cautious, he jumped over the rusty barrels by the side of the building, cracking his shin against a broken board. Regaining his balance, he spun around the corner and crouched in front of the doorway, his pistol moving in precise synchronization with his eyes as he zeroed in on his target.

The Doll-Maker, having heard the crack of wood and the quick thud of a body hitting the outside wall, immediately grabbed the short iron pipe by the coffin.

"Freeze!" Philips warned.

The Doll-Maker threw the pipe like a war-axe, then charged. Philips was able to squeeze off one round before the pipe cracked into his shoulder, shattering his collarbone.

The bullet ripped into the side of the Doll-Maker's belly, but its force wasn't powerful enough to halt her attack.

Before he could raise the gun with the one good hand he had left, she had him. One huge arm lifted him up by the neck while the other twisted his wrist until the pistol dropped from his grip. With a mighty jerk, she snapped his head back and he fell limply to the ground.

Ignoring the searing pain in her side, she limped back to the table, a river of blood following her every step.

"Mary beckons," the woman taunted, looking down at the girl. "Hear her cries of torment?"

. . . Gretchen . . .

A cold wind suddenly swirled through the building. The loose wall boards creaked in grotesque harmony with the chilling cry.

. . . Free me, Gretchen . . .

The Doll-Maker grinned. It is good, she thought. The child works with me, even from the land of spirits. She is close. And Mictlancihuatl is with her. She carries the child's pleas in the wind, her voice from the underworld.

"Heed thy sister's call, little one." The Doll-Maker picked up the golden knife. "Or this blade, the tongue of the goddess, Mictlancihuatl, will lick the skin from your body."

Gretchen closed her eyes and said nothing.

"So be it," the Doll-Maker growled. Again, she ran the blade over the girl's chest, crossing the first wound with another.

Writhing up against the ropes, Gretchen pleaded futilely for mercy.

"The pain of the living should not be yours," the Doll-Maker sang out. "To receive mercy, one must give mercy. Go back. Go back to thy true body." The woman pointed at the coffin. "There. There is thy place. Let your sister go. Free her from the doll."

The girl gritted her teeth. She would never go back. Not there. Not to that cold black place called death.

"Xipe," the Doll-Maker entreated. "God of Sacrifice. Taste the blood of thy victim." Wiping her hand over the child's wounds, the old woman lifted her fingers to her mouth and licked them dry.

"Mictlancihuatl," she cried. "Thy child refuses to return. Call to her, Goddess of Darkness. Beseech her to give back what she has stolen."

Looking back down at the girl, the Doll-Maker let the bloody knife drip on Gretchen's lips. Another blast of wind shook the building.

. . . Gretchen, your place is here . . .

Above them, the roof swayed precariously.

. . . Here with the dead . . .

. . . Let me go . . .

"Do you not understand, little one? The life you have stolen will no longer be one of joy . . . or comfort. You are mine now. I will not kill you. But I will cut the skin from your body, piece by piece, until every nerve, every muscle screams in torment."

Again the old woman drew the blade across the girl's chest, this time following the curve of her ribs.

It took twelve men to move the tree enough to let their vehicles pass.

"Let's go," the chief commanded. Doors slammed and engines revved as, one by one, they followed his squealing lead up the muddy road.

After two more long but shallow incisions, Gretchen could no longer bear it.

Anything was better than this hideous torture.

Anything . . .

Even death.

"Mary," she pleaded. "Make the pain go away. Please!"

"Take her back." The Doll-Maker spun around and drove the knife into the heart of the corpse. "Mictlancihuatl, open the gates to the land of the Dead. Thy child awaits."

Lifting the soft-sculptured doll, she shook it over the living girl's body, then the corpse's.

"See, Mictlancihuatl. See through the sacred eyes of the doll. Show this child the way back. Let the soul of the innocent one go. Free her from her prison in limbo."

The nine candles suddenly exploded in flames and went out. A freezing wind blew through the building, shaking its rotting foundations.

"Omotéotl, Lord of Lords, god of the Universe, quicken the transfer. Aid your daughter, Mictlancihuatl. Help the child free herself."

The entire building swayed as if the full weight of

343

the sky had fallen down upon it. A section of the roof creaked and tumbled down on the trailer.

A grotesque scream pierced the darkness.

Then silence.

Moments later, a soft moan drifted across the room.

The Doll-Maker held the doll against her huge breasts, exhausted, a large pool of blood growing around her feet.

The little girl on the table opened her eyes and started to cry.

"She's gone," Mary whispered weakly. "I can't feel her at all."

"Hush, baby," the Doll-Maker soothed. "Everything is all right now. You are free."

She quickly untied her bonds and hugged the trembling girl.

"Shhh, baby. Your sister can hurt you no longer. You did well, child. It took great courage to face the darkness and hold the hand of Mictlancihuatl."

Opening a small wooden box, the old woman dipped her fingers in the salve and spread it across the child's wounds.

The throbbing pain in Mary's chest was gone almost instantly.

As if awakening from some horrible nightmare, Mary peered up at the Doll-Maker, dazed.

"What . . . what am I doing here? Who are you?" she asked, disoriented but not afraid. Whoever this woman was, she had saved her from the place of eternal darkness. "Thank you. I was so scared, but . . ."

"Be still, child." The woman gently stroked her

small head. "Rest. It was a long journey back."

Six cars swerved to a halt, one after the other, at the foot of the twisting path to the lumber camp. The chief quickly gathered his men around him.

"We'll go in two's. Jack, you take your partner up behind the camp. The rest of you, circle to the left and right. I'll come up from the front with Striker. And be careful, Philips is out there somewhere too." He unstrapped his holster and removed the revolver. Michael reached back into the squad car, grabbed the pump-action shotgun, and clicked off the safety.

As soon as they began to tighten their web around the camp, they heard a voice cry out from the doorway to the mess hall.

"She's in here," Philips warned, still too weak and dizzy to move. "In the mess hall."

"I see it," another yelled. "The Winnebago. Inside that building." His flashlight directed the others.

Chief Daniels ran back to his vehicle to get his bullhorn. Barbra jumped out of the passenger door and blocked his path.

Her questioning gaze spoke for her.

"She'll be fine, Mrs. Foster. Don't worry. We've found her now."

Praying he was right, he grabbed the bull-horn and ran back up the hill. Michael dashed around the flattened out-house and joined Barbra by the chief.

Like spokes on a fire-wheel, every available flashlight was centered on that one building, probing the windows and the cracks in the planks.

"Mrs. Perez," the bullhorn crackled loudly. "We have you surrounded. Let the girl go. And come out with your hands on top of your head."

A small voice broke the long silence.

"Mommy?"

Barbra felt a sudden jolt of life in her dead limbs.

"Mary? I'm here, Mary. I'm out here," she cried gratefully.

When she attempted to run up the hill, Michael held her back. Spinning around, she beat at him with her fists. "Let me go, damn it! My baby's alive. And she needs me!"

Michael quickly checked with the chief. He shook his head negatively. Michael held tight.

Suddenly all the lights shifted to the doorway. Barbra stopped struggling and squinted to see into the shadows of the building.

Carrying the child and the doll in her arms, the Doll-Maker stepped out into the blaring yellow-white circle of lights.

"Put the girl down, Mrs. Perez," the chief urged over the bullhorn.

In the glare, Barbra could see long lines of blood on Mary's pajama top. Her knees buckled, but Michael scooped her up before she fell.

In the sudden, cold silence, she could hear the clicking of revolvers as a dozen hammers were cocked back.

"Mommy?" Mary called out again, unable to see with all the lights in her eyes.

Barbra bolted free and ran toward the child. "Mary! Mary, I'm coming!"

Half the officers immediately squatted, arms extended, revolvers aimed and waiting.

The Doll-Maker stepped toward the galloping woman and let the child down.

Barbra swept her child up in her arms and backed away.

Philips forced himself to his feet and jumped the woman from behind. With his one good arm, he tried to twist the Doll-Maker's wrist behind her back, but was knocked flat against the wall of the building.

"She's got a knife," someone yelled.

A dozen shots rang out.

Mary spun around, shoving herself out of her mother's embrace.

"Don't kill her!" she pleaded, dashing back to the old woman's aid.

The Doll-Maker, her massive flesh riddled with holes, swayed and dropped to the ground. Blood bubbled out of the corner of her mouth as her lungs began to fill with the fluid.

Mary threw herself over the huge woman's chest to protect her. She could feel the warm liquid rushing out against her cheek as she clung to her, crying fitfully.

"Do not weep, child." The Doll-Maker coughed.

"Don't die," Mary whispered, choking back her tears. "Please don't die."

The Doll-Maker patted the girl's shoulder weakly. Feeling her life quickly passing from her, she fought against it, trying to form her last words.

"The doll," she grunted. "It is yours now. Love it like your own child."

Frantic, Mary tried to stop the flow of blood by plugging the bullet holes with her palms. "Don't die. Oh please, please, don't die."

"Look, child," the Doll-Maker spit out, between gulps of blood. "Look to the doll. And remember. I will be with you . . . always. Look to the doll, child. The doll!"

Mary felt the old woman's final breath wash warmly across her face.

A moment later, she was dead.

Picking up the doll, Mary hugged it against her cheek.

"I'll take care of you," she whispered in its ear, her tear-soaked eyes riveted on the Doll-Maker. "We're safe now. No one can hurt us anymore."

THE BEST IN GOTHICS FROM ZEBRA

THE BLOODSTONE INHERITANCE (1560, $2.95)
by Serita Deborah Stevens

The exquisite Parkland pendant, the sole treasure remaining to lovely Elizabeth from her mother's fortune, was missing a matching jewel. Finding it in a ring worn by the handsome, brooding Peter Parkisham, Elizabeth couldn't deny the blaze of emotions he ignited in her. But how could she love the man who had stolen THE BLOODSTONE INHERITANCE!

**THE SHRIEKING SHADOWS OF
PENPORTH ISLAND** (1344, $2.95)
by Serita Deborah Stevens

Seeking her missing sister, Victoria had come to Lord Hawley's manor on Penporth Island, but now the screeching gulls seemed to be warning her to flee. Seeing Julian's dark, brooding eyes watching her every move, and seeing his ghost-like silhouette on her bedroom wall, Victoria knew she would share her sister's fate — knew she would never escape!

THE HOUSE OF SHADOWED ROSES (1447, $2.95)
by Carol Warburton

Penniless and alone, Heather was thrilled when the Ashleys hired her as a companion and brought her to their magnificent Cornwall estate, Rosemerryn. But soon Heather learned that danger lurked amid the beauty there — in ghosts long dead and mysteries unsolved, and even in the arms of Geoffrey Ashley, the enigmatic master of Rosemerryn.

CRYSTAL DESTINY (1394, $2.95)
by Christina Blair

Lydia knew she belonged to the high, hidden valley in the Rockies that her father had claimed, but the infamous Aaron Stone lived there now in the forbidding Stonehurst mansion. Vowing to get what was hers, Lydia would confront the satanic master of Stonehurst — and find herself trapped in a battle for her very life!

THESE ZEBRA MYSTERIES
ARE SURE TO KEEP
YOU GUESSING

By Sax Rohmer

THE DRUMS OF FU MANCHU	(1617, $3.50)
THE TRAIL OF FU MANCHU	(1619, $3.50)
THE INSIDIOUS DR. FU MANCHU	(1668, $3.50)

By Mary Roberts Rinehart

THE HAUNTED LADY	(1685, $3.50)
THE SWIMMING POOL	(1686, $3.50)

By Ellery Queen

WHAT'S IN THE DARK	(1648, $2.95)

Available wherever paperbacks are sold, or order direct from the Publisher. Send cover price plus 50¢ per copy for mailing and handling to Zebra Books, Dept. 1788, 475 Park Avenue South, New York, N.Y. 10016. DO NOT SEND CASH.

THE BEST IN REGENCIES FROM ZEBRA

PASSION'S LADY   (1545, $2.95)
by Sara Blayne
She was a charming rogue, an impish child—and a maddeningly
alluring woman. If the Earl of Shayle knew little else about her,
he knew she was going to marry him. As a bride, Marie found a
temporary hiding place from her past, but could not escape from
the Earl's shrewd questions—or the spark of passion in his eyes.

WAGER ON LOVE   (1577, $2.50)
by Prudence Martin
Only a cynical rogue like Nicholas Ruxart would choose a bride
on the basis of a careless wager, and then fall in love with her
grey-eyed sister Jane. It was easy for Jane to ignore the advances
of this cold gambler, but she found denying her tender yearnings
for him to be much harder.

RECKLESS HEART   (1679, $2.50)
by Lois Arvin Walker
Rebecca had met her match in the notorious Earl of Compton.
Not only did he decline the invitation to her soiree, but he found
it amusing when her horse landed her in the middle of Compton
Creek. If this was another female scheme to lure him into marriage the Earl swore Rebecca would soon learn she had the wrong
man, a man with a blackened reputation.

DANCE OF DESIRE   (1757, $2.95)
by Sarah Fairchilde
Lord Sherbourne almost ran Virginia down on horseback, then
he silenced her indignation with a most ungentlemanly kiss.
Seething with outrage, the lovely heiress decided the insufferable
lord was in need of a royal setdown. And she knew the way to go
about it . . .

*Available wherever paperbacks are sold, or order direct from the
Publisher. Send cover price plus 50¢ per copy for mailing and
handling to Zebra Books, Dept. 1788, 475 Park Avenue South,
New York, N.Y. 10016. DO NOT SEND CASH.*